MW00513273

Praise fo

Book One of The Illusion Trilogy

"For such a young writer, it was very good... **I could see glimmers of true talent in this book.**"

-*New York Times* Bestselling Author, Tawni O'Dell

"The most creative book I've read in a long time!"

"I'm so impressed with Ms. Rodgers' *Illusion*. A **page turner** that is geared toward young adults, **it is a great read for anyone.** Definitely one to add to your to-read bookshelves!"

-Dana Faletti, bestselling author of *Beautiful Secret*

"Captivating!"   "Compelling!"   "I couldn't put it down!"

"**Wow, what an impressive new young writer who already has stirred things up in people's minds and hearts in her first book** *Illusion*! **Readers will get lost in her intriguing and inspired writing style.** This is one fantastic read, and I could not put it down. This is saying a lot from someone who does not normally read these styles of books and this genre. You see I am a business man and a number one best selling author of my own business book. I normally tend to read fact based business books. **But this author and these series of books has just changed all that.**"

-*#1 Amazon Bestselling Author*, Stephen D. Rodgers

Praise for Echo
Book Two of The Illusion Trilogy

"Nadette has **taken something ordinary and made it extraordinary** with the Illusion Trilogy, which is precisely what makes storytelling so wonderful. Nadette Rae Rodgers has wrapped **everything a good story needs into this beautifully written package**."

-Holly at *Nut Free Nerd*

"Even better than the first!"

"*Illusion* and *Echo* are an **imaginative and romantic journey into the world of dreams** and teenagers. Rodgers perfectly captures the teenage experience and voice. With the first chapter of *Illusion*, Nadette Rae Rodgers draws the readers in and keeps them guessing all the way through to the last chapter of *Echo*. She leaves readers eagerly awaiting the third installment of the trilogy!"

-Em Lyons Bouch, author of *Moving the Chains*

"Echo is a book that even when you're not reading it, you find yourself thinking about it."

-Nino at Enchanted Readers

"Marvelous!"   "I wish Zach Walker was real!"   "Page-turner!"

"Addison and Zach's story is like a fine wine: it gets better with time. The second installment of The Illusion Trilogy is a wonderful addition to an already exciting world."

-K.J. Reitsma of *Finding Fairyland*

"Intriguing and surprising!"

"In this second installment of the Illusion trilogy, Rogers does not disappoint! Echo will certainly keep its readers on the edge of their seats. I its readers on the edge of their seats. **I promise you will not want to miss this one!**"

-Emily at *The Obstinate Owl*

Also in The Illusion Trilogy:
Illusion (Book One)
Echo (Book Two)

Also by Nadette:
Hoo Loves You (a Hoo Loves You children's book)

Coming Fall 2018:
Hoo's Birthday Is It? (a Hoo Loves You children's book)

Sweet Dreams

Book Three

Nadette Rae Rodgers

Printed in the United States of America

ISBN-13: 978-0-692-15542-4
LCCN: 2018952284
Kindle Direct Publishing
Columbia, South Carolina

To all the dreamers out there, I hope that you follow your dreams and pursue your passion, whatever they may be. I pray the very sweetest dreams come true for you!

"You may say I'm a dreamer, but I'm not the only one. I hope someday you'll join us, and the world will be as one."
-<u>Imagine</u> by John Lennon

"I promise to be the warrior who fights all your nightmares and the messenger who brings all your sweet dreams."
-unknown

Prologue

She sits there, on the old rickety bed, back slightly slouched --

just slightly -- and her dark, slightly graying hair falling down her back in gentle waves.

She turns page after page in a book, not really reading -- or grasping -- the words printed on each page. She prefers this story for its pictures. Happy ones. Full of color and smiles and animals.

The book she reads is actually meant for a child, which she hasn't been in a very long time. This woman wasn't a child for long either. The way her life was, she had to grow up quicker than most. That's probably what got her here.

She rocks slightly as she reads. It's barely noticeable, but if you watch her long enough, you'll see the small, rhythmic back and forth, back and forth of her frail body.

If you watch her long enough, you'll also notice the ever-so-quiet humming. She hums a familiar tune -- a lullaby, one she used to sing her baby to sleep with. *Her baby, oh, how she missed her baby.*

She still sees him when she dreams, you know. And in her dreams, he is three-years-old, with dark hair and dazzling blue eyes that light up when she tells him, "It's alright. Mommy's here."

In her dreams she sings him to sleep. But once he's asleep, she doesn't leave. No. She quietly walks over, turns out the light, then settles in the old wooden rocker her mother used to rock her in. Then she would sit quietly and watch her baby boy sleep soundly. And she'd wait until the nightmares came for him. And when they did, she'd do what she could to block them out. She hated to see her child so scared and upset.

She can't remember what happened to her little boy... just that something did. But that's nothing new. She can't remember much at all these days, which she sees as both a blessing and a curse.

A lady opens the heavy door just then, startling the woman out of her day dream. The lady has kind eyes and very curly hair.

"Hello! How are you today?" the lady asks her, still hovering in the doorway.

"Fine. Who are you?"

"I'm your nurse, hon. My name is Nancy. I was here just a few moments ago. I'm back with your snack."

"Oh. All right."

"Are you still hungry?" the lady asks.

The woman sits there, pondering this question as if it were a life-changing one.

"I'm not sure," she finally tells the nurse.

"It's chocolate pudding. You like chocolate pudding," the nurse assures her.

"I do? Yes. You're right. I do."

"Okay, honey. Well, I'll set it here. But you also have a visitor."

"Oooo. I love having visitors!" she coos.

"I know you do. Would it be all right if he came in now?"

The frail woman nods enthusiastically.

The nurse motions behind her, and a young man steps in her room.

She notes that he had short, dark hair and dazzling blue eyes she had seen before somewhere.

"Hi, Mom," he says.

She looks around the room, afraid. Was someone else in here that he was talking to?

But he just steps closer to her and repeats, "Hi, Mom. How are you today?"

"Your young man is quite the charmer," the nurse says. "He brought donuts for the whole staff again. You sure raised him right."

Who? My son is dead, the woman thinks.

The boy sits down on the edge of her bed, comfortable, like he's been here before. Has he been here before? she wonders.

The nurse steps out, leaving her alone with this boy. She can't remember how it is she knows him… just that she did.

"So, listen," he starts. "I have some exciting news to tell you."

"Oh, I love exciting news!" she says, sounding like a child.

If only I could remember this nice young man's name, she thinks. Such a pity.

Part One

Fighting Nightmares

1

- Zach -
Sunday, April 10th, 2022

I knocked on the front door, surprised at the way my hands were shaking. *Get it together, Zach,* I warned myself.

The door swung open.

"Hello, Zach," Mrs. Smith smiled warmly at me. I hadn't seen her in a while -- probably not since Addison's birthday dinner this past year. School's been insane lately with my senior thesis and my internship.

I cleared my throat. "Hello, Mrs. Smith. How are you?"

Her smile faltered a bit as she no doubt wondered why I seemed so nervous. "Addison isn't here right now..."

"I know."

"Okay... Zach, is everything alright?"

"Yes, ma'am." I looked around before finally getting my question out. "Is Mr. Smith home?"

She nodded.

"Can I speak with him?" *Wow, I sounded so formal and uptight. This wasn't a business deal.*

In that moment, she looked like she was going to cry. "Bob!" she called behind her.

Great. She knows.

"Yes, Anne?" Mr. Smith called from his home office.

"Zach is here," she said, unable to hide her smile and anxiousness. "Come on in," she told me.

"Thank you," I replied and kicked off my shoes like I always did in their entry way. Every time, like now, Mrs. Smith tells me I don't have to, but that was one thing my mother ingrained in me as a kid. "Take your shoes off in someone's home, Zachary," she'd say.

I rubbed my hands on my pants and then lifted my head. I walked into Mr. Smith's office, with its dark cherry, wooden desk and leather back chair. I sat down in a fancy chair he pointed to that Mrs. Smith no doubt put there, and he eased his laptop closed.

"What brings you here today, son?" he asked me.

The short answer to that question? Addison. She's what brought me to where I was right then.

The more specific answer was that I had something to ask her father.

This is it, Zach. Just ask him, I told myself.

"Well, Mr. Smith... I have something I've been wanting to ask you for a while. But first I wanted to thank you."

"For what?" he asked, clearly not catching on as quickly as his wife had.

"For Addison. For how you and Mrs. Smith raised her. She's incredible; the strongest woman I've ever met. She saved me and made me who I am today. I know I would've gone down a really different path if it weren't for your daughter."

At this point, a knowing grin spread across his face.

"I'm in love with your daughter, sir. I can't imagine a life without her in it. And that's why I'm here today... I was wondering...er... I'd really like your blessing and permission, because I really respect you, and you and Addison are so close..." Deep breath. "I'd like your permission to ask her to marry me."

We both jumped just then as something clattered to the ground just outside the office.

"Annie?" Mr. Smith called out.

She popped her head in the doorway, a dish towel in one hand, a shard of a broken dinner plate in the other.

"Were you eavesdropping?" he asked her.

"Oh, don't look so surprised. Of course I was."

He just looked at her as I sat there not sure what was going on.

He wouldn't say no, would he? I wondered.

Mrs. Smith shook her head, "Bob, this is our only child you are talking about -- my baby -- you can't blame me for getting a little excited... Now, are you going to give this wonderful young man an answer?"

"I was just about to," he told her and then turned to me. "Zach," he started, sounding serious.

Is he saying no?

"You are exactly what we had hoped for for our daughter, young man. You have my blessing, son."

"And mine!" her mom chimed in.

I stood, and Mr. Smith shook my hand. "Thank you, both of you. Really."

"This is so exciting," Mrs. Smith squeaked.

"Now, Annie," Mr. Smith warned. "Don't go saying anything to Addison."

"Pft. I wouldn't do such a thing." Then she turned to me. "I have the perfect thing. I'll be right back."

2

-Addison-
Tuesday, April 12th, 2022

"**S**o, what does it mean?" Sophie asked me, brown eyes twinkling. She looked anxious, worried.

"It *means* that you and Todd are getting serious," I replied in a tone that said *how-are-you-seriously-not-getting-this-one?*

"Okay, but what about the bit about all my teeth falling out before he came to pick me up?" she added, as if this would change my previous answer.

"You're the one who's about to be a dental hygienist. You tell me. Are you not flossing twice a day, Soph?"

"I'm serious, Addie. What does it all mean?"

"Sophie...it was just a *dream*," I pointed out, stressing the word "dream." Now, for someone like me -- a dreamer -- saying "it was just a dream" is not helpful and rarely applies to my life. My dreams are intense, vivid, and take place in a whole other world. A world "normal" people like Sophie here could never even begin to understand. But since I'm talking to Sophie, and not another dreamer, I leave all this out during our frequent "what does my dream mean?" conversations.

I met Sophie during freshman orientation four years ago, and we have been friends ever since. It's sometimes surprising because of our very different majors and interests, but somehow our friendship just works, and she's always making me laugh.

She was, however, *fascinated* by my major choice and the mind. She thinks it's *so cool* I chose psychology and am focusing my studies, when I can, to dreams. She was constantly telling me *how cool* my classes must be, even on days when I was struggling to remember my mnemonic devices for my neuroanatomy exam and didn't find psychology that *cool* myself. Sophie was also always asking me questions, most often about dreams and dream analysis. And like today, I would appease her and answer all of her questions. She'd always remark what a good memory I had to remember so many *fascinating* things about dreams. Little does she know most of the things I tell her I never read in a textbook or was taught in a lecture.

Dreams are my life. They're all I know. To her, they are fascinating little movies that play in her head while she sleeps -- sometimes, because she doesn't remember most of her dreams. To me, it's another me, a dream me, living in a dream world, trying to make it in the real world the rest of the time. To her, dreams mean you're stressed or you're happy or you're angry. To me, though, dreams mean so much more.

But then, sitting in the coffee shop on campus -- our go-to hangout place -- she twirled her light hair into a bun at the top of her head, let it fall down her back, and dropped her hands into her lap, looking over at me.

"I *know* it was 'just a dream,'" she said with a sigh. "But you're always saying how important dreams are. You even made it the subject of your thesis. Can you just tell me what it means like you usually do?"

Then I sighed and took a sip of my chai tea. "Okay. One, the dream as a whole means you and Todd are getting pretty serious. And you really like him, but you're nervous, because last time you got close to this point with a guy, you got your heart broken, and it sucked. *But you like him.*"

As I was explaining all of this, she was nodding with this look in her eyes as if she never in a million years would have drawn that conclusion.

"And the teeth thing?" I continued, "That tells me you're afraid of where the relationship is headed. You don't want to grow up or go to the next level because you're scared. Losing teeth is a symbol for that, a fear of changes and growing older. So my advice...is that you just take things slow and see how you feel. It seems like things are going well for you and Todd. Don't feel like you have to rush into anything. Take a deep breath and enjoy it."

"Wow," she said. "You are *so* good with dreams! That is exactly what I've been worried about. But like I never would have gotten that. You just know *so much* about dreaming."

I smiled and sipped more of my drink.

If you only knew, Sophie. If you only knew, I thought as she began telling me about some craft she saw online that we just had to try sometime.

* * *

The clock ticked on and on, making me more and more anxious with each passing second.

What's taking so long? He shouldn't be in there this long, I thought, cracking each knuckle, a new nervous habit of mine.

I pulled out my phone and typed:

Jess, what's the holdup?

A beat later she responded:

I really can't do my job with you constantly checking in.

I began replying and barely typed out the word "but" when she texted again.

I thought putting you in separate rooms would help...

Jess, Zach, and I have been studying our dreams for the past year. We've been training and working together since high school, and we surprisingly all make a really great team.

Except for when Jess claims we "distract" each other, and she now won't let me in the room while Zach is dreaming.

I made my senior thesis focused on dream analysis, so we get to use some of the labs and equipment here at my university. This means we have access to computer programs, books, and the electrodes and monitors needed where we can evaluate brain wave activity and sleep patterns.

This is taking a while, I thought, knowing Jess was only monitoring one dream.

Even when a dream of yours feels like a whole day or hours, it's really only a couple of minutes.

Unless, of course, you're like me, and you're in a coma for three whole days. Then your dream feels like a month of craziness that never actually happened. But that's a different story, an illusion in my mind, an echo of the past, a very small part of who I am and what has made me *Addison Smith.*

I am a dreamer.

I live partly in this world, earth. And my mind is often in what we call the dream world. It is a vivid, color-filled place, everyone has been there before. It's where we all go -- briefly -- when our heads hit the pillow each night.

Some people, though, are "special," and a little piece of us resides in this other realm. It is ingrained in us, deep within the core of who we are.

I am one of these "special" people; as is my boyfriend since my junior year of high school, Zach Walker. He is an amazing, incredibly attractive young man who despite his rough upbringing is the kindest, most loving human being I know. Most dreamers have "gifts" or "powers," and his main one is view changing. He can make any nightmare seem like a dream with a smile, a flash of his beautiful blue eyes, or a touch. Just by holding my hand he can block out all of the bad dreams and fill my mind with only lovely things.

Apparently, I'm more special than most. I'm still trying to decide if this is a pro or a con in life. I'm told I'm a "natural" dreamer. Things that take Jess weeks to master, are skills I pick up in one try.

My main "gift" is dream-sharing. But if you ask me, it sounds more like a curse than a gift. If I'm thinking of a bad dream, I can transfer it directly into someone else's mind. *Great gift, right? Share my pain with others.*

But Zach is always telling me that his family always thought dream-sharing was a myth until he met me. I guess it's a very sought-after skill.

It also means my dreams are intense and often terrifying, so it doesn't always feel like a "gift."

Being a dreamer is--

Suddenly the door flew open and Jess yelled in, "I need you. Get in here."

"What?" I barely asked before I was already running into a small, all white room, staring at my boyfriend sitting in a chair like one you'd see at a dentist's office. It was a chair I myself sit in every other day while he waits in the other room.

He looked fine, sleeping soundly, face in neither a smile or a frown.

"I don't know what happened. It won't stop. Everything was fine and then..." Jess was saying, looking frazzled, which was very unusual for her, as I noticed the wild beeping coming from the monitor.

The beep is supposed to be steady.

"What happened?" I yelled at her over the noises.

"I don't know!"

"We have to wake him up," I said, pointing out the obvious.

"I tried. He won't snap out of it."

The beeping was not helping at all, I couldn't focus. *What happened? How do I fix this?*

The monitor showed his brain waves as being all over the place, erratic, crazy. Something was seriously wrong.

What I had learned in class about the human mind wouldn't help me now. No, this was in a dreamer's world, uncharted territory as far as most textbooks were concerned.

I rushed over and grabbed his wrists searching. His pulse was racing, *This is bad. This is very bad,* I thought or said, I wasn't sure.

"Zach," I tried, shaking him. "Wake up. Please."

Nothing.

I turned to Jess. "I'm going in."

"I can't let you do that," she said strongly.

"Seriously?" I put my hand out. "Give me those."

She reluctantly handed over a set of wires attached to the monitor, and I stuck them on my temples, pushing back my hair.

"Addie, don't do this," she begged.

"I have to." I climbed onto the chair beside him and closed my eyes.

My other "gift" is that I can dream myself into other people's dreams -- dream travel. I've used it before to save Zach in the dream world and many times in high school and more recently searching for answers about this life we live.

If Jess thought I wouldn't go in to try now, she's crazy.

I took a deep breath, pictured Zach, and was off, my mind soaring through the other realm trying to find the dreaming mind of the man I love before something tragic happened.

3

- Zach -
Monday, April 11ᵗʰ, 2022

My mom is still living at The Haven. That fact kills me every time I think of it. My mom doesn't need to be there. She doesn't *deserve* to be there.

It's weird to visit her.

I do because I love her -- I mean, she's my mother. But it's strange to picture a younger, more put-together version of her reading me stories or baking cookies while singing old songs and dancing around the kitchen, and then show up at The Haven and see her like *that.*

My mom loved to dance. She'd dance anywhere and everywhere -- whether music was playing or not. I remember seeing her dance in the living room with my dad when I was a kid. The older I got though, and the "sicker" she got, my dad wasn't there to dance with her as much. And when he was around, he'd say no and go into his den to read.

So, my mom would grab my hand and pull me around the living room. We'd dance and sing and laugh. She'd say over and over, "I just love this *and* I love *you*, Zachary."

When I was really young, I'd laugh and dance with her, just as happy as could be. But then I got a bit older, and I no longer thought it was "cool" for an eight-year-old boy to dance in circles with his mom. So, I'd act annoyed each time she asked me and tell her dancing was "dumb."

Then one day she stopped asking me altogether.

And soon, she wasn't there at all.

Now, I'm twenty-two, and I wish I hadn't acted that way. I wish I wouldn't have taken for granted any time with my mom, because I didn't realize how little time we had.

I know that I should be grateful. She's alive, after all. Some people actually *lose* their mom when they "lose" their mom.

But in a way -- and I know it's selfish -- but in a way, I feel like this is harder.

My mom has become the child. I didn't really think that would happen in my teens and early twenties; I didn't think I'd have to watch my mom act so childlike, so dependant, this soon.

Although, I guess that's better, to have some hope and some chance at a relationship after thinking she was dead for ten years.

Like I said before, I should be grateful...

But it's hard when she's sitting right in front of me like she is right now in her little room at The Haven. She sits and tells me stories, but she doesn't really know who I am. She thinks her son (me) died when he was eight. Meanwhile, I was told my mom had died when I was eight.

Mitch and my father really covered all their bases with that one. We both thought the other was dead. It was genius of them really, to come up with such a plan. It worked too. That's what sucks.

My father couldn't handle either of us.

So he ditched both of us.

He got my mother locked up for being insane and sent me off to live with my uncle, Mitch, claiming he was so filled with grief he needed some time away. Later, I found out he had no intention of ever coming back to raise his eight-year-old boy. Nope. He had already signed the papers "granting" Mitch guardianship of me.

When I first found out about all of this I was furious. At everyone. At Mitch. At my dad. At my mom, mostly. How could she go along with pretending to be dead? Why didn't she ever call?

Which I now know is because she thought I was dead and was constantly getting a ton of medications that kept her in a daze.

That's cruel, I'd think. *Who does something like that?*

But later I realized why they told her what they did.

My mother loved me; I know she did. And if she loved me even *half* as much as I love Addison, I know she wouldn't have gone down without a fight. Her dreams were bad, and she needed help from The Haven. They knew she wouldn't have gone if there was any chance at all of her being able to stay home and help me with my dreams. She never would've gone otherwise. I wouldn't go. I would never leave Addison.

Now, I have the chance to make new memories, even if my mom doesn't remember them tomorrow. So I visit her as often as I can; and some days, like today, Addison comes with me.

And I try to take the chances I have with Addison to dance with her, like at the school dances or during a snow squall in the town square. I know how much my mom loved it when my dad would dance with her, and I can tell Ad loves dancing, too. So I dance with her. Even if that seems "dumb" or "not cool." I dance with her because it makes her smile -- and man, I love that girl's smile.

Like right now, when she flashes a smile at me and holds my hand a little tighter.

"That's such a sweet story, Mrs. Walker. Your son sounds so great."

I shake my head, bringing my mind back to the present, where Ad and I are visiting my mom, and my mom has been telling us the same few stories over and over.

I didn't even have to hear the story to know it was yet another one about me as a little kid, because she still doesn't know who I am now, or maybe she won't let herself believe it's true.

"He was!" Mom agrees, smiling to Ad.

Then, quickly, the smile fades, and her face becomes serious.

"What's wrong, Mrs. Walker?" Ad asks, leaning closer to her.

My mom looks around as if she's afraid someone will hear or walk through the door at any minute.

She leans toward us and whispers, "Are they coming for me now?"

"Who? The nurses?" I ask.

"No. *They.*"

"Who is 'they'?"

"You know," she says. "*Them.*" She looks around, still seeming scared, and nods at me like it is so obvious and I should know who she's talking about.

But I don't know.

Each time we are here she starts going on and on about "they" and "them" and that we should "be careful because they are dangerous."

Then, just when we are close to getting a real answer out of her, she starts shaking and yelling. Then her nurse runs in, pushing us out the door, saying mom's just late for her nap and daily medication, "that's all."

Every.

Single.

Time.

So now I just have one question:

Is this "they" she screams about real, or is she just crazier than I thought she was?

Either way, I'm worried...

4

- Addison -
Tuesday, April 12th, 2022

*H*e is dreaming about his mom when I find him. It doesn't take long to locate his mind within the dream world. Just like it doesn't take long to find his face in a crowd. But, man, today felt like forever searching for him, even though it was seconds.

I panicked. The monitor was going all crazy, and Zach wasn't responding. Each second felt like minutes; each minute felt like hours.

In his dream now, he is really young, maybe six or so? His mom, stunning and happy, is picking him up and spinning around a little kitchen with pink and blue tiled floors and white cabinets.

I wait and watch the dream Zach is seeing in his mind right now, trying to figure out what about this dream set his mind off a minute ago.

It seems like a good dream to me.

But then she sits him down on the countertop, his little legs swinging and kicking the cabinets, making his tennis shoes light up blue and red.

"Now, listen to me, Zachary," she orders in a very chipper voice. She sounds like she's talking to an infant about puppies or something cute and happy like that. But then she continues, in a happy-as-ever voice, "You watch out for those mean people, okay? Don't let them take you. Okay?"

"Okay, mama," he says, looking happy.

What people? I wonder.

"You'll tell me if they're mean to you, won't you?"

"Yes, mama," he responds.

"Good. You're all I have, baby," she says with a tear in her eye.

"Don't be sad," he tells her, compassionate as always.

"I'm okay," she reassures him, not looking "okay."

"Can I go play with my cars now?"

She chuckles, "Yes, sweetheart."

He hops down and runs into the other room. She turns, opens a white cabinet, and pulls out a yellow pill bottle with a white twist cap. She quickly twists off the lid and drops one into her hand.

Oh, no, I think, praying she isn't going down the same path Sandy and so many other dreamers take. *You can't do this, I plead,* knowing she can't hear me. *You can't leave Zach; he needs you. Don't take the pills.*

It's as if she hears me, even though I know she doesn't. She clutches the pill in her shaking hand and takes two steps to the left, reaches out, and opens her hand. The white pill drops from her grasp and falls down the sink. She turns on the faucet, water rushing out, and then flips a switch on the wall. The garbage disposal whirs to life, grinding the pill out of existence.

Something tells me to look at the rest of the dream, so I look all around, taking the whole room in.

Then I spot him.

He's hiding behind the post in the doorway to the other room, just watching quietly.

Meg turns around, and he dashes out of sight as she simply walks to the refrigerator and gets groceries out to start cooking dinner, never realizing her son was watching.

"That's when she was at her best," I hear from behind me.

I turn around and see Zach standing there, a hazy grey filling the space around him. His eyes are brighter in the dream world -- as if that is possible -- but they're even brighter and blue-er in dreams. And right now they shine, and he almost shines, too.

"What do you mean?" I ask him. "Why are we here?"

"She stopped taking the pills. She said they made her 'feel funny.' But my dad got mad because he saw the pill bottle was still full weeks later. He yelled at her one night saying we didn't have the money for all her medical stuff, especially if she was going to just let them sit there and not do any good. He told her she had to take them. They would make her 'normal.' I was watching then, too, and she looked so defeated. He slid the bottle across the table and sat there until she took one. Then he got up and walked into the office to go work, and she walked over to the sink and spit it down the drain. Then she did that every day. From time to time he'd shake the pill bottle to make sure she was taking them. And since the pills kept disappearing, he thought she was taking them. But she wasn't.

And that's when she was at her best and happiest. She was more like the mom I knew before. I forgot about it, though. Until just now. It's the pills."

Now, he was looking past me, watching the dream continue. We had been here for a while, longer than we usually go into a dream when we are experimenting like this.

"Zach, I think we should go," I warn.

He just nods and starts walking into the grey haze.

"Zach," I call, following him.

We woke up laying on this big reclining chair like one you'd see in a dentist's office. I blinked and quickly tried to adjust to switching realms so quickly.

"Oh my gosh! Are you two okay? I was freaking out!" Jess yelled, rushing over to us.

"I'm fine," Zach said. He sounded so rough and harsh.

I turned and gave him a look.

"What?" he asked in a tone equally as annoyed as before.

"Are you okay?" I asked him.

He ripped the wires from his head and abruptly got out of the chair.

"I said I'm fine. I'll see you tomorrow," he said to me, softer on the last part.

"Zach, come on. What just happened--"

"I need to go somewhere. I'll see you tomorrow."

Then he left.

"Okay, what was that?" Jess asked me as she pulled a stool out from under the metal desk beside her and sat down. "Trouble in paradise?" she joked, raising her precisely and perfectly done eyebrow at me.

"I have no clue what just happened," I admitted, removing my own wires.

"Well...maybe give him some time to cool off and be alone. Memory dreams can be traumatic and hard to process." She stood up and grabbed her sparkly notebook. "Ready to get started with your session?"

"Shouldn't I go check on him?" I more-so said than asked.

"I wouldn't. Just give him some time and call him later."

"Okay, I guess you're right."

I sat back in the chair, and Jess began asking questions about my dreams this past week and checking things off her list. But I wasn't focused. My mind was on Zach and the fear I had when that monitor went all crazy before.

Loving someone is scary. It's even more terrifying when you don't know what to do to help them. Or if you even can.

* * *

On my way home that night, I decided to stop by my Aunt Carrie's new townhome not too far from campus.

I walked up the many steep steps and knocked on her cherry colored front door. "Your front door is your first impression to people visiting or driving by," she'd always explain, "and I want mine to scream 'A fun-loving, wild-child lives here!'"

A beat later, the front porch light flipped on, illuminating the space around me. As I heard the lock clicking open, I could see -- and hear-- her new puppy jumping and pawing at the side-light window.

"Well, this is a lovely surprise!" my aunt said, pulling me in for a hug the second the door swung open. "How is my favorite girl?"

Daisy, her fluffy little snowball-looking dog, barked.

"I'm sorry," Carrie said to Daisy. To me, she added, "She's a sensitive dog, this one. I think she's just jealous of you. I told her she was my favorite girl this morning on our walk. Now, she hears me saying it to you. Poor thing." Aunt Carrie shook her head and looked at the puppy with pity, which is funny because that dog honestly has the best life.

I bent down and scratched the top of Daisy's soft head. "Hi, Daisy," I cooed.

"I just made a pot of macaroni and cheese! You are just in time!" she said excitedly and pulled me into the kitchen, telling me to make myself at home.

I sat down and took off my cardigan while she pulled two bright blue bowls out of the oak cupboard.

"So," she started, divvying up the noodles, scooping every last bit into the bowls, "to what do I owe this wonderful surprise visit?"

I reached out, taking the bowl from her. "Thanks," I said, not realizing until right then how hungry I had been. "I knew you'd have food," I told her.

"Addie, is everything okay?" she asked and took her seat across from me.

"Yes."

But then I realized lying to her, and myself, wouldn't get me anywhere. "No," I replied with a sigh.

"Tell me," she said, not in a demanding way, but in a firm you-can-trust-me sort of way.

It was great to finally be able to talk to Carrie about dreams after the trip a few years ago. That trip changed a lot of things, but one major change was my relationship with my aunt. We were a lot closer now than we had ever been. So, if I could talk to anyone about all of this and have them understand, it was her.

"Things went...wrong today," I began. Then I recalled everything that happened in Zach's dream and right after.

After I told her all of this, she was quiet for a bit.

"What 'mean people' was Meg referring to?" I asked Aunt Carrie.

Instead of actually answering my question, she replied with another question, "Do you remember Becky?"

I nodded.

Of course I remembered Becky. How could I forget her?

5

- Addison -
Sunday, June 10th, 2018

*M*om, Jess, Aunt Carrie, and I are strolling down the streets of a little town in southern France. We've been here for three days now. It's the most incredible place! I can't find the right words to describe the feeling you have just walking these streets. It's like setting foot on the sanctuary makes you feel lighter, like whatever burden you've been carrying around is just lifted instantly and completely. I feel...whole here.

I haven't had a single nightmare the whole time we've been here, you know. Aunt Carrie says it's good, that I needed a detox within my mind, a break from it all.

That might be the best thing that came from this trip so far -- being able to talk to her. It's like Carrie showing up opened this door for us. I feel like we can talk about dreams now. In three days, she's already told me more about dreaming and her past than she's ever said my entire life.

"Oh, my gosh! Look how beautiful these are!" Jess called, pulling us over with her to a little shop set up on the side of the street.

She placed something in my hand, it was cool to the touch. I picked it up between two fingers and let the string dangle down, holding it out in front of me. They were rosary beads; beautiful, sparkling rosary beads, with pearls and colorful gems.

"These are incredible," Jess told the young girl, who was manning the booth, in perfect sounding French.

"Merci," the girl replied with a sheepish smile.

"Where are these from?" Jess asked her.

The girl began a conversation with Jess, while I looked at the other things she had to sell.

I was still holding the blue rosary in my hands, when I found another one, just like the first, but in different shades of pink. I gently picked that one up as well.

Jess came over to me a second later. "She made all of these herself," she said. "Can you believe that? She's only fourteen."

"Seriously? These are amazing."

I decided to buy the pink one for myself because I really liked the colors. I couldn't put the blue one down though. I handed the girl, Nicolette, Jess says her name is, both rosaries.

She looks at me, overjoyed. "Thank you, Miss," she says.

There's a twinkle in her eyes, not just happiness, something else. I wonder if maybe she's a dreamer too.

I'm not sure what I'll do with the second rosary, but I tuck it in my pocket for now.

* * *

As we continue our walk down the brick streets on our way back to where they have the healing waters, Aunt Carrie surprises me and just starts talking; about dreams, about being with Mitch before, about her own trip years ago, about everything.

The three of us walk slowly beside her, hanging on every word. You can tell my mom wasn't expecting this either. You could also tell she never realized just how bad things had gotten for her little sister. You could almost hear her heart breaking for Carrie in that moment.

"How did you do it?" Jess asks. "How did you get rid of them?"

Aunt Carrie just looks at Jess with a sad smile. "Did I?"

It's the most cryptic thing my aunt has ever said. "Did I?" What does that even mean? For years all I've heard is that Carrie got rid of her dreams. Carrie made them stop. If you're a dreamer, you either leave that world entirely and get rid of the dreams (which I still don't know how to do), or you go insane. I've always been told my aunt was one of the lucky ones -- that she had this secret, like the fountain of youth but for dreamers, and everyone wanted to know what it was.

No one says anything. You can tell we all want to say something, but we don't know what that something is.

"We had better hurry up, girls," my aunt tells us, as if she did not just throw the biggest plot twist nonchalantly into our conversation. "We don't want to miss our time slot."

So, we all follow her down the sloping hill, past the beautiful church, around the bend with the statue in the mountainside, and over to the baths.

All of the websites and travel guides said that you cannot come here without bathing in the special and holy waters. These waters are known for their healing, and God only knows my mind could use some of that.

As we sit on the cold, metal benches waiting for our turn, I look all around me, watching the people who take the seats here as well. Everyone has something in their lives that needs some healing. I may not know everyone's story, but I do know they have one. So I sit, and I watch. And as I see people being pushed in wheelchairs or walking with prosthetics or even those who sit on the benches with a look on their face that this place is their last hope, I'm thankful for everything I *do* have in my life.

A woman sitting across from me waiting her turn catches my eye. Her hands are folded in her lap, and she is praying, mouthing her prayer quietly to herself. Her hands shake a bit as she prays. Her eyes are closed shut and tight, like she's focusing really hard. Her long, wavy black hair falls down over her shoulders, and she reaches up to brush it back behind her ear.

I wonder what her story is, I think to myself. Why is she here? What does she need healing for?

I'm still watching her a minute later when her prayer is done. She unclasped her hands and opens her eyes.

And in that instant her eyes lock with mine from across the open area.

Oh, no, I think, worried she saw me and knows I was staring. That was so rude of me, I think.

But I'm fixed in place, my eyes never leaving hers.

So then why won't I stop staring?

Her mouth turns up at the corners, forming a slight smile. She seems so welcoming and kind. I know nothing about this woman, but I can tell that she is kind, that her soul and heart, though broken, still manage to pour out light and goodness.   There's something about this woman...

A volunteer tells the woman just then that it is her turn, her time slot, her chance for healing.

She gets up, still holding eye contact with me, and smiles. Then she looks up at the sky and mouths the word "please." And then she's gone, walking into the building that houses the baths filled with the waters.

"Addie?"

I shake my head. "Sorry, what?"

"You okay?" my mom asks.

"Yeah, I'm fine."

But I'm not fine. I need to know more about that lady. I need to know what she knows, what her story is, and why she seemed so...familiar. It isn't like I've met her before; I doubt that I have. It's more like I feel like I know her, even without knowing her.

An hour later, we're sitting outside where a service is about to begin. Jess is telling my mom what she thought of the baths.

Aunt Carrie nudges my arm with her elbow. "Hey, kiddo."

"Hey," I reply, only half paying attention. I'm still in a daze.

"What do you think?"

"Of what?"

"Of the baths? Of this place? What are you thinking about?"

"I'm not sure. It was weird."

"Weird?" she asks.

"Not bad weird. Weird like... out of body experience for a minute. I can't describe it. Good weird though."

"Hmmm."

"Hmmm, what?"

"Do you feel any different?"

"Aunt Carrie," I say, "I don't think it's an instantaneous cure. I mean, maybe for those stories we heard for physical healings, but I don't think they all are. I mean, I don't feel any different."

"Really?"

I don't say anything. I just look at her.

She looks away, turning to face the front, as the music starts playing. "I do."

What does that mean? I wonder.

But before I have much more time to ponder this, I see movement out of the corner of my eye. I see the woman from before, taking her seat in a pew.

"I'll be right back," I whisper to my aunt without even knowing what I'm doing or where I'm going.

I walk over and stop to the side of the pew the lady is sitting in. The woman looks up and smiles. I point to the open seat next to her and she nods.

"Bonjour," I say.

She just nods again.

In as good of French as I can manage, I ask her how she is, where she's from, and if she speaks any English.

She says that she is good and thanks me for asking. She's from not too far from the town. And she does know some English and begins to talk with me in that way.

"I'm Addison," I offer.

"I am Becky."

"Hi, Becky. It's very nice to meet you."

"And you, Addison. What brings you here?" she asks.

"I guess I was looking for a miracle."

"Sometimes you can't go looking for miracles. You have to let them find you," she says.

I shift in my seat, unsure what to say, and I feel the rosary, scrunched up in my pocket. I pull it out and unfold it.

"Here," I tell her, gently placing the beads in her hands.

"Why? Why me?" she asks after a minute or two just looking at the rosary.

"I want you to have it. A gift. I--"

Before I can finish she rests her hand on my arm and says, "Thank you, Addison, for your kindness."

In that moment she locks eyes with me again, and I realize what it is that made her seem so familiar.

It's that twinkle in her eye, that light and darkness that's common in people who have a gift, but that gift sometimes brings heartache.

Her hand is still resting on my arm when she closes her eyes.

My mind is filled with dozens of images. A garden of vegetables. A family, with her sitting amongst three children who all have her smile. A graveyard. A boat. Her shivering in the cold. Her looking in a mirror, with someone standing right over her shoulder, their face covered by a mask or the shadow from a hood or something.

I blink and stare at her, my eyes wide and my jaw on the floor.

"I-I –" I stammer but cannot find any words.

"Take care of yourself," the woman says with a knowing grin.

She knows about me, too.

She holds up the rosary, "I will pray for miracles to find you, Addison Grace."

Chills run up my spine as I realize I never told her my full name, just my first.

I can't even say anything. I'm so stunned. Years from now, I know I'll look back on this moment and kick myself for not asking her more questions, finding out more about her and her dreams. But I'll never be able to change the fact that in this moment, I just sit there as the lady, Becky, gets up and walks away, taking my rosary, and some of my dreams with her.

She wasn't just a dreamer, I realize. She was a dream-sharer.

She was just like me.

I stand slowly, watching the procession pass me and continue down the aisle. Then I walk back to my seat, slide in beside my aunt, and say, "I need to tell you something."

6

- Zach -

Tuesday, April 12ᵗʰ, 2022

*T*hat's it, that has to be it, I thought, putting my car in drive and jamming my foot on the pedal. I drove and drove, speeding down the route I took every week to go see my mom.

I can't believe how long it's taken me to figure this out!

It's got to be the medication they have her on. Of course, at a place like that there would be something twisted going on. It's just like it was back with the pills before. Dad would flip out if she didn't take them, saying she was only hurting herself and that she'd just keep getting worse without them. But she was getting better. He said it was the pills. But it wasn't the pills. It was her not taking the pills.

I need to get her out of there.

The light in front of me changed to red, like it passed right over yellow just to stop me. And of course, the light stayed red for what seemed like forever.

Come on! I slammed my hands on the steering wheel.

Finally, it turned green, and I sped off and turned down the street that led to my mother's "home" for the past fifteen years. But this "home" is killing her, slowly. Breaking her spirit and wiping away her memory.

Those pills keep her numb, unaware of what's going on around her. She's in her own little world.

I find a spot right away -- there's never anyone here, and I threw the car in park, jumped out, and rushed in the door.

"Mr. Walker, you don't usually come on Tuesdays?" the receptionist said with a questioning look and a cautious tone. I knew I must have looked insane, the way I ran in here, when I usually walked in with a smile and donuts. She probably had her hand reaching for some button, just in case I said something crazy. Just in case I turned out to be exactly like my mom, and this was just the start of it. Just in case she needed backup and the men in the white scrubs would come out and hold me down and bring me to my own room here at The Haven.

"I need to see my mom."

"Visiting hours are over, Mr. Walker," she said, not in a stern way, but in a confused way, as if I should know this by now, after visiting for so long.

"I need to see my mom," I said again.

"Mr. Walker, I'm sorry, but I cannot let you go back to Mrs. Walker's room. She's just gone down for her nap."

Just gone down for her nap? This woman is talking like my mom is a three-year-old.

I started walking toward the door, the one I know she has to buzz me in to. I tried the door knob anyway, maybe it was open. No luck.

"Mr. Walker," she said more forcefully than I have ever heard or thought possible. "You need to leave. Now."

"No, I need to see my mom. Now."

And then she did it, she hit the button behind the desk.

Within seconds two guys came out from behind the door. But they weren't in their scrubs here to admit me. No, they were in their security uniforms.

They stood there for a second, arms folded across their chests, staring me down and trying to assess the situation.

"Fine," I huffed, and lead myself out so they wouldn't have to.

I needed a plan. I needed a way to get her out of there, to help her. And I was worried I didn't have much time.

* * *

I walked over to my dresser and pulled open the second drawer. Sitting on top of my t-shirts was the notebook.

After I talked with Mr. and Mrs. Smith and they gave me their blessing to propose to Ad, Mrs. Smith told me she had "the perfect thing". I wasn't really sure what she was getting, maybe it was some family heirloom for Addison? I had no clue. But I wasn't expecting her to come back and hand me a small composition notebook.

"Here," she had said, placing it in my hands. "I think it's time you read this."

"What is it?" I asked her, looking at the black and white cover, with the words *"Addison's Hopes & Dreams"* written neatly in Addison's slanted handwriting in the little white box in the center of the cover.

"Take it home and read it. She showed me this a couple years ago. I never knew she had it until then. She's been writing in it since she was fourteen, she said. It's got everything you need to know for your future together. I think it's time you have it."

I just stared at it for a minute. "Will she know?"

Mrs. Smith, knowing what I meant, shook her head. "No," she said. "She keeps it under her bed, but she rarely adds to it anymore, almost all the pages are filled up anyway. I don't think she'll notice for a bit."

"Okay," I said, still not sure what this notebook was all about. But I took it home anyway.

It's been two days, and I hadn't read it yet. But now seemed like a good time, I needed a distraction.

So I grabbed the book, walked over to my bed and sat down.

I opened it up to the first page.

This dream journal belongs to:

Addison Grace Smith

Below that was a list of years, the handwriting changing as they went on, and I assumed it was all the years she added to this book.

Under that it said:

Thank you, God, for my amazing life. And thank you for everything you have in store for my future, no matter what it is.

Then I started flipping through the pages. At first I assumed this would be her dreams she's had, a book where she wrote down all the nightmares and good dreams, too, that she's had over the years, a list of dream meanings and interpretations, because I know she gets into that stuff.

But no, as I turned the pages of her notebook, I realized that these were her dreams for the future. Hopes and wishes she's had over the years. Pictures of dresses with the word "prom" written in bubble letters across the top of the page. One of them actually looked pretty similar to the dress she wore. *She looked amazing in that dress,* I thought as I flipped to the next page.

"My dream house!" it said with a date next to it from 2014. There were printed out pictures of light blue houses with darker blue trim and shutters. They all had white picket fences and big trees in the front yard. It made sense that she'd want a house like that. That girl loved blue, anything blue made her happy. *I want to get her that house,* I decided. *I want to get her a house like these ones to make her happy.*

Throughout the other pages there were quotes she liked and pictures from high school of her and Cammie or her and I. Pictures of her family, the ocean, her trip to Europe.

A list of places she wanted to visit on one page and a map of the world with stars to mark the places she'd been on the opposite page.

There was a page with her favorite movies and books.

Looking at this was... really awesome. It's like Addison, and everything she wants in life and loves is all over these pages. I pictured her sitting in her room cutting out all these pictures and pages from magazines and filling this book with her ideas for the future. I think it's really cute she did this, and I'm really happy her mom gave it to me.

Then I turned to the next page. "For when I say yes," it said it cursive writing across the top.

There were pictures on the page of engagement rings. There were a few different styles, but they were all silver and had a similar look.

She had her ring size written in the corner of the page, and it was highlighted in pink highlighter. I let out a laugh. Only Addison would have a detailed book, with exactly what she's looking for in a ring, down to the size. *That makes this easier for me!*

The rest of the pages had pictures of grad schools she had looked into with a star by the one she's attending this fall. There were shoes and purses she must like. Couches, tables, and other things were on a page she titled "Things for My Dream House." Pictures of little kid's clothes and other kids' things filled another page.

I decided I would go look around for rings tomorrow. Addison had clinicals and wouldn't be asking to meet me anyway. I would go to my usually planned visit with my mom, calmer this time, and then I'd go get my girl her dream ring.

7

- Addison -
Tuesday, April 12th, 2022

"**S**he was a dream sharer, just like me," I told Aunt Carrie, now back from my dream memory and sitting at her kitchen table with a still-steaming bowl of macaroni and cheese in front of me.

"How could you tell?" she pressed.

"I could see it in her eyes. Then she showed me dreams."

"But how can you be sure?"

"I'm sure."

"But how," she asked again, with a slight grin on her face.

"I can't explain it. I could just tell."

"And there are others."

"Other dreamers?" I asked.

"Well, yes, of course. There's at least twenty in our town alone." Twenty? Who were the others?

She continued, "There's other dream sharers though. I mean, we had heard about them growing up. I had never seen dream sharing in action until you though. But I don't know why I always assumed that was it. That there were no other dream sharers."

"Do you think there's more?" I asked.

"Sure, I do. You just haven't met them yet."

I was about to ask how I would find these people when Aunt Carrie spoke again, "Do you know how I found out about you?"

Found out about me?

I shook my head.

"Well, you were about five. Maybe six. You were telling me about these dreams you had been having about clowns--"

"I hated clowns!"

"I know you did," she agreed. "So I would ask you questions about them, when your mom left the room or a few times when I picked you up from kindergarten in the afternoon. Annie would have flipped if she thought I was putting that 'crazy dream nonsense' in your head when you were so little. But I had to know if my suspicions were right."

"What suspicions?"

"You know how you said you could just feel it, that Becky was a dreamer?"

"Yeah..."

"The day you were born, I was so excited. I stopped by the store and got more pink balloons than I could fit in my little car at the time. I came rushing in the hospital room, with ten thousand pink 'It's a Girl!' balloons trailing behind me. And there you were, cradled in your mom's arms. Both your mom and dad didn't even notice I came in. They were so enamored with you, not even an hour after you got here. It wasn't until your grandpa looked at me and asked if I had bought every balloon the store had and where would they put so many balloons in this little room, that your parents even looked up. I told them congratulations, and they told me your name -- I had suggested 'Grace' by the way for a middle name -- and then I got to hold you. My first little niece. You were so teeny-tiny and perfect, and I held you as you slept. But then you started to wake up, and I got really nervous because I hadn't really even held a baby 'til you showed up. But then you opened your eyes and looked right at me. I couldn't pull my eyes away from yours. You didn't cry either. You had just woken up, but you didn't cry yet. You just stared right back. And that's when I knew -- I could feel it with everything inside of me. You were a dreamer, and you were special. Then your mom, taking you back, said 'Isn't she special? Isn't she just a dream?' and I thought to myself, 'You have no idea, big sister.'"

"You could tell that early on?"

"You are a dreamer, Addison. That's not some magic power that is bestowed on you on your sixteenth birthday at the strike of midnight. It's ingrained in you, a part of you. It's been there your whole life."

"Well, I don't know if I want it."

"Oh, don't say that."

"Everyone always says I'm special because of what I can do. But what good is any of this if I can't do anything about it or make anything better?"

"But you can, Addison Grace. Don't you get that?"

"How can I, Aunt Carrie? I've been a dreamer my whole life you say and still I know nothing. I haven't done anything."

"But you have so much potential. Come on, Sweet Pea, I need you to see that for a minute."

"Aunt Carrie--"

"No, listen to me. You've been given a gift. And you, my dear, out of all the people on this planet, have the grace and the compassion to do something about the way the world is."

"But what do I do?"

"You'll know what to do when the time comes."

"How?"

She smiled. "The same way you knew Becky was a dreamer. The same way you knew Zach was your person. The same way you knew you could trust Jess again. The same way you knew I was a dreamer too, from that very first moment. You'll just feel it. You'll know."

Yeah, but that doesn't help me right now, I thought.

As always, it was like Carrie could read my thoughts because then she said, "I know that doesn't help you right now. But give it time, and it will. I believe in you-- more than I believe in many other things on this earth. You're going to move mountains, Addison. You just have to believe first that you have that power, that ability, that heart to do that." She pointed to her mind and tapped her head three times, then did the same over her heart. "Don't think about it too much. Just dream. Dream with your heart first, then think it through."

What am I going to do? I wondered. How am I, just Addison Smith, supposed to move mountains?

Dream with your heart first, her words echoed in my mind the rest of the night.

So later that night, back at home, I laid my head down on my worn, blue pillowcase and closed my eyes.

Dream with your heart, she had said.

Ok, I thought, and cleared my mind of everything that was weighing it down. I focused on breathing, in and out, in and out, until I fell asleep, dreaming with my heart first, and a clear mind.

8

- Zach -
Wednesday, April 20th, 2022

Today I stopped by The Haven. It wasn't a time I usually visit, but I know it's within visiting hours at least. My one class got cancelled this afternoon, and I was really happy about that. But then I realized my mom's whole life now is one big schedule. I've even gotten in the habit of visiting at the same time on the same days.

She never gets surprises anymore. She used to love surprises.

So today I stopped by at a random time with flowers for her. *Hopefully she likes these,* I thought, as I picked some out at the local supermarket. They were pink, and I remembered she always liked pink.

"Mr. Walker?" the receptionist asked, looking surprised.

"Hi, Kelly." I reached forward and took the sign-in sheet.

As I was signing my name and writing down my information as I always did, she said, "It's not *Tuesday* or *Saturday*. It's Wednesday, sir."

"I know," I said nonchalant. I glanced up at her. "How's she doing?"

"Pretty well, today, I think."

"That's good," I replied with a nod and then went back to filling out the form.

As I wrote the final digits of my phone number, I saw something -- something I never thought I'd see-- printed right above the seven I was writing.

I froze as I read the combination of letters and numbers -- a combination that matched exactly the letters and numbers I associated with one person.

Visitor:	Contact:	Resident Visiting:
James Kenneth	931-555-2632	Sally Kenneth
Mitch DeMize	787-555-8191	Meg Walker
Zach Walker	787-555-317-----------------------	

Mitch was here?
Mitch is in town?
Why would he come here?
When did he come here?

I looked over at the time and date stamped beside his name. *Today. Around ten this morning.*

What was he doing here at ten this morning?

"Sir?" the receptionist asked.

I shook my head and looked up. "Yes?"

"You can go back now," she told me. Then I saw that the door was already wide open, waiting for me to go back. I hadn't even heard the buzzing noise when it opened. I wondered how long I had been standing there like that.

I pulled my phone out of my pocket, pretending to check something, and quickly snapped a picture of the visitors list while the receptionist was looking for her timestamp.

"Thanks," I said and handed her the clipboard.

Then I stood up tall and walked through the doorway-- the same doorway my uncle walked through earlier today.

* * *

"So," I started, leaning forward trying to keep her attention focused. "Tell me about your mother."

I knew from Mitch that the gene for dreaming (if there truly is one) got passed on to him and my mother through their mother. Their father was apparently a horrible man, very unkind, especially when it came to my grandmother's dreams and nightmares. Mitch said my grandmother was crazy, that her dreams had gotten the better of her pretty early on, but that he loved her anyway. She was his mom after all. And trust me, sitting in a place like this, with my mother acting the way she was, I knew the feeling.

"My mother?" she repeated.

"Yes. What was her name? What did she look like?" I asked.

"Her name was Mary," she told me with a far-away-look to her eyes, as if she truly was looking past me into her past. "Oh," my mom said, reaching up and running a hand through the ends of her hair. "my mother had the prettiest hair. Jet black and straight. She looked like she had walked out of a dream."

As she said the word "dream," I could see her eyes fill with fear.

I searched quickly for a safe topic. "What was she like?"

"She was kind. So kind. She had a lovely voice, too. She would sing me to sleep when I was little. Beautiful songs and rhymes."

This seemed to be working, I thought to myself. She was doing much better with questions from her past than right now. Maybe I could get more answers this way. Start further back and work my way to now.

"What songs were they?" I asked.

She thought about it for a few minutes, sitting there on the edge of her bed with the tip of her finger pressed to her lips as she thought. "My sweet little baby," she began to sing, quietly.

Immediately, with the tune and the words, I recognized the song as one she had sang to me when I was little.

"I dreamed of you for oh so long," she sang. "Now you're here, a dream come true, oh my child how I dreamed for you."

She rocked back and forth with her eyes closed tight as she sang this song to me, just like she had years ago.

I had forgotten about that song. It was so long ago that I had heard it, after all.

Her eyes snapped open. "Do you know my brother?" she asked me, looking excited.

"Yes, I do."

"Oh! Good! He is a good man. Isn't he a good man?"

I tried so hard to bite my tongue, not to say anything, just nod and agree with her. *Good man? Yeah, sure.*

"My brother was the only person who cared about me."

"It sounds like your mother cared about you a lot," I pointed out.

"No..."

I waited, wondering if she would add more or just leave it at that.

Finally, she spoke, "Well, she used to care about me. But then she couldn't. It wasn't her fault. They took her spirits. They took her heart. And finally, they took her."

This was my chance!

"They?"

"Yes, *they.*"

"Who is *they?*"

"Don't you know?" she shook her head, like something was such a pity. "Well, if you know my brother, you certainly know who they are."

What?!

"Why do you say that?" I questioned.

"Well, he went off to find them. I'm sure he did."

"Went off to find who?"

"Them!" my mother almost yelled. "The mean and horrible people who I know took my son away! I know it!"

"Is Mitch working with them?"

"Oh, no! Heavens no! He went to stop them. Someone needed to stop them."

"What were they doing?" I asked once she had seemed to calm down a bit.

"They are the people who haunt the dreams of dreamers, turn their dreams into nightmares. That's their job. Everyone who dreams like us knows who they are."

"Dreams like us?"

"Yes, boy. Keep up."

I was shocked at this change in personality that was happening. She was getting annoyed with me for not knowing the answers. However, the more frustrated she was getting, the more information she was telling me. Even if it was slipping out accidentally, every bit helped.

She continued, "Dreamers like us. You dream. I dream. We all dream. Some of us just dream the right way. Some of us don't."

I had never said anything about dreaming to her, never told her I was a dreamer.

"How do you know I dream like you?" I asked her.

"What a silly question!" she huffed.

"I'm sorry?"

Was I mistaken? Did I tell her I dreamed like I do and I just don't remember it?

Then she reached out and wrapped her frail fingers around my wrist. Her hands were so cold, like ice. But that wasn't the weirdest thing about what she did.

The weirdest thing about it was that when she wrapped her hand around my arm, a picture popped in my head.

It was a younger version of herself with long curled hair and a nice dress on. Mitch was there and so were what I assumed would be my grandparents. Mitch looked so much like his father, and my mom looked more like a combination of the two of them. Her eyes though, were exactly like her mom's.

Then my mom pulled her hand away. "See," she said simply.

I did see. I saw what she had dreamt once before or a scene that was a memory of hers.

I did see something I had never seen or realized before.

My mother was a dream-sharer.

Just like Addison.

Someone with the types of natural skills my uncle spent years searching for, and here my mother was one of them all along.

No way, I thought. *This is crazy.*

But then a thought hit me. I know the way dream sharing works because of Addison. She just showed me a dream. But Addison can show dreams to non-dreamers. She's shown them to her mom and Cammie many times. The fact that my mom just shared a dream with me doesn't mean I'm a dreamer.

"What did you just do?" I asked, playing stupid, wanting her to explain it to me.

"I stole one of your dreams."

"Huh?"

"You must really love this girl," she said, ignoring the fact that what she had just said was crazy. "Protect her then. Make sure they don't come for her."

Then the door opened a crack and my mom's nurse Nancy popped her head in. "Meg, I have your medicine."

"Oh, alright," my mom agreed, sitting up straighter and cracking her knuckles.

I reached in my pocket, grabbing the little box I had in my pocket.

Could I really swap it out without her noticing? I wondered, eyeing the nurse.

She set a grey tray down on the night stand by my mom's bed. On it was a bowl of red gelatin, a glass of water, a napkin, a spoon, and a small paper cup with a single white pill resting inside.

Do it, Zach, I told myself. *This was the plan all along. It's the pills. You know it's the pills making her this way.*

Nurse Nancy turned around to grab the clipboard of notes from the bottom of my mom's bed. She clicked her pen a few times then tapped it against the clipboard.

"How are we today?" she asked, still looking at the notes.

"Good," my mother replied.

Of course "good" because you haven't had your "medicine" yet today, I thought.

I pulled the box quietly from my pocket and shook out one small white mint. The mints were shaped similarly to the pill.

I stuck the mint in the cup and took the pill in my hand, wrapping my fingers around it and sliding my hand back into my pocket.

I looked up just as Nancy was finishing her notes.

"Good, I'm glad, Meg," she told my mom with a smile. "Take your medicine, dear," she ordered.

Please don't say anything. I crossed my fingers she would just take the "pill" and not point out that it was different.

She did, as I had hoped. She took it.

"Good. Thank you, dear," Nancy said, putting the clipboard back. "I'll be back in a bit, okay?"

"Okay," my mom repeated.

I forced a smile and a nod at Nancy as she left the room.

It has to be the pills, I told myself.

9

- Addison -
Thursday, April 21st, 2022

It was your typical Thursday night. After my night class ended --
early as always with Dr. Greene-- I stopped by Sal's to grab some
takeout. French fries, of course, and chicken tenders off the kid's
menu. Some nights you're just hungry for what you're hungry for, so
you order off the kid's menu for you and your boyfriend even though
you're both twenty-two.

I got back in my car, turned the key in the ignition, waited for
the car to warm up in this cold weather, and breathed in the warm,
comforting smell of Sal's.

Just what I need, I thought, trying to push away the thoughts of
my day and all the exams and papers I had coming up soon. *All of
that can wait for an hour.*

Ten minutes later I was pulling into parking spot 23B, which is
actually the space reserved for the older man who lives across the hall
from Zach. He doesn't have a car, so his parking space has kind of

become mine whenever I'm here. He said it was alright, but that might have been because I brought him over a batch of chocolate chip cookies a few weeks ago.

Not able to resist the wonderful smell any longer, I reached in the bag and took out a French fry. Just one, delicious, warm, salty fry. Then I scrunched the paper bag back down, grabbed my things, and headed inside.

"Hey, you," Zach greeted me at his door with a kiss and grin when he saw the bag of food. "Oh good! I was starving!" he said, taking the bags from my hands and letting me in.

He set the bags of food down on the counter and then walked back over to me, stretching out his hands to take my slightly snow-covered winter coat.

"How was your day? Greene let you guys out pretty early again?" he asked, hanging up the coat.

"Yes! He always does. Honestly, I think he thinks the class is only an hour, so I'm not saying anything."

"I wouldn't! Less lecture time for you guys. How 'bout the rest of your day?" he asked.

There was something different about the way he was acting. Not that he doesn't usually ask me how my day was -- he does -- but it was the way he was talking. It was a big difference from last week when he rushed off from our dreaming practice with Jess. After that day, he wasn't quite himself for a bit. He was quieter than usual. It was weird. And he wouldn't talk about anything related to dreaming. He didn't even meet Jess for their next session; he just never showed up.

So I was giving him a bit of space this past week. We still saw each other, but not as much. We still talked every day, but it was more about school or general everyday things. Nothing at all about dreams.

I wasn't sure what had changed to cause the shift in attitude there was tonight, but I certainly wasn't complaining.

"It was pretty good. Just getting kind of nervous about the test on the stages of brain development on Monday," I answered, following him into the small common room area of the apartment.

"Don't be nervous about it. You're really acing that class. You're gonna do amazing!" he assured me, grabbing my hand with one hand and the bag of food with the other and walking me over toward their brown leather couch.

There wasn't much to this room; I mean, there's just a bunch of college guys living here. Just a sofa, a coffee table, a bookshelf type thing holding up the TV, and the TV and gaming systems his other roommates brought from home.

"Did you sneak some already?" he asked, gesturing to the bag of food.

"Don't I always?" I responded while batting my eyes at him.

He just laughed and took out all the contents of the bag and put them on the coffee table.

We talked about school and some exams and projects we each have coming up soon while we ate. A little bit later, the TV was on and Zach was absentmindedly flipping through the movie choices, not really looking at them.

I reached out my arm, snatching the last French fry from the paper bag, and then curled back into the spot where I felt so comfortable and fit so perfectly next to Zach. As I chewed the now-cold fry, something dawned on me that I honestly hadn't thought of in a while.

I swallowed and stared at the screen, watching the titles roll by. *Should I ask him?* I wondered.

Honesty and openness, I reminded myself. *Those are keys to a good relationship.*

"Zach?" I asked, clearing my throat and resting my hand on his chest.

He looked down at me. "What's up?"

"Do you think it's weird we never hear from Mitch anymore?"

"Weird?" he asked, like he was testing out the word in that context.

"Yeah."

"Ad, I think that's a good thing. Don't you?"

"I do. I mean, I did. But it's also weird. Think about it, he wouldn't leave us alone for so long, and suddenly he just goes off the grid completely? Where is he? What is he up to?"

"What makes you think he's up to something?"

"Zach..."

"Right." He sat up straighter and shifted so he was facing me. I sat up too and crossed my legs, pulling a pillow around and holding it in front of my stomach. "But," he continued. "couldn't he just be traveling or something?. Maybe it isn't something bad."

"Zach, come on. It's been years!"

"Well, maybe he's changed."

"Changed?" I repeated, testing out this word in this context. "Mitch can't change. I don't think he's capable of it."

"*Everyone's* capable of change," Zach said with a pointed tone.

"What does that mean?"

He huffed out a breath of air. "Just that everyone changes sometimes. We shouldn't write off the possibility that people can change."

"Well, I'm not writing off *everybody*," I said. "I'm writing off *Mitch*."

"That's fine," he replied, sounding totally fine with that.

"Well, then, what's the issue?" I asked.

"There is no issue. I just don't want people thinking change, for the good or the bad, doesn't happen. Mitch changed for the bad. But some people can change for the better."

"Zach, what's going on? Please just talk to me," I pleaded with him.

"Nothing's going on."

I just looked at him, knowing he'd tell me eventually.

"I just...I think that if people can change one way, maybe they can get back to how they were. And maybe it wasn't even their fault that they changed to begin with."

"Zach," I started, resting my hand on his arm. "Hon, who are you talking about? Who can change?"

He just stared at his shoes, sneakers like always.

"Zach?"

Still looking down, he said, "I think my mom needs help. I think she's still in there. I think she could change and get better if we just get her out of there."

"You know they never let anyone out of there," I said, trying my best to sound sympathetic while also being the voice of reason here. I mean, it's *The Haven*. Once you check in, you don't get checked out.

"That's just it though."

"What is?"

"There's something in the water there," he told me, now looking at me again.

"The water?"

"Not the water, water." When he saw I was still confused he added, "The pills."

Then suddenly it all clicked into place. *The dream the other day when we were with Jess-- it was about the pills his mom used to take. That's why he got so upset and has been acting so strange.*

It's the pills.

"What can you do though?" I asked.

Clearly he had been thinking about this a lot because he answered as soon as I asked. "I'm going to help get her out of there."

"How though?"

"I don't know yet. But she needs to stop taking those pills. I think once she does, she'll see everything clearer."

I thought about all of this for a minute or so. *What could we really do to get her out of there? Is that even possible?*

But then I realized that if Zachary Walker said he was going to do something, it would get done.

"Okay, I'm in."

"In?" he asked.

"I'm in," I repeated. "Whatever you need. Whatever I can do. I'll be there and I'll do it. Whatever gets your mom back home, I'm game. I'm behind you completely. We're in this together."

"Thank you," he said smiling, even more than usual. "That's why I love you so much."

Then he pulled me back over to him and kissed me.

I could kiss this guy forever, I thought, smiling and then kissing him back.

10

- Addison -
Thursday, April 28th, 2022

S ophie had called me about an hour ago, but I was in a lecture and missed it. After the lecture, I was getting a coffee from the little coffee cart on the cobblestone walkway near the library, when I got a bunch of texts from her in a row.

> **So sorry!**
> **Just realized you were in class.**
> **My bad.**
> **Ignore my voicemail.**
> **I forgot you had class...**

I swiped my student card, paying for the coffee, and stepped out of the way so the girl behind me, someone I recognized from a communications course I took last semester, could order her coffee. She smiled at me and said hello, and I did the same.

What's up? I replied.

Those little dots popped up and she was typing a response for what seemed like forever.

Are you busy?

"Here you go. One caramel macchiato," the kid who usually works here at this time said to me, handing over my coffee.

"Thanks," I told him.

When I started college, I didn't care much for coffee. But now, after all of the early morning lectures and late nights cramming, I *really* liked coffee.

I switched my phone with my coffee in my right hand so I could type easier.

Coming was all I said.

My classes were done for the afternoon, so I had a bit of time to kill before I met with Jess. It was the last time we had planned for our dream monitoring sessions. I'm not sure what we are going to do once I turn in my final paper this Friday.

It has been so great that they let us use the space and the equipment. Every once in a while I bring Sophie in (since she's just so fascinated by dreams and is totally willing to participate) so that there are some more "normal" numbers, heart rates, REM cycles, and things like that. I convinced Zach's one roommate to come from time to time, too. He has some strange sleep patterns-- lots of energy drinks.

Jess said she thinks she has enough data to keep working on it, try to get us some answers. I'm going to keep researching and studying as much as I can, but it will be hard to try to balance it all. It will also be hard without the access to everything in the lab.

It was kind of a weird feeling, walking this path to Sophie's apartment, knowing that this week, the last week of classes before finals start, was probably the last few times I'd be walking this way.

Gosh, that's weird.

Four years goes so fast. And it's funny, too, because after high school, you think time can't possibly move quicker than it seemed to in those four years. Then you set foot on your college campus, blink, and you're graduating from there, moving on to the next phase of your life. For some people, it's a job. Out in the real world. And that's a scary thought. But for others, like me, it's more years of schooling. And that's even scarier, because you know that those next however many years -- though in the process they'll feel unending -- will pass even faster than college did. Time is just such a strange thing. It's hard to grasp the concept of time, especially when these past four years felt so long, yet went by so quickly.

I mean, *I'm turning in my last paper this Friday.* Isn't that insane? Then next week, I have final projects and final exams, and then that's it. Graduation.

Zach starts his job in a few weeks, which is also crazy.

Okay, I warned myself as I climbed the many stairs to Sophie's dorm hall, *enough thinking about college ending. Just calm down, knock on Sophie's door, and put it all aside for a bit.*

Before I could even knock on the door, it swung open. Sophie was standing there, waving her hands in front of her face, partially fanning herself and partially just shaking out her hands, while jumping up and down a bit.

"Soph, what's wrong?" I asked, stepping inside and closing the door behind me, kicking off my taupe ballet flats by the door.

"I am freaking out, Addie! Freaking!"

"What's going on?" I asked.

"Just thank you so much for coming," Sophie sighed, pulling me in for a giant hug in the middle of her dorm.

She tried being a director for her dorm hall floor during our sophomore year. In the first two weeks, during all the orientation activities for the new freshman students, she absolutely hated it. She contemplated quitting-- a few times actually. But her parents told her that she had to stick it out at least a year.

Sophie's family could not really afford for her to go to our college and live there, but she was too far away to have any other choice. So, when she saw the flyer looking for resident directors (and saw that there was a stipend involved), she applied.

By the end of that first semester though, Sophie was completely in her element. She was amazing with those girls! Every one of them started coming to her for advice or homework help. She planned fun things for the weekends with the girls on her floor. Honestly, she was doing so many good things in her position, and you could tell all of the girls just loved her.

So now, even as a senior, she has stayed as the resident director of the same dorm building, and each fall she helps the freshman girls transition into their lives in college.

She also gets a dorm room all to herself! She decorated it super cute actually. Everything is mint green and gold, her favorite colors. She has twinkly lights and photographs over all of the walls, and music is always playing in the background.

"Of course," I told her, settling in to her white fuzzy papasan chair and moving the mint green "I'd Rather Be Napping" pillow until I got comfortable. "Soph, come on. What's going on?"

Now she was pacing in front of her little table and chairs set, wringing her hands through her hair.

"Okay, calm down. What happened?" I told her.

"I really just needed someone to talk to. I'm so sorry I called you during class... I know you don't have your phone on. I should've thought of that."

"Really, Sophie, it's okay!"

So, there we were, minutes later, with her sitting (finally) on the couch and myself in the papasan chair, talking about our futures. Sophie had yet to get a solid job offer. She had spent weeks sending out application after application and hasn't heard back yet. She was getting really frustrated (and rightfully so) because she has stellar grades, has had some great connections, and worked her butt off all semester at a prestigious internship. Nothing seems to be panning out for her yet though.

"What am I going to do?" she asked, looking up at the ceiling and shaking her head.

"Sophie, lots of kids don't have jobs yet," I pointed out. "Besides, you have resumes out to a bunch of companies, who would all be lucky to have you! Plus, you just had an interview last week!"

"Yes! Last week. Actually over a week. They said they'd get back to me within a few days. That has to be a 'No' then, doesn't it? I mean, they obviously hated me."

"Oh, come on! Why would you say that?"

"Because it's true. I waited too long to start applying for jobs, and they could tell. They know I didn't plan ahead enough. They know I slacked off."

"Sophie, you did *not* slack off. You were working as an *intern* all semester."

"They wouldn't hire me either," she said, reaching for a tissue.

"It's not you, though. That branch is closing," I told her, trying to get her to realize that a lack of an offer had no reflection on her performance in the internship, as she always thought it did.

"Everything is."

"Everything is what?" I asked, confused what she meant.

"Closing."

I sat there, waiting it out, knowing her well enough to know she would continue to explain her point soon.

"Everything is closing, coming to an end. I can't do anything to stop it. The branch-- I loved working there. But the branch is closing. It'll be gone in two months. School. Well, it's not closing, but I won't be here anymore. I love it here. I won't get to see you all the time. You're moving on. All of my friends are moving on. Todd's moving on too. He got a job out in Michigan. So that's obviously ending too. Everything's ending, and I'm just stuck here..."

I took a breath. "I was honestly worrying about the same thing on my way over here."

"You were?"

"Of course! It's ending for all of us. And it scares me. A lot... But don't worry
about things with Todd yet. You don't know what will happen. Maybe you'll get a job in Michigan too?"

She looked around the room, her eyes falling on the same picture hanging on the wall that mine did. It was one of the two of us that we took in the first few weeks of school. We had a break from class and it was a really nice day out. So we ate our lunches outside on a striped blanket she had. "This is just lovely," she said that day. "We need to do this more often!" It was the first picnic lunch of many throughout the years.

In the picture, you could see our sandwiches and bags of chips spread out in front of us on the blanket. We are both smiling, squinting in the sun, and looking up at Sophie's phone as she took the photo of us.

"I did hear back from another company..."

"That's great!" I told her, looking away from the picture and back at her.

"They want an interview."

"That is awesome! What company?" I asked.

"Well... that's the thing. It's a small company, you probably haven't heard of them."

"Really? Where is it?"

"It's back home. My mom has a friend who works there, and she passed my information along."

"Oh..." I said, realizing that then Sophie would be back in her hometown, hours away from here. "Well, you are going to do amazing! Really! You'll knock their socks off in the interview and they'll just have to give you an offer. That's awesome, Sophie." I was trying to sound as positive as I could and not let the fact that I wanted Sophie to stick around, like she had planned on doing, change the fact that she had a great company interested in hiring her.

"Yeah, I guess..."

"How do you have everything all figured out?" Sophie asked a while later, eyes now dry from tears and tissues scattered on the floor.

"I don't."

"Yes, you do," she argued.

"I have no clue what the future holds..." I admitted.

Four Months Later...

11

- Addison -
Sunday, August 28ᵗʰ, 2022

"Cammie, please. Calm down," I begged, yanking my arm away from her.

She reached out and grabbed my arm again, trying to pull me along. "Addie, I love you, but we are going to be late."

"Late? Cam... we are over an hour early for dinner, okay? Chill."

Geez, Cam is wound so tight tonight, I thought to myself as I finally freed my arm from her grasp and reached for my shoes.

"Really?"

I stopped dead in my tracks, hand frozen on the heel of my black ballerina flats. "What?"

"Are you really going to wear those shoes?"

"I was planning on it."

Cammie sighed. "Oh, Addie, Addie, Addie. When will you learn?"

"I thought we were late, Cam?" I asked with a grin. Honestly, Cammie could be in the middle of a crisis or running incredibly late for something, but if it involved boy-talk or anything fashionable, she will drop everything and take as much time as necessary to help me out.

"Oh, we have a few minutes." She turned, surveying my closet. "Here, try these."

"Cammie, those are really high, and dressy. Don't you think?" I asked, looking at the sleek, patent leather heels.

"Oh, please! You'll look amazing. Plus, you have to look fancy tonight."

"Why? It's just dinner with some friends from Madison High."

She looked like she had said too much, her eyes wide like a deer in headlights. "Just put them on!" she groaned.

"Fine," I said, taking the shoes from her and bending over with one hand on her shoulder for balance and the other strapping on the heels.

"And, uh, why don't you throw on some lipstick. That *red* is nice," she said in a sly way that really meant, 'I've wanted you to add the lipstick for the past half-hour but only decided to mention it now.'

"Which one?" I asked.

"I'll get it!" she yelled and ran off to my bathroom to retrieve the lipstick.

"Hey!" I called when I lost my balance the second she tore off to get it.

"Oh, sorry," she replied coming back with a tube of lipstick I had bought with her a few months back. "This one. The red you bought for your date with *Zach*," she told me with a mock swoon at his name.

A few months ago, Zach and I had a big dinner planned for our fifth anniversary of being together. Cammie insisted she come back from school a few weekends before the dinner to help me find the perfect look. She insisted also, that I buy the red lipstick she currently held in her hands, because red was Zach's favorite color and apparently I can pull off the red-lipstick look, whereas she supposedly cannot and will therefore live vicariously through me.

"Okay, but that's it," I said, applying the lipstick while looking in the little mirror in my room.

"You need jewelry. Oh wait! No, you-"

"Can we go now?" I asked.

She finally stopped looking around my room to see what else she could dress me up in and looked over at me. "Oh, Addie! You look gor-ge-ous!"

"Thank you, darling! You do, too!" I said as I grabbed my purse and she rushed me out the door.

Cammie had offered to drive us to dinner, but once we got in the car she turned to me and said, "If you're going to make me drive, the least you can do is run a quick errand with me."

"Make you drive? Cammie, you practically begged to drive!"

"Details," she said with a flip of her hand.

"But, yes, I will run an errand with you. What is it?"

"Quick question," she said, changing lanes and changing conversation, "did Zach say he's meeting us there?"

"Yeah, at the restaurant in like an hour. Which is why I have no clue why you rushed me. It's only fifteen minutes away."

"Good. And I rushed you because of the errand I have to run!"

"Okay, well, where is this errand?"

"We have to stop at school."

"School? As in Madison High?"

"Yes, Addison."

A light changed quickly and she had to practically slam on the breaks. She muttered under her breath something about being late and stupid lights ruining everything.

I turned to her. "Cammie, are you okay? You're freaking out and we have tons of time."

"I just have to stop at the school first," she said as if that should answer everything.

"I know. We have time to stop there." I looked out the window, watching a car slow down beside us, the driver also seemed aggravated he had come to a red light. "Cam, what are you stopping at Madison for?"

She tapped the steering wheel a few times with her thumbs. "What?"

"Why do you have to stop at school?"

"You know how I was president?"

"Yes, how could I forget?"

"Well, the five year reunion is coming up soon, which is my job to plan. The new secretary was supposed to leave a binder for me with the, uh, contact info of all the students from our graduating class. There were so many of us, you know, it's hard to keep track of everyone's contact info after all these years. Plus I need to grab some papers anyways."

"Oh! The reunion! Oh, my gosh, has it really been that long?" I asked, looking at my reflection in the side view mirror. That fact made me feel instantly older.

"Not yet. But almost. It's in the early stages of planning right now." I could feel her turn and look at me. "You look beautiful, by the way."

"Thanks, Cam," I replied, still staring at my reflection. *Where did all the time go?* It felt like just a little bit ago I was graduating and hopping off to Europe. Now, I'm back home. I've graduated college and already started grad school.

"Finally!" Cammie cried as the light turned green.

Soon enough we were pulling up to our alma mater, Madison High, in all it's red, white, and black glory.

She pulled in a "faculty only" parking space. "One of the many perks!" she said with a wink as she shut off the car and got out.

Cammie decided nursing was not for her and actually, changed her major, multiple times over the course of the four years. She is not really one for needles, so it didn't take too long to realize it wasn't the best career path for her. I honestly think she would have made a great nurse, but this might just suit her even better than any of us could have thought.

"Well, come on, you're coming in with me!" she ordered me, her door still open.

I quickly unbuckled my seatbelt and got out. "Yes, Miss Fuller. Whatever you say."

She just grinned and locked the car over her shoulder, not even looking back. Then she swung her set of keys around her finger and stopped it on the new one, the shiny silver key that just got added to the key ring. The key they made for the new faculty member.

Miss Cameron Fuller, the new mathematics teacher, algebra II to be exact, at Madison High. The timing was perfect, to be honest.

Mr. B decided it was time to retire -- we were all surprised he was even there this long to begin with but were even more surprised he actually retired -- and there was a new position open that they had to fill quickly mid-year.

Lucky for them, an alumnus --Cammie -- being the overachiever that she always has been, graduated early and happened to be living back home in Madison looking for employment. She was hired instantly and has loved every minute of it. She's incredible at her job, too. The students all love her, and she seems to make math really fun for them all.

I smiled as she unlocked the side door. I was really proud of her. She really has found her calling in life, I think, and she seems so happy it makes me really happy for her.

"Alright, so we just have to go back to my room, Kelly was supposed to leave the binder and some copies of some worksheets on my desk," Cam explained as she flipped on only one of the hallway lights, making it look kind of bright, but also kind of eerie.

Honestly, it was crazy being back here.   Cam checked her phone. "Oh, shoot. Gracie needs me to check she fed the fish," Cam sighed and looked up at me, shaking her head. "You know, I'm still surprised they okayed that one. She has this whole aquarium in the science room but always needs everyone else to go feed the fish for her."

I just smiled and nodded, like I totally understood her world of teachers' lounges and bus duty. I'm still in the world of term papers and observations.

"Do you mind grabbing the binder for me?" She placed her set of keys in my hand. "This key. It's the same room Mr. B had. Just go down the hall, make a right, and--"

"I remember where it's at," I told her, smiling.

"Perfect!" she replied, seeming honestly a bit too happy to be going to feed a bunch of fish. "Meet ya there in a jiffy!"

"Okay!"

Then I turned and made my way down the hallway, heading to where I used to have math class.

I looked over and counted the lockers, 582, 584, 586...587. That one was mine back in the day. I tried to open it just to see what it was like now, but it was locked. I wondered who had my locker now.

Just as I was pondering if number 587 belonged to a guy on the football team or a girl in the drama club, I felt like I stepped on something.

I looked down and bent my leg up, trying to look at what was now on my shoe.

What is a rose petal doing here? I peeled it off my shoe and held it for a second.

Then, when I looked just a bit ahead of where I stood, I saw there were actually a ton of red rose petals scattered on the grey tiled floor of my high school.

Oh! I thought, realizing the first week of classes was coming up, which also meant the Welcome Back dance. *It's probably this weekend,* I thought. *That's so cute.*

But as I kept following the little trail of rose petals, making my way to my old math class, I saw a candle on the ground, the little flame flickering and giving the hallway a warm glow.

As I kept walking, there were tons of candles and rose petals, and I began to think this maybe wasn't for the dance after all.

What was going on? I wondered.

I paused for a second, looking around at this place I spent four years of my life. Right over there, to the left, is the little nook where, in a dream, Zach pulled me aside, knowing something was wrong, to ask what happened to my ankle after I had sprained it in another dream. This very hallway is where we would walk to classes playing twenty questions, getting to know each other so many years ago.

And this hallway is also where we...

I looked around, down at the candles and petals.

Oh. My. Gosh...

This is where we met...

I realized I was still holding that first rose petal. I held it a little tighter in my one hand, the key to Cammie's new classroom in my other, and I kept walking down the rose petal, memory covered hallway.

But I was too busy looking at the petals and candles and reliving the memory of both times I met Zach right here, in the dream world and reality, to notice the guy standing there, arms outstretched, ready to catch me because he knows me so well, when I turned the corner.

12

- Addison -
Sunday, August 28th, 2022

I crashed into him.

Before I could fall over, his one arm steadied me and his other caught Cammie's keys that I had just dropped. *Wow, his arms are like rocks!*

"I'm sorry," his deep voice made me smile. I was staring in his eyes, in the middle of the hallway, just exactly like things happened back then.

Only this time, he steadied me, standing me back on two feet. Although, I must admit, my knees felt about as weak as they did that first moment, too.

But this time, instead of introducing himself, he fixed his very nice tie -- a blue one I had bought him for Christmas last year because it matched his eyes -- and then... he bent down... on one knee.

Only one.

I knew what that meant.

My hands were shaking, and his face got a little red like it does when he gets nervous, which I find insanely endearing.

"Addison," he started.

"Yes..." I said, taking a deep breath, knowing my life was going to change, for the third time, right in this hallway.

"Over five years ago you stumbled into me right here. That was part of a dream, part of some elaborate scheme that my uncle dreamt up, that, on the one hand, I wish he never had because it caused you so much pain. But on the other hand, the selfish side of me is so grateful that he did. Because I met you."

I smiled at him, and honestly there was a tear in the corner of my eye threatening to spill over. I would not have traded anything his uncle did back then, because everything he did brought us to where we are today. And let me tell you, it's a pretty amazing place to be.

"Then," Zach continued, smiling, "all of my dreams, and that whole dream scheme, actually came to life, and instead of stumbling into me, you ran after me, attacking me and kissing me right here in front of everyone -- which I must tell you, I loved." He stopped, grinning, and then continued, "And so..."

"Yes..." I said, growing impatient because I just really, really wanted to say "yes" for a third time tonight, hopefully in response to the question I could feel coming.

"I thought this would be the perfect place to ask you this." He reached into his jacket pocket -- he was wearing a suit, by the way, a very classy looking suit, with the tie I bought him -- and pulled out a very tiny black velvety box.

A jewelry box.

A jewelry box the size of a...

He flipped it open, facing it out to me, revealing a silver, very sparkly, round-cut diamond that was resting on a band covered with tiny diamonds.

My hands flew up, covering my mouth. *Oh, my gosh,* I thought, *this is really happening.*

"Addison Grace Smith," he said in his smooth, deep voice that still got to me.

"Yes!" I squealed.

His shoulders dropped a bit. "Ad, you have to let me ask," he said laughing. "I had this whole great thing planned out."

"Oh! I'm sorry! Keep going!" I replied and shrunk back a bit and covered my mouth again.

"Ad, I love you. It's insane how much I love you. Growing up, I never thought I'd be here, proposing to a girl I would do anything for, would die for. I mean, I was raised by cynical Mitch. And I thought it would be easy all those years ago when I met you to follow through on Mitch's plan. But the very moment I met you, I knew I was screwed. The first time you smiled at me, I was a goner. Honestly, I've known I wanted to marry you for a very long time. I sometimes think maybe we are still in that crazy dream world. Maybe I am dreaming that a kind-hearted, beautiful, strong, talented, amazing woman like you would still be with me after every stupid thing I've done. But I'm hoping that maybe you'll let this perfect dream keep going, and you'll be with me every day in my dreams and in my life."

He took a deep breath and then flashed his signature grin, blue eyes shining. "Addison Grace Smith, will you marry me?"

I screamed "Yes!" And when I say "screamed", I mean I *screamed* it.

He stood up, and for the second time in this very hallway, in this very spot, I jumped into his arms.

I knew there was a huge smile on his face, that lovely smile I'd come to know.

I knew that it was him kissing me now, in the middle of the hallway.

I also knew that every single person who had stared at me five years ago with the "new kid" could never have possibly imagined how insanely happy that "new kid" would make me.

I knew that what Zach and I had was real.

I knew that as long as we were together, life would be like the sweetest dream of all.

I knew that there was nothing I wanted more in life than being his wife and building a future with him.

This was certainly no illusion, I thought, as I kissed him again and again with the happiest of tears streaming down my cheeks.

This was real.

13

- Zach -

Sunday, August 28th, 2022

And there we were, standing in the middle of the hallway of Madison High. I was holding the ring in one hand and her in my other.

She said yes! I thought to myself, still in shock. Not necessarily the fact that she said yes, I had hoped she would. It's more the fact that she's mine. *I mean, have you seen her?*

She pulled back and just stared at me, smiling this huge, goofy smile.

I pulled the ring from it's spot in the box and took her left hand.

"Ahhhhh, it's so pretty!" she squealed, biting her lip and switching between staring at the ring and back at me.

"You like it?" I asked.

"Like it? Honey, it's gorgeous!" she said extending her hand to look at it.

"It looks good on you," I told her, trying to sound smooth and regain some composure here.

She smiled and batted her eyes at me. She looked back at her hand, wiggling her fingers around and looking at the ring in different lights.

"Oh, baby, it's perfect!" She looked back at me. "You're perfect! Oh, I'm so excited!" And as she said that, she grabbed my face and pulled me in for another kiss.

Then Cammie screamed and came running over from her spot around the corner. Addison turned and saw her and rushed over. They were holding hands and jumping and screaming, and I just stood there laughing.

"Look!" Ad yelled and held out her hand.

"It's gorgeous! I made him show it to me last week for approval," Cam admitted. "He did good," she said approvingly.

"You knew?" Addison asked her, looking back at me.

"Of course I knew! He needed help getting in the school and distracting you today."

"Oh...that's why you insisted we paint our nails last night!" Addison said laughing and pointing a finger at Cammie.

Cammie walked over to me. "Good job, Zach. That was really sweet. You better always be that sweet, do you hear me?"

"He is," Ad said walking up and sliding in right next to me.

"Alright, you two crazy kids, have a good time tonight, okay?" Cam told us, flicking on the rest of the lights in the hallway and blowing out some of the candles.

"Wait, what about dinner?" Addison asked, clearly confused.

"Oh, honey," Cammie replied, shaking her head. "Sometimes you are so oblivious."

"What are you talking about?" Addison asked.

I stepped in now and explained, "Cam and I came up with that as a distraction and to make you think there was something else going on tonight. Then you'd think this was just a quick stop on the way to dinner."

"But Jess and I talked about it this morning."

Cam laughed. "I knew you'd ask her about dinner, so I let her in on the secret."

"Oh, you guys are good!" Ad said.

"We do have a reservation though. But just us," I told her.

"And that's my cue," Cam said, pointing to the door. She hugged Addison, then me. "Congratulations," she told us both and then walked out.

"Well, you just thought of everything, didn't you?" Addison said, turning to look up at me.

"I try..." I answered, shrugging my shoulders like it was no big deal.

She moved in front of me and brought her face really close to mine. I thought she was going to kiss me again, but instead she just yelled, "We're getting married!"

I couldn't help but laugh. "We're getting married!" I yelled back to her, not even hiding my smile.

* * *

On our way to dinner, I told her we had to make a quick stop, because if I knew Addison, I knew she would want her best friend to know right away.

I took a left, pulling into her neighborhood. "What are we doing?" she asked.

"Stopping to tell your parents," I told her, passing the one house three up from her that always (no matter what time I drove by) had all of the boys in the family outside shooting hoops, and sure enough, they were there playing right then.

"Oh yay!" Addison said, and I could tell she was trying to hide her excitement.

Before I even had the car completely in park and off, she was unbuckling her seatbelt and jumping out of my car. And at that same moment, Mrs. Smith was opening the front door and rushing out onto their covered porch with Mr. Smith following behind.

I got out and made my way up their front steps as Addison was screaming and jumping up and down with her mom the same way she had with Cammie. The only difference was Mrs. Smith looked like she was about to cry or maybe already was.

"Congratulations, son," Mr. Smith said, clapping me on the back and shaking my hand.

"Did you know this was happening tonight?" Ad asked them.

"Yes," her mom told her, picking up her hand to look at the ring. "Oh, let me grab my camera! Stay right here!"

Her mom rushed back in the house and came back not even a second later with their family camera. You knew it was going to be an important picture when Mrs. Smith brought out the big guns instead of just using her phone to snap a picture.

"Oooo! Stand right here," she said, positioning us in front of the big tree in their front yard.

Ad placed her left hand on my chest right over my tie, so you could see the ring. We both smiled.

Flash! Flash!

Then she reached up and kissed me on the cheek. More flashes as Mrs. Smith clicked away.

"Oh, I'm just so happy for you both," her mom, my future mother-in-law, said, wiping at her eyes and putting the lens cap back on the camera.

Her father just gave a knowing smile to the both of us.

"Well," I started, checking my watch. "We had better get going to make our reservation."

"Where are we going?" Ad said, sounding like a little kid.

"Zambini's if that's alright?"

She looked at her mom, "He really does love me!"

"Yes, he does," her mom agreed, smiling and standing next to Mr. Smith as he wrapped an arm around her shoulder.

They seemed happy, for Addison and just in general. I've always thought that. They remind me of my parents early on, before things got bad.

I hoped Addison and I would be happy like her parents are, married for twenty-five years and seeing our kids happy and starting their lives.

Two hours later we were sitting at a round table at the fancy restaurant Addison loves, Zambini's. She loves to come here for special occasions like birthdays or big anniversaries. I thought I'd surprise her tonight with reservations here.

I called ahead and told them we'd be celebrating our engagement, so they had champagne at the table when we arrived. I chuckled when I saw it. Champagne makes Ad really talkative-- and I mean *really* talkative.

We had a table with one of those booth seats that wraps around three quarters of the table, but the two of us were squished together in the center.

"This is incredible!" Addison gushed, her mouth full.

"It's awesome," I agreed, taking another bite of the chocolate cake the server had just brought out to us. One slice. Two forks. "Congratulations" written on the white plate in chocolate sauce.

"Can we please have chocolate cake at our wedding?" she begged, wrapping her arm around mine.

I laughed. "Yes, babe. We can."

"Can we get this exact chocolate cake? I'm in love with it!"

"I thought you were in love with me?" I teased.

"I am! But I am currently in love with this cake as well. And my ring. And this night. And you. And the fact that you planned all of this out!"

She took another bite of the cake. "I just *love* this cake!"

"Me too, Ad. Me too."

14

- Addison -
Sunday, August 28ᵗʰ, 2022

*T*onight was a dream, a literal dream. I couldn't believe how much Zach did for tonight.

I kept reliving every second from this night as I brushed my teeth, getting ready for bed. As I moved my right hand back and forth, I lifted up my left hand, admiring the way the light hit the diamond and it sparkled.

Diamond! I have a diamond ring! Because I am getting married! To Zach!

Like I said, tonight has been a dream.

I crawled in bed a few minutes later, twisting my hair up into a scrunchie on top of my head. I pumped some strawberry lotion on my hand from the bottle on my nightstand like I do every night. I started rubbing in the lotion, rubbing my hands together, but then crawled right back out of bed.

I knelt on my shaggy rug beside my bed, resting my elbows on my comforter and folding my hands.

Thank you, God, for this life, my life up until now and everything you have in store for it from this day forward. I don't deserve half the good things in my life, but I thank you for every one of them. It's just...thank you.

I reached up and grabbed a little card I got at a gift shop at the sanctuary. It had a prayer written in French on one side and English on the other. I prayed that and then crawled back into bed, turning out the lamp beside me.

* * *

I'm dreaming in fast forward. It's like in romantic movies, at that certain point, when there's a montage of the couple's life so far together. My dream is all of the moments of my life since I met Zach, and they play in my mind like a movie montage.

And it's a wonderful montage.

But then it gets to the point where we are in life right now, tonight, and then the dream shifts. That typical grey haze coats the scene, weighing down my mind.

It gets eerie. Quick.

No, not tonight. I don't want this. Things have been so good. I've barely had any nightmares these past few months. The trip didn't cure me completely, but it definitely gave me the tools to battle these dreams. And I have been, I've been doing so well.

Wake up!

I try to snap my eyes open, and I do, but I don't see my room. I see the same grey, foggy space.

I try to sit up, but I'm frozen. Paralyzed. Sleep paralysis, I bet.

I'm telling my body to sit up, my feet to move, my arms to move, or even just my fingers to wiggle. Nothing.

Help! I want to scream.

But I know it's no use. No sound will come out either. I'm completely frozen in place.

It's never been this bad before.

My heartbeat is speeding up. I'm beginning to sweat.

Let me go! I scream in my mind.

Who am I yelling at? I don't know.

I just need to move, I think, trying again to sit up to no avail.

The scene begins to zoom in, panning from faraway to closer and closer, cutting through the fog.

What is this? I wonder.

And suddenly, the shapes all take form, the scene coming together better, until I make out what it is.

It's a graveyard.

What is this dream? I want out of it!

It continues to zoom in and move forward like a camera in a movie, making its way through a graveyard scene. I'm just lying there, waiting for some monster to pop out from behind a tombstone and scare me.

It's eerie and cold-- yes, I can feel the cold.

I feel a chill run the whole way up my spine, but at the same time I can't feel it, but I know it's there. I feel so weird, so out of place, so helpless.

Just then, something that never happens in dreams happens. I can read.

I can read the tombstones.

Here lies Maggie Tate. Mother, sister, wife, and dreamer. April 3rd, 1887 - April 3rd, 1902.

The scene zooms off of that tombstone and onto another, which I can also read.

R.I.P. Stephen K. George. October 19th, 1947 to May 4th, 1964. "I dream..."

Before I can read the quote, another tombstone appears.

Forever in our hearts, Jason Day. Beloved son, quarterback, and dreamer. June 26th, 1999 - December 20th, 2016.

The dream continues to show me grave after grave. Each one reading the typical name, quote, and dates. But then, just before the words vanish, the word "dreamer" appears in the list of ways the individual was known, or the word "dream" shows up in their quote.

The dream quickly zooms in on another grave, a newer looking one, with fresh flowers in front.

I tried to read the name, but this time it was fuzzy, just barely out of focus.

Zachary D. Walk–

And then, right then, my body decided to snap out of it and wake me up.

I sat up in bed, heart racing, head spinning. I was trying to think of any other way, any possible way, that combination of letters could end differently. That it had to be a coincidence my fiancé (as of five hours ago) had the first name "Zachary," middle initial "D," and last name beginning with "Walk." *Right? It was just a coincidence.*

It's just a dream anyway, right? That can't be real.

Maybe it was in the future... like seventy years in the future. Some of those dates were so long ago. *It would make sense to have some in the future, too, right?*

But what if it's the near future?

Okay, I can't think that...

Just calm down, I told myself.

But it wasn't working. I was freaking out.

Why did all of those graves have dreamers names on them? And why did it have to end with the one dreamer's name I could never bear to see on something like that?

It can't be real. Or a premonition. Or a sign.

It just can't be.

But that awful image kept appearing in my mind, making me want to throw up.

What happened to forever?

We are supposed to have forever.

15

- Zach -

Friday, September 2nd, 2022

"**S**o the other night I asked Addison to marry me," I told Charlie, my buddy from my engineering classes in college. He also got a job in the area, so we meet for drinks at Sal's sometimes to catch a game.

"No way! Bro, that's awesome!" he took a swig of his beer. "She say yes?" he asked, pretending to be surprised.

I just drank my beer and laughed. *Charlie, always the sarcastic one.*

"How'd you afford a ring like that?" he asked a few minutes later, nodding at the picture of Ad and me from last night that was now on my phone.

Our waitress brought up a basket of fries and set them down. Charlie nodded at her. "When did they get waitresses this hot around here?

They all used to be old," he loudly "whispered" across the table when she left.

I grabbed a fry and poured some catsup on one of those little appetizer plates.

"Seriously! Is this a new thing in Madison? I mean, *dang*, what happened?"

"Don't know, Charlie."

"You're telling me you haven't noticed?" he asked, leaning on his elbows on the table.

"Nope."

"Wow, she's got you hooked," he said with a low whistle, grabbing some fries for himself.

I shrugged. *I was fine being hooked.*

"Anyway, how'd you get a rock like that, bud?"

"I've been saving up," was all I said. I didn't tell him that I'd been saving up for years. I didn't tell him I've always known it would be her; or that I thought she deserved the best, so I've been saving for years so I could get her the best ring.

"So glad I'm still solo," Charlie said. Then, mid-fry, he seemed to remember how this conversation started, and he coughed and said, "But congratulations, Walker! That's great! Really."

"Thanks, Charlie."

I took another sip of my beer, finishing it off. The waitress came back, asking if we wanted another round. I just shook my head no, but Charlie, for any excuse to talk to this girl, started asking her for recommendations. Which led to, "are you new around here?", which later led to "what time do you get off tonight?" Meanwhile, I was catching the final period of the local minor league baseball game on the screen above Charlie's head.

The screen looked a little blurry. I blinked a few times.

That's weird, I thought when it didn't clear up. *I didn't have that much to drink.*

"I'll be right back," I said, but of course neither Charlie nor the blonde waitress noticed or cared.

I walked back toward the bathroom, feeling off. *Maybe something was up with the food?* I wondered. But then I remembered I have felt, not dizzy, but just off for the past few days, and then on and off leading up to that.

I got to the restroom just in time to throw up.

What is wrong with me? I thought.

* * *

We're driving. I have a convertible now. A red one. The sun is shining, wind blowing, music blaring.

Addison is in the seat beside me, beautiful and perfect as ever.

"What happened to our forever?" Addison asks me, still smiling. I have to think about the question for a minute because her expression and tone do not match what she's saying.

"What do you mean, babe?"

"You promised. You ruined it."

"What did I do? I can fix it," I said, throwing the car in park.

Why would I stop in the middle of the road?

"I don't know," she says.

She gets out of the car, slamming the door behind her.

"Addison!" I call after her.

And then, she collapses, right there in front of me. She's walking, and then suddenly she's not. I jump out of the car, but I can't reach her fast enough. She's already on the ground, lying there.

"Addison!" I scream.

What just happened?

"Addison, no!"

She's just lying there. Not moving.

No, no, no... This can't happen. It can't.

"Ad, wake up. I love you. I don't know what I did, but I'll fix it. We'll fix it. We'll be okay! I need you to wake up."

"You're the one who needs to wake up, son."

I whip my head around to see my uncle standing over my shoulder.

"What did you do to her? Why couldn't you just leave us alone?" I scream at him.

"I didn't do anything. I'm here to help you, believe it or not."

"Stop talking then and do something! Help her."

"She doesn't need help, Zachary. You do. I need you to wake up. Right now." His voice is deep and firm, like he is not playing around now and actually cares.

"Stop it. I'm not dreaming."

"Yes, Zachary. You are."

"No, I need to do something."

"Zachary, you are dreaming. Wake up now."

It isn't that simple though. I can't just wake up because he says to. Especially if this is real, because it feels pretty real. You can't just wake up from real life.

I hear a slow and steady beeping, coming from somewhere down the road. *What is that?*

"Wake up."

I just turn my attention back to Addison, shaking her shoulders and telling her over and over again to wake up. Something had to happen dream-wise, that's all. I can fix it.

"You can't fix this, Zach. You just have to wake up."

"Fine," I spit back at him. "I'll 'just wake up'." I use air quotes with my fingers, acting like he's so in the wrong here.

"Good. I'll see you soon."

"Whatever," I say to him.

Then I kiss her forehead, smoothing back her light hair, and I take a breath.

Wake up, I tell myself.

It won't work.

But it did.

I woke up, with Addison right next to me, holding my hand, her head resting on my shoulder. She was fine, so it really was a dream. She was okay, and that was all that mattered.

But the beeping sound was still there, louder now. Slow and steady, picking up pace a bit now.

What was that noise?

16

- Addison -
Friday, September 2nd, 2022

Cammie, Jess, and I were all planning to hang out tonight. Zach had a guy's night planned, so I planned a girl's night. However, what started out as us all getting dressed up and going out to dinner and a movie, turned into my parents' house with sweatpants, greasy takeout, and binge-watching the latest season of our favorite TV show.

I was on my way home from running some errands, so I swung by Sal's, running in to grab our mobile order -- Sal's had recently stepped up their game and accepted mobile takeout orders, so obviously we had to try this out!

There happened to only be one spot left in the parking lot, and I recognized the car to the left. It was Zach's.

I thought he and Charlie were going to the new burger specialty restaurant in Madison, but as always they ended up at Sal's. *Should've guessed.*

I put my car in park, grabbed my keys and phone, and headed into Sal's.

Yum! I breathed in. You could smell the food the second you walked in the door. It was like you were transported somewhere else, stepping through those green-painted double doors. Suddenly, you're in a small-town, good-old-days diner and pub mixed into one. The smell of his classic French fries wafting right up to you as soon as you stepped foot into his establishment. I can't imagine anyone coming in here and not staying to at least try something fried -- his specialty.

"Hiya, Addison!" Kimberly called to me as I walked up to the hostess podium.

"Hello," I greeted her back. Kimberly was a few years younger than me. She grew up in my neighborhood. "How's softball?" I asked the town's star player.

"Not too bad! Just working on conditioning and all that. My coach thinks I can get a scholarship to college if I keep working this year and next year!"

"Kimberly, that's amazing! Way to go!" I said, remembering all those summers I saw her outside playing catch or baseball with all the neighborhood boys.

"Thank you!" she smiled. Then she grabbed a menu from the bin behind her, turning back to me. "Table or booth?" she asked.

"Actually, I'm just grabbing take-out," I told her, peering around behind her to see if I could see Zach and Charlie.

"Hmm," she said, looking through a small stack of papers and also scrolling on a tablet. "You know, this new system keeps messing things up. Let me go check in the back and see if it's ready."

"Okay. Thank you, Kimberly!"

She left and headed for the back, and that's when I saw him. Charlie, ever the flirtatious one, hitting it up with one of the waitresses here. I swear, you couldn't take Charlie anywhere without him leaving with multiple phone numbers or "dates" planned already.

I walked over to their table. Zach's coat was there, but he wasn't.

"Well, well, well! Look who it is!" Charlie exclaimed, looking away from the girl just long enough to notice me walking up. Then he turned to the waitress, "This is my buddy's wife."

"Hi, Charlie," I said, leaning my hip against the side of the booth a bit and putting my phone in my pocket.

"Sorry. It's his fianceé," he corrected. Then he lowered his voice, "Although, they already act like an old married couple, so I think the term *'wife'* is more fitting."

"Do not," I added.

"But, I mean," he said, turning his attention fully back to the girl. "I think weddings are so great. Beautiful things. And marriage. Wow."

I rolled my eyes at this, and the waitress batted hers, totally buying everything Charlie was saying.

I cleared my throat a bit, "Hey, Charlie?"

"Yes, Addie?" he said with a look and a tone that said butt-out.

"Where's Zach?"

He sat up, looking around the booth. "Dude, I don't know." He looked at the waitress. "Did you see him leave?"

"No," she answered, looking very fake-concerned. "Well, listen, I've got to get back. But here's my number. Use it, okay?" she told him, handing over a napkin with writing on it.

Wow. Like I said, Charlie was Charlie. Always getting the girls.

The waitress walked away, Charlie watching after her until she turned the corner and went to wait on another table. I'm sure they were wondering where their fries were and what was taking so long.

"Well," he said, turning back to me. "Have a seat. He'll probably be back in a second."

"No, that's okay. I'm just grabbing some take-out."

He nodded. "I'll be right back," Charlie told me, jumping up and heading over to the little screen the wait staff punches the orders into just as the waitress walked over there.

I walked back toward the front door, wondering what was taking the order longer than usual tonight.

I could see Charlie telling the waitress something that must have been hilarious because she was laughing and slapped his arm playfully. She nodded enthusiastically and then went back over to her other tables. Charlie walked over toward the restrooms.

I looked up. The baseball game was on the TV screen above me. Our team here in Madison isn't that great. My dad loves baseball though, so he will watch any game he can. He roots for our local team and pretends they're amazing, even though they haven't won a game in years. *But, hey, at least we can say we have a team, right?* And tickets are a steal, so it's a go-to gift for Dad.

Just then, as the pitcher was winding up, staring down the batter, time went into slow motion. The doors to the bathroom swung open and Charlie was running out of them, looking all around.

He spotted me and ran -- in what still seemed like incredibly slow motion -- toward me. "Addison!"

"What?"

He was breathing really heavy and his face was all red and splotchy. "Zach's passed out. Something's wrong."

"What?!"

"I don't know! I went into the bathroom and he was just laying there in front of the sinks."

"Oh my gosh!" I started running after Charlie to the back of the restaurant.

The waitress came up, "Charlie?" she questioned, wondering what was making him and I run through the restaurant. He stopped to explain it all to her and told her to call for an ambulance.

Ambulance? No, he's okay. It's fine. He's probably dreaming or something. Charlie just can't tell the difference because he doesn't know.

But then I had a flashback to that time things went haywire with Jess. And another few times after that when Zach's dreams had been...off.

I needed a way to tell him things would be okay, to tell *myself* things would be okay. I took a breath, closed my eyes, and tried my hardest to find his mind in jumbled mess of my own.

There was nothing. It was like looking at a blank television screen.

Where is he?! I wondered and worried, not finding his mind anywhere.

Oh, no, I thought. *Either he wasn't dreaming or something was really wrong.*

Something was wrong; I could feel it. I should've been able to see his mind when I thought about him, but I couldn't.

Please no.

* * *

An hour later, Charlie and I sat in the waiting room of St. Gregory Memorial Hospital. They wouldn't let us back yet. They had to "assess the situation," which is a load of crap if you ask me.

"Why can't we just go back there? I'm just sitting here. I can help."

"Addison," Charlie said softly, just barely above a whisper. "It'll be okay. Just let them do their job, okay?"

I had to admit, Charlie had been so helpful, driving my car over here in case I needed it, while I rode in the ambulance with Zach. I swear I blacked out that whole ride though. I just kept praying and praying that he would be fine. Anyway, he'd been much calmer and way better in a crisis than I ever would have thought.

"It'll be okay," he told me again. "Zach's a tough guy."

A bit later, as the medical drama continued to play on the screen across from me -- terrible choice of shows for a waiting room, let me tell you -- the side door opened and a nurse popped her head out. "Addison Smith?"

"Yes!" I jumped up, rushing over to her. "How is he?"

"We are having him prepped for some tests," she explained, while still standing in the doorway.

"Can I come back now?" I asked, poking my head over her shoulder, trying to see him or anything that would let me know he was okay.

"Not yet, miss. Family only."

I sucked in a breath. Family only? I glanced down at the brand-new ring on my left hand. Doesn't this count? I wanted to ask her.

"What tests?"

"I'm sorry, I can't--"

"This is his fiancé," I heard coming from behind me. Charlie walked up, rested a hand on my shoulder, and looked the nurse in the eye. "Can't you tell her anything? Is he going to be okay?"

"We're prepping him for some testing right now," she repeated.

"What tests?" I repeated.

"We want to rule out a few possibilities first." She then rattled off a few of those possibilities, quickly and matter-of-fact, as if those could be real possibilities.

"No," I said.

"Thank you," Charlie told her, pulling me back to the uncomfortable blue-grey chairs.

"No," I said again.

"I'm sure that's not it, Addison. They just want to rule out those things."

"Because it's an option! They think it's a possibility!" I yelled at him.

"Come on," he instructed, tugging at my arm, pulling me up to a standing position. "Let's get some fresh air." Then he ushered me out the door.

The cold air smacked me in the face instantly. So did the reality of what was happening, what she just said. What they had to rule out. Because they were worried it was a possibility.

Something's wrong with his brain.

Aneurysm, she said like it was so simple.

Tumor, she said like it was "just something to rule out."

No...

I looked up, letting the weight of those words sink in.

It can't be. He's only twenty-two.

Charlie stood off to the side, close enough in case I needed him, but far enough to give me space.

Suddenly the ring felt incredibly heavy on my hand, foreign there. Which is understandable because it hadn't been there til a few nights ago.

A few nights ago.

That's it.

We just got engaged.

He said forever.

We needed more time.

But in that moment, all I could think about was those stupid two months.

I'd give anything to have those two months back... I thought to myself, or maybe prayed.

17

- Zach -
Saturday, June 30th, 2018

Addison gets home today!

She's been in Europe with her mom and Jess since graduation. Her aunt even surprised her and met them in France.

I can't wait until she gets home. It's been so weird not having her around. But I'm really happy she got to go. I think she needed this.

Part of me hopes she found whatever it was Carrie went there looking for years ago. Part of me hopes she found some sort of cure for her dreams.

But the other part of me-- the part I'm not proud of, the part that reminds me more of my father and of Mitch, the selfish part-- hopes she didn't. Dreaming is our thing. *If she got rid of her dreams like Carrie did, what would happen to us?*

I don't want to think about what that would mean, so I grab my keys and my wallet and head out the door. Her flight doesn't get in for hours yet. So until then, I thought I'd go visit my mom again at The Haven. Maybe things will be different with Mom today. Maybe.

* * *

Mom had a freakout again today while I was there. She kept screaming and yelling that someone was coming after her. "They were coming" and "they" would kill her because of the things she's seen in her dreams.

The nurses asked me to leave, so I did.

And I drove here.

I look around the lacrosse field, a place I spent many nights for games and many days for practice. Lacrosse was the one consistent thing. Despite the constant moving around with my uncle growing up and the switching of schools, Mitch always signed me up for lacrosse.

He told me growing up that everyone needs an outlet, a way to blow off steam. He used to play basketball when he was younger. I've heard he was pretty good. He probably could have gotten a scholarship or continued to play past high school. But of course, life got in the way, his dreams got in the way, and my uncle spiraled down the path he did.

But still, one thing Mitch was adamant on was having a sport to play. Every time we moved to a new area, he would check if the school had lacrosse, either as a team or a club activity. He knew I liked the sport. He knew I was decent at it. For all of Mitch's wrongs in raising me, he did always get me to practices and games before I could drive. He would always be there in the bleachers, watching the game.

I remember once seeing him reading up on lacrosse and watching videos so he could help me and give me pointers as I was just starting to learn how to play.

"I can tell you anything you want to know about the game of basketball," he had said. "But lacrosse? We both are going to have to learn that one, kiddo."

So lacrosse was one thing --besides dreams-- that we had to talk about, something we had in common, a sure topic.

I'm not planning on playing in college. I mean, I may join an intramural team if they have it, but it won't be the same as it used to be.

Everything seemed to be coming to an end.

Except Addison...at least there was always her to rely on.

As if on cue, my phone buzzes in my pocket.

I'm home!!!!!!!!!!!!! she texted.

Another four messages popped up on the screen:

Where are you?

Get over here!!

Please!

Missed youuuuuuuuuuuuuuuu

I reply that I'd be right over. I spin my keys around with the new lanyard Addison got for me that has our college's name on it as I walk to my car.

It takes me less than ten minutes to get to her house. As I am driving down her street, nearing her house, I see her. Her hair looks lighter and longer, falling over her shoulders as she sits on the front stoop, knees up to her chest. She is shaking her legs, bouncing them up and down a bit and also biting her nails -- two signs she is either very nervous or very excited -- when she sees me pull into her driveway. She jumps up, screaming, and starts running toward me as I throw the car in park and get out.

"Ohmygoshlmissedyousooooooooomuch!" she squeals, her words all running into one.

I laugh and tell her I had missed her, too. Then she jumps up, and I catch her in my arms. She wraps her legs around my waist and her arms around my neck and kisses me on my cheek.

We stay like that, me holding her, in her front yard, for what seems like forever but also not long enough at the same time.

She hops down, back on the ground, and then presses herself against me. "Hi," she says, looking up at me.

"Hi," I say back.

Then I kiss her and she kisses me back like she is making up for being away for half of the summer.

When she pulls away she says, "I got something for you! Come inside!"

"Okay, just a sec," I tell her, reaching in through the open window of my car to grab the grocery bag from the front seat.

"What's that?" she asks, bobbing up and down with her hands behind her back.

A grin spreads across my face. "I have a surprise for you, too!"

"Really?" she squeals.

"Yes, really!"

I'll admit, I'm not very good with wrapping gifts or anything like that. So, yes, her surprise is just wrapped up in a plastic grocery bag. But I figure she won't mind. This isn't a *big* gift or anything. It is just something I've been wanting her to have and I thought today would be a good day to give it to her.

The lacrosse team was getting new jerseys this upcoming season -- some big donor dropped a boat load of money to get all new equipment and uniforms for the lacrosse team. I guess he had played on the team years ago and recently made it big. Because the team is getting all new jerseys, coach got them all cleaned and said all the seniors could take their jerseys as a parting gift. He also got us t-shirts printed with the school emblem and our names on the back.

I'm not sure if it is too cheesy or not, but I decided to give Addison my jersey. We watched a movie a while back and the main guy had given the girl his jersey to wear, and I remember Ad sighing and saying, "Isn't that the sweetest?"

When coach handed me mine, I remembered that moment and decided I would give it to her.

We walk inside and I kick off my shoes by the door. I say hello and chat with her parents for a bit. Mrs. Smith keeps starting to tell me about something they had seen in France, but then halfway through a story she just waves her hands and says, "Oh, well, I'll let Addie tell you the rest!"

Ad had been holding my hand while we talked, and now she tugs on it and starts walking toward the basement steps.

"I'm glad you guys had a good trip," I say to her mom.

"Thank you. It's good to see you, Zach!" she says to me, and then tells Addison to make sure I try the macarons they brought back, "especially the blue ones."

"I will!" Ad calls, pulling me downstairs.

The second we got downstairs, I pull her closer and she starts kissing me again. "I missed you," she says between kisses. "I have so much to tell you!"

She jumps back, gets an excited, knowing look on her face, and then says, "So...what's in the bag? Is it a present for me?"

"Yes," I reply, handing it to her.

I watch her as she plops down on the couch, untying the knot at the top of the bag. "Lovely wrap-job, Z," she says with a glint in her eye.

"Oh, you know, I'm just so crafty."

"Obviously."

She unties the bag and slowly pulls out the jersey, eyeing the fabric in her hands with a questioning look as she takes it out and holds it up.

She just looks up at me, over the jersey. I can't read her face. *She hates it,* I thought. *She was expecting a real present, not my jersey.*

I start rambling then, trying to save the situation in case she doesn't like it. I tell her how we got new jerseys for the team and everything. I tell her I wanted her to have my jersey.

A slow smile spreads across her face. "It's like that movie!"

Whew, she likes it!

"Oh, thank you, Zach! This means so much to me." She stands up and pulls the jersey over the top of her white t-shirt.

"It looks way better on you," I tell her.

"Why, thank you!" she exclaims, striking a pose. "Okay!" she says, clasping her hands together. "Your turn!"

She walks around behind the couch and comes back with a small white paper bag with a blue Eiffel Tower stamped on the front of it.

"Here," she says, handing it to me with a big smile.

As I start to undo the tape on the back of the bag and open it, she says, "Oh, and there is also a whole box of macarons for you upstairs! Don't let me forget to give you those!"

I smile, "I've never had a french macaron before!"

She puts her hand on my arm, saying, "You will love it! Absolute heaven in a cookie."

"Can't wait," I tell her.

"Okay, open it! Open it!"

Inside the bag is a little piece of paper, a card-type thing. It has a picture of a mountain side with a lady standing in a divot in the mountain. It looks like the place Ad had emailed me a bunch of pictures from. *This must be that super holy place she talked about in her emails, the place she said changed everything.*

On the paper, on the back, it reads: **I prayed for you at the grotto.**

Also in the bag is a very tiny little jar-looking thing, filled with water.

Looking incredibly excited Addison says, "*That* is it."

"Is what?" I ask.

"The water, silly!" she says with a laugh.

Water?

"The water I emailed you about," she explains, blue eyes shining. "It has all these healing properties. It's a miracle. It really is. The card is saying that I used my *one special prayer* there for you, for your dreams, I want yours to go away too, and --"

"Wait a second... your dreams...did you get rid of them?"

I am surprised at myself for the sharpness in my voice just then. *Wouldn't that be a good thing? Don't I want that for her?*

"Well, not exactly...well... I'm not sure yet. Something is definitely different with them though," she says to me, looking down and looking sad. "But anyway," she starts, excited again. "I think you should drink this." Then she chuckles a bit, "You have no clue how hard it was getting all this water back! We had to put it all in these tiny bottles so the airport security wouldn't take it away. We only have a little bit, but I want you to have all of this bottle."

"Okay..."

"Go ahead," she says.

"Go ahead what?"

"Drink it, silly."

"Drink this?"

"Yes. Of course. That's what you do with it."

I turn the jar around in my hands, looking it over. "Ad, I don't know too much about holy water. Mitch wasn't really one to take me to church on Sundays or anything. But, I do know you don't drink it. Wouldn't that be like sacrilegious or something?"

"No! This holy water is special. You are *supposed* to drink it and it will heal you. There's all these incredible stories of people who were blind and then could see after they drank it, or people who get bathed in it and couldn't walk before but now they can."

"But, Ad, those are all physical things. I don't think I need this."

She looks upset. "Yes, you do. We both do. Like I said, I got it for your dreaming."

"But, Ad... it's water."

She draws back and looks at me almost as if I had said or done something crazy. *Isn't it? Isn't it just water?* It sure looks like water.

"It is not *just* water." Her voice is tight, clipped.

"What's in it?" I ask, holding up the jar.

"Water!" she half-yells.

"Exactly," I point out.

"No. Not exactly. Zach, it is just water. But it is also not just water. Get it?"

I don't. I don't get it. I just sit there looking at this jar that was both water and not water. I am so confused.

"Listen, Zach. It is really important to me. I spent weeks at this place, learning about it, hearing people's stories and talking a lot with Carrie about dreams. I really think this will help. And besides the dreaming thing, this trip was a big deal for me. Being there, standing there, it was like everything in my life had been leading me there."

It seems really important to her that I drink this, so I guess it couldn't hurt. It seems like it was just water.

"Okay," I say.

"Okay?"

"Yeah, I'll try it."

I start unscrewing the lid to it. *How could water change anything?* I thought and a small laugh escapes from my throat. I instantly regret it.

"Well, wait just a second, Zach." I freeze and look up at her.

"What?" I ask. "I thought you wanted me to take it?"

She stands up and is looking down at me. "Only if you believe in it, Zach."

Great. What am I supposed to say here?

She stands there, waiting for me to speak.

"Listen, Ad..." I sit there for another second, trying to choose my words carefully. "I don't necessarily believe in *it*. It is water. No one understands how our dreams happen the way they do, they just do, okay? So I don't really think there is anything out there, *even magical water*, that will help that. I just don't. I've lived this way my whole life and so has all of my family. You just have to deal with it. You can't just hope, wish, and pray it goes away. But..." I take a breath and stand up, taking her hands in mine. "*But* I believe in *you*, Addison. So if you want me to try it, I will."

"Don't do me any favors," she says bitterly, pulling her hands away.

What is happening here?

"Ad, come on."

"No, Zach. You come on."

"What do you want me to say, Addison? What do you want me to do? Just tell me and I'll do it. I'll drink this water, okay? Is that what would make you happy?"

"You just don't get it, do you?" she says. There were tears welling up in her eyes, her beautiful blue eyes. In this moment I hate myself for being the reason for those tears. I had clearly done something wrong here.

Trying to salvage this, I say, "Exactly. I don't think I fully understand it. So let's just sit down and maybe you could start over and explain it to me again." I sat back down on the couch and patted the seat next to me.

"Not everything is so black and white with a specific answer to it, Zach."

"I know." I scooch over, showing her there's plenty of room on the couch and she should just sit down and talk it over with me.

But instead of sitting down, she takes a deep breath and tucks a piece of hair behind her ear. "Zach... what do you believe in?"

"You."

She rolls her eyes. "That's not what I mean."

Being honest here, I feel like any other moment, if I would have said I believed in her she would have gotten that swoony look on her face and said I was sweet or something. I don't understand how she is upset by that statement. It's true. I do believe in her. I believe in us.

"What do you believe in?" she asks again.

I sit there, at a loss for words.

"Do you believe in God? Miracles? Any of it?"

"Addison... you have to understand the difference in our lives for just a minute. You grew up going to church. I didn't. You went on this life-changing experience while I was here delivering pizzas and trying to scrounge up enough money to go to the college we want to go to. You had two parents there for you your whole life, and up until very recently, I thought my mother was dead. So I'm sorry, but I haven't ever really thought about stuff like that. I didn't think it mattered, okay? But I know all of that stuff is important to you. I just don't know what to do or how any of it works."

I let her think it all over, as she stands there very quiet.

"Why haven't you ever told me that?" she questions, looking hurt.

"Ad, come on. It never really came up. We haven't really talked about this deep stuff before. I mean, we were dealing with my uncle and just high school and everything else."

"Well we should have talked about it."

I feel like someone just punched me in the gut, knocked the wind out of me. *What is she insinuating?*

"Would it have changed anything?"

"I don't know..."

What? Now I'm getting upset. I've been trying to see this all from her point of view, I really have. I have been trying to understand, to listen. But now she's trying to tell me that things would be different way back when junior year when we used to play twenty questions if I would have said, "Why, no, Addison, I don't really believe in anything." Because at the time it was the truth. I didn't believe there could be anything good in this world, *anyone* good. Then I met her. And Addison is all good, all whole, all beautiful, despite all of her nightmares.

But -- and this may be arrogant-- I think *I am* good, too. I try to do the right thing. I work hard. And maybe half of any sort of goodness I have is because of her. But I'm fine with that. I would give her all of the credit, honestly. But, still, I'd like to think I'm a good person. I'd like to think I helped her through all of that stuff. I thought she loved me for me. Isn't that enough?

"So, what? If I would have told you all of this before you wouldn't have been with me?"

"I said I don't know, Zach..."

"How could you not know?" I yell.

"Because!" she yells back. "It's something incredibly important to me. I just traveled halfway across the world for this. Don't you get that?"

"Just, Ad. Just. You *just* travelled halfway across the world. You never used to be so invested in all of this."

"What's that supposed to mean?"

"It means before this trip I don't think you would have cared so much. Otherwise you *would* have brought it up to me. And besides, Ad, we're kids, okay? We don't know anything yet. We are both still figuring this all out. I'm not saying I would *never* believe in all of that stuff. I just said I never had a reason to before all of this."

I set the jar of water down on the ottoman and stand up, reaching for her. "Addison, please."

She won't look at me. *Why won't she look at me?*

"I think that maybe..." her voice trails off then, and she closes her eyes tight. A tear rolls down her cheek. I gently brush it away, but she turns her head away from me.

"I think that maybe," she starts again. "Maybe we both need some space. You know, to figure things out."

"What?!" I yell. "Addison, come on. You don't mean that!"

"Look, Zach, I know it wasn't as important to me before, but it is now."

"Addison, let's talk through this. Please."

"I think we both need time to think about it. I don't think talking through it will help. I don't want you just saying whatever to make me happy. We haven't really been apart, so maybe it'll be good for us to figure out who we are by ourselves and then see."

"And then see what? Addison, no. I know who you are. I don't need space to see that."

"*You* need to figure some things out, too, Zach--"

"And what do you mean 'we've never really been apart'? What were the past how many weeks? You were gone. We could only talk when you finally were in wi-fi and only over emails."

"Zach, please. Don't make this any harder." She steps away.

"Addison, please just tell me what just happened. I'll fix it."

"You can't fix everything right this second, Zach. Things need time."

"Okay," I breathe. I walk closer and kiss the top of her head, breathing in the smell of the mint shampoo she always uses. "Fine. I'll give you some space. I'll call you in a couple days."

"Sure," she says.

I do call her. Three days later.

She doesn't answer.

18

- Addison -
Friday, September 2nd, 2022

*I*t's been about an hour now. We are still waiting for the test results to come back. I hope they come back okay. They *have* to come back okay. I *need* them to come back okay.

I put my phone up to my ear, waiting as it rang and rang.

"Addie? What's up, honey?" my mom's voice asked on the other end.

"Mom," I croaked. "Something happened to Zach. We're in the hospital. I don't know what's happening. I–"

"Addison, your father and I are leaving right now, okay? I will be right there as fast as I can. It will be okay. It will be okay, Addie," she said, soothingly.

I said "okay" and wiped my hand across my face to somewhat dry the tears.

I stood up, rather unsteadily, and made my way over to the coffee machine. Has it ever seemed odd to you that hospitals always have those dispensers for coffee? The vending machines for coffee? I've never seen one of those anywhere else besides a hospital. It's like in the midst of all the craziness, anxiousness, and sadness that hospitals bring, you then have to sit there and pound your fist on the side of this stupid machine that won't pour out any coffee into that stupid paper cup.

I just need some coffee! I wanted to yell-- at the machine, at someone, at nothing. *Someone help me get some coffee!*

Even in that moment, I knew it wasn't really about the coffee. I don't even really drink it that much. I just needed something to do besides sitting there. I can't help if I'm just sitting there.

I took a deep breath. In and out. In and out.

It wasn't helping.

I looked up and looked around the corner.

Chapel a sign read with an arrow.

Now, *that* was what I actually needed.

I forgot about the coffee and my dollar and headed in the direction of the chapel. When I found it, I gently eased open the door. There was no one else in there, and I was thankful for that.

The room had about twenty chairs all lined up in rows. There were two thin, rectangular stained glass windows on the far wall. At the front was a table and a podium, both made of very dark wood.

I sat down in one of the chairs in the back. I knew no one else was in there. I could have sat in the front. But for some reason I just sat down in the back.

My mind was racing. I felt dizzy, like I couldn't breathe.

Air. I needed air.

This wasn't happening. Please, God, tell me this wasn't all happening to us.

I twisted my ring around and around my left finger with my right thumb and middle finger. My nails were all chipped, and I started chipping away at my thumb nail, little flakes of polish falling to the ground.

I stood up. I needed to do something, *anything,* to hep Zach. I started cursing myself for not going the medical route like I had wanted to years before. *If only I were in med school, I could know what was going on,* I thought. *Why did I have to pick psychology? That can't help me right now!*

I reached up, ran my hands through my hair, and then just gripped my hair really tight behind my ears. I was pulling my hair and curling tighter into a ball, as if that would help me feel better.

Why won't they tell me anything?

I felt like I had been here for hours.

Waiting.

Crying.

Falling apart.

Not with him.

I let go of my hair and sat up, brushing some tears away. Then I just started talking -- because that's just what I do when I'm nervous and scared-- I talk and talk and talk. So I took a deep breath and just started rambling, to myself, to God, outloud or maybe just in my mind. I don't even know.

"This wasn't supposed to happen. This can't happen. I keep telling myself not to jump to the worst case scenario. But, come on, what good case scenario could there even be when a healthy guy who's only twenty-two passes out suddenly? There is no good case scenario there. People don't just get sick and pass out. Zach doesn't do that. No matter what the doctors say, I'm not ready for it. There isn't anything they could say that I'm prepared for. The other day, when he asked me to marry him, that, I was ready for. I would marry that boy today. That, I am ready for. I'm not ready for any of this. I know the vows say "in sickness and in health," but I never thought that would happen before we even made our vows. We aren't even married yet. We just got engaged. We were talking just yesterday about the house we want someday. We were looking through my dream book, and he told me that he would do anything and everything to get me that light blue house someday. A house with navy blue shutters, a picket fence, a big driveway for our kids to ride their bikes in, a big backyard that would fit a swing set and a treehouse, because Zach said he always wanted to build his kids a treehouse someday. God, you can't let this happen now. He didn't get to build that treehouse or buy me that house yet. What about our kids? He would make the best dad in the world. I want to be able to see that. I want to see his blue eyes in our little boy someday. I want to see our little girl with his smile. That would be adorable. We need more time. This isn't supposed to happen until we're both old and gray and our kids are all grown up and living their own lives or have kids of their own. This can't happen now. We're too young."

I let out a sound that was somewhere between a scream and a cry. It was a horrible sound, even to my own ears. Low and guttural, and like you could hear my heart breaking. I didn't even know a sound like that could come out of me.

"Please, God, please. I'll do anything. I really will. Just let this nightmare be over, please. I've lived through so many nightmares already, I don't think I can handle this. Please just let this all be over. Let me wake up from this horrible, horrible dream and have everything be okay. I'll help other dreamers. I'll take whatever pain he's in instead of him. He's such a good person. He doesn't deserve this, any of it. He deserves to be happy and healthy."

I bowed my head, tears escaping and rolling down my cheeks. *Please help me. There has to be an answer here. There has to be a way to fix this-- a way to help Zach.*

I had a flashback to my dream a few nights before, the one where his name was inscribed on that grave...

I didn't even want to think about it. There's no way that could happen. *That can't happen. Not for many, many years.*

I need a sign. I need something to tell me this will all work out. Please...

I realized I had still been holding Zach's jacket, grasping it for dear life the whole time I've been here. It was leather and black. *Zach always looked so good in this jacket,* I thought.

A chill ran up my spine.

It's cold in here, I thought, sliding my arms into his jacket. It felt warm, wrapping around me. I breathed in the smell of him, the cologne I got him last year for Christmas from that store at the mall that he likes.

His jacket felt so big on me. I curled into myself a bit more, hugging his jacket tighter around me. It reminded me of when I used to wear his jersey around, the way it was so long on me, almost like a dress, and I felt like I could just curl up in it.

I felt it then... a flashback coming on. Not just one where I think of a picture from a previous dream like I did just seconds ago. A real dreaming flashback. One where I am fully transported to the dream realm. One where my mind goes off somewhere else and my body stays put, while the dream from the past plays out.

* * *

He stands up, walks closer to me, and kisses the top of my head. He lingers there for a few minutes, and this time I let him. But it's killing me inside.

"Fine. I'll give you some space. I'll call you in a couple days," he says sounding so distraught.

"Sure," I mutter.

Then he is gone, and so am I. I'm just gone-- a mess of tears and aches and more pain than I ever thought I'd be feeling.

How did this happen? I wonder. *How did I go from the best experience of my life to feeling like the floor just dropped out from under me?*

I got home from Europe not even two hours ago and the biggest fight of my life has already happened.

How could he not care? How could he not understand?

I sink down on the floor in front of my couch, quite literally crumbling to pieces. I never thought I'd be this girl. I never thought I'd fall apart over a guy.

But Zach isn't just some guy, I remind myself.

Then I start questioning everything that just happened, wondering why I said what I just said. I was the one who told him to leave. I was the one who said we needed space. I don't want space. I want the way things used to be. *What did I just do?*

I grab the bottle of water from the ottoman, turning it over in my fingers, just staring at it. *How did all of that just happen from this tiny bottle of water?*

But it isn't just water, I remind myself.

I set the water back down. I curl up tighter, trying to form a ball and block the world out. My fingers feel the material of his lacrosse jersey, and I start to cry all over again.

His jersey feels so big on me. I curl into myself a bit more, hugging his jersey tighter around me.

I cry myself to sleep.

He does call. It takes him three whole days.

So, I don't answer.

* * *

My eyes snapped open, and I was lying on the floor in front of the chair I had just been sitting on in this hospital chapel room. I was curled up in front of the chair, in the same position I had been in when I cried myself to sleep in that dream.

This hasn't happened in years. I haven't dreamed of something and woken up somewhere or in a position I wasn't in when I fell asleep. That is one of the things that got better from the water.

My dreams did not go away completely. Everyone dreams. I didn't get rid of them. Neither did Carrie, not really.

There's a difference between what people have always said happens and what really happens. I think us dreamers thought that "getting rid of" your dreams meant they were just gone. *Poof! You're healed!*

I think it's deeper than that. They may not go away, but you're given the tools to handle them, to fight them, and to help others.

My physical nightmares definitely went away after that journey. I would no longer wake up injured or on the other side of the room. After that trip, I still had dreams, but they stayed that way -- dreams, in my mind.

Why did it just happen again though?

I curled my fingers around his jacket sleeves. Again I'm hit with the same thought as before, *I'd give anything to have those two months back.*

I looked around the hospital chapel, the light blue walls feeling like water flooding all around me.

I reached in the pocket of his jacket, finding his phone there. I pulled it out and immediately smiled. He had made the picture of us from the other night, the engagement, his lock screen on his phone. *That's so sweet.*

I'm still not sure what made me unlock his phone in that moment, but that's what I did. I opened up his camera roll and began scrolling through the few pictures he had. Most of them were photos I had taken on my phone and sent to him or ones my mom had taken on our nice camera over the years and I uploaded them for him.

I looked at that picture, the one from our engagement, for a long time.

We looked so happy. *How could this just be a few days ago?*

I actually don't think I've ever smiled that big in a picture before. I don't think I've ever smiled that much in one night as I did the other night. I still couldn't believe all the thought he put into it all.

I still couldn't believe I was sitting in a chapel in a hospital...

I took a breath and said a small prayer, under my breath, very quietly. It was one I remembered from when I was little.

Then I opened my eyes and realized I had accidentally scrolled to the next picture. I was about to turn off his phone and go back to saying the rest of the prayer and then go back outside to find Charlie, when I read it.

It was the sign-in sheet for The Haven.

Why does he have a picture of this?

That's when I saw the name signed on the sheet.

Mitch DeMize.

Oh my gosh, I thought. *He's in town? He visited Meg?*

Without thinking, I grabbed my phone from my back pocket and began dialing the numbers on the picture beside his name.

This is it. This was the sign.

I sat there, my legs shaking and my heart racing. *Please answer,* I thought which is something I never thought I'd say when calling Mitch.

Ring...Ring...Ring...Ring...Ring...

"Hello?"

"Oh, thank God! Mitch!"

"Who is this?" a gruff voice responded.

"Mitch?" I asked.

"Who is this?" he said again.

"Mitch... It's Addison. I need your help."

I could actually hear the shock in his voice as he said, "You need my help, now?" He sounded way too happy.

"Mitch, I swear. Don't be like that. I need you to listen to me."

"What? Do you finally want to join my side of things?"

"I'm serious. I need your help."

He seemed to think about it for a minute. "How did you get this number? Why are you calling me?"

"Zach's in the hospital."

His voice was finally all serious when he repeated, "Zach's in the hospital?"

"Yes."

"What happened?" He sounded worried. He should be.

"I don't know. He was out to dinner with Charlie, and then he passed out or something. They're running all these tests. And now looking back, his dream sessions have been all weird lately. I think something's really wrong. These doctors won't know what to do. His mind is probably different. Or there's something wrong they can't see or don't know to look for."

"Addison, slow down. Tell me. What hospital are you at?" he demanded.

I told him, and then I did the worst thing possible. I started to cry. I was crying to Mitch of all people on this earth. I couldn't control it either, I was just crying so hard.

"I'll be there in twenty minutes."

"Okay," I said between sobs. "Please come. He needs you."

The phone went silent. He had hung up.

The realization set in then. *I just called Mitch DeMize for help.*

Then another realization set in.

An eye-opening amazing one. It felt like my mind was pulling itself back into the dream again, back into that moment years ago.

That's it!

Why didn't I think of this sooner?

I picked up the phone, dialing my mom's number.

"Mom! Did you leave yet?" I asked, talking a mile a minute.

"Yes. I was just about to call you. We are coming as fast as we can, sweetie, but there seems to have been some sort of accident blocking the highway."

I told her that I needed the box. She muttered under her breath that she should've thought to bring it herself. My father was in the background trying to talk out a way to turn around and go back, but there was no way they could safely.

"That's okay," I said, racking my brain for what to do.

"We will be there soon. It will be okay," my mom repeated again.

After I hung up, I jumped up and ran out of the chapel, colliding with Charlie right outside the door.

"Charlie!"

"Hey, Ad. Nothing yet. They said it shouldn't be much longer though."

"Charlie!" I yelled again, grabbing him by the shoulders and shaking.

"What?"

"I need you to do me a huge favor. Huge. Okay?"

"Anything."

I shoved my car keys in his hand. "Go to my house. Just go on in. It's this one," I told him, pointing out which key on the ring went to the house. "In the front living room, there's a built-in bookcase. There's a box on one of the shelves. It's blue with butterflies on it -- the box is, not the shelves." I was babbling now. "Just bring it back here, okay? Be quick. I need it."

"Yeah, of course," Charlie said, closing his fingers around the keys. "Sure you don't need me here?" he asked.

"No. I really need that box."

"Okay. I'll be back as soon as I can."

He turned to leave and I remembered why I had to send him in the first place. "Charlie!" I called out.

"Yeah?"

"The highway is crazy right now. There was an accident or something. Go Brandt then Washington then-"

"Then Delilah Avenue. I got it, Addison. Don't worry," he said and then rushed off toward the exit.

"Thank you! Thank you!" I called and then made my way back to the waiting room.

I needed that box. Now.

19

- Addison -
Friday, September 2nd, 2022

*M*y legs shook as I sat in the uncomfortable blue chair in the waiting area.

Not family.

That was crap. I wanted to see him. I *had* to see him.

I looked all around the waiting room. There were only two other people in the room. The woman was clutching her arm while the guy beside her filled out the paperwork. She looked like she was in a lot of pain. He looked worried.

I really hoped Charlie got back quickly with that box. It could change everything.

"Addison!"

I knew that voice.

I whipped my head around, turning in the plastic chair.

There he stood.

Mitch DeMize.

I stood up and just stood there, not moving, not walking toward him, just standing insanely still.

"Addison," he repeated. "How is he? What happened?"

"I-I..."

"It'll be okay. Just tell me what happened. Has anything else been going on?"

I had a million questions running through my head right then. *Why did I call him of all people? Why is this happening? Why is he acting so calming and helpful? Why did he show up?*

"Why did you go to The Haven the other day?" I asked, surprised at myself that this was the first question I managed to ask him.

"She's my sister," he replied as if it was as simple as that.

"I know, but why did you go just the other day?"

"I've been visiting more than that. I come back from time to time to check in on her, on you guys. But I just moved back here permanently about a week ago." He paused and placed both hands on my shoulders, willing me to focus on what he was about to say. "We can talk about all of that later, Addison. You need to give me some background information here. Anything you know that's been going on with him lately. Anything you can tell me will help. There's so much they won't find and won't tell us here, so I need you to tell me."

"Okay," I said sitting down.

Mitch shook his head and nodded at the couple sitting just a few seats away.

For a second I wondered if they'd even hear us, or if they'd even care. But Mitch gave me a stern look, and I knew he was right. Even if they didn't understand everything we would say, it was too dangerous to talk about dreaming around non-dreamers. So I stood and followed him down the hall.

There was another waiting area, much smaller, a few yards down the hallway. It was just a couple of chairs lining the wall. There were hospital rooms down a bit, but it seemed unoccupied at the moment.

Mitch whistled under his breath, a low and almost sad-sounding noise. "This hallway brings back memories," he said, sounding somber. I wondered what had happened here, what had happened to him.

So we sat down in the chairs and I racked my brain for any clues in the past few weeks that would've said something like this could happen.

I explained to Mitch in as best detail as I could muster what had happened that night at Sal's and also what had happened before in the dreamscape with Jess and what he had been dreaming about.

"Wait, are you sure it was a dream? Or was it a memory?" he asked me, his voice low.

"Is there really a difference?" I asked. A lot of dreams stem from memories anyway.

"Big one," is all he said.

I tried to think about it. Zach had been talking more like it was a memory. "I think it was more of a memory," I told Mitch.

"Well, I remember seeing Adam freak out on Meg multiple times about taking the pills. To be honest, we both thought they would help. Zach is right though, the downside is they made her drowsy and, quite frankly, out of it. But I assumed she was taking them."

"Mitch," I said.

He seemed to remember that the pills and Meg's dreams weren't exactly what we were worried about at that moment. "Right. Okay, so..." he began mumbling to himself and stood up, pacing back and forth in front of us.

I'm a nervous pacer, too; I get it. Sometimes when things get crazy, you just want to walk back and forth in a very small area. I do that, too, so I shouldn't have gotten so upset. But sitting there watching Mitch pace back and forth was driving me nuts. "Mitch," I barked. "Could you sit down! You're not helping."

He stopped, his shoes squeaking against the floor. He just looked at me.

I instantly felt bad. He did come. He was trying to help. This wasn't his fault. "I'm sorry," I told him, focusing my gaze on the floor.

"It's alright." He took a breath and sat down. "So, I'm going to go in there. Hopefully he's still sleeping, and I can see what's going on in that brain of his."

I nodded.

He stood up and walked down the hall, rounding the corner and just walking right on back through the double doors. No one stopped him. No one questioned who he was or what he was doing back there. The nurses just stayed at their station and let the forty-year-old man with dark sunglasses and a leather jacket walk right on back.

Maybe he really could help...

* * *

Not even ten minutes later, Mitch came walking back toward me. I was still sitting in that same chair. I sprang out of the chair.

"What did you find out?"

The corners of his mouth turned up into a smile for a moment so brief, I may have dreamt it. "I'll go into more depth later, but something is up. I'm not sure what. I have some theories. None of them are good."

It felt like a knife drove into my stomach when he said that. Mitch was so matter-of-fact. *"None of them are good"* he'd said in a way you wouldn't know he was talking about his own blood.

"But," he continued. "Some of them are fixable, if my studies have been correct these past few years, which I will explain to you both soon."

"Both?" I asked.

"He's up."

He's up. Two words that on their own don't seem that significant, but after a day like today and a history like ours, those two words meant the world to me.

"He's up? Is he okay?" I asked, tears welling up in the corners of my eyes.

"Yes. Room 205. You should go see him. He's groggy, but he should be good for a bit. I'm sure he wants to see you."

I nodded enthusiastically and then rushed off on the direction I had just seen Mitch come from.

201, 202, 203...

Come on!

204...

There it was. 205. I didn't even knock, just opened the door and walked right in.

The second the door closed behind me, I froze. Right where I was. I assumed I'd just run over to the side of his bed and hug him and kiss him and just be there with him. But the sight of Zach lying in that hospital bed made me stop dead in my tracks.

There were tubes coming out of him and other tubes pushing liquids into him. There was a beeping noise coming from a machine. He looked so small. He looked so different.

I couldn't handle it. I couldn't move any closer. I just stood there and looked on while my fiancé laid there in an emergency room.

"Addison!" he whispered. I thought maybe he had seen me, had heard me come in. Now he saw how cowardly I was being, standing by the door, too afraid to come in. I felt like I was going to be sick. *What if Mitch and I couldn't fix this?*

But I realized he was half-asleep. He squirmed around a little bit and then quieted again.

I walked in and settled into the chair next to his bed. I wrapped my hand around his. His eyes fluttered open and locked on mine.

"Thank God you're here," he said.

"Thank God you're awake," I replied.

"Are you okay?" he asked me, his eyes wide.

"Am I okay?" I repeated. "Zach, I should be asking you that question."

"You didn't collapse in the middle of the road?"

"Zach, I think you were dreaming that. That didn't happen. I'm okay. I'm right here. I'm not leaving, okay?"

"I'm sorry I ruined it."

"Zach, what are you talking about?" I asked. He looked and sounded so shaken up, so unlike himself. His eyes were wide and a more muted grey color, as opposed to the vibrant, heart-breaking blue they usually were.

"I dreamt about when we --"

Broke up. I knew that's what he had dreamt of, because that's exactly what I dreamt of, too.

"I know," I cut him off, kissing his forehead. "Me too."

"I'm so sorry," he told me, gripping my hands tight.

"Zach, that was forever ago, and --"

"I am so sorry. I was so stupid."

Through my tears I said, "It's all okay now. Everything's going to be okay."

20

- Zach -
Saturday, July 14th, 2018

It is pouring down rain as I sit at my computer, looking at the "Welcome!" email from my "future home." It has a list of things that are suggested to bring with you to a college dorm. To be honest, the list isn't worth crap. There is barely anything on it besides the obvious and also some cheesy things like "an attitude to learn!" and "good roommate behavior!", neither of which will help me figure out what to buy at the store in an hour.

I am still crashing at Mitch's place until move-in day for college. It works because it's still his mailing address, so when the college wants to send forms and information, it all checks out. Either way, I'm eighteen and can sign for most things for myself. The rent here has been paid through October, and by then I'll be settled in at school.

For now it's working. But still from time-to-time Billy's mom insists that I have to go over for dinner. I think she thinks Mitch is still here, though. She just thinks he can't cook very well. I'll never pass up a good, free dinner, so I always go when she asks me.

Like tonight. I'll be heading over to Billy's in about a half hour. His mom is making a pot roast, which sounded amazing. She really is an incredible cook!

My stomach growls. If I wasn't so hungry, I wouldn't even go. It's been two weeks since Addison broke up with me. I really don't want to sound like a wimp, but it has really sucked. It's so weird to go from seeing someone so often to not seeing them at all. I have tried calling a few times. I've tried texting her. She just won't answer.

I haven't gone over there, even though I have wanted to, because I know that'll only make things worse.

It sucked though, not seeing her. What sucks the most though is that I still can't really figure out what happened or where things went so wrong.

A half hour later I was sitting on Billy's couch arguing with him over the real reason he lost the previous round of his newest video game. He was very close to searching online for any known glitches causing players to randomly lose-- he was always blaming losses on glitches-- when his mom popped her head in the family room.

"Hey, William?"

Billy cringed. He hated being called William or any variation of the name besides Billy. He never told his mom though. He said she picked the name, so that would be like saying he didn't like her or her opinions. So he just lets her call him William. But only her.

"Yeah?" he hits pause on the video game and looks up at her.

It is weird sometimes how much of Billy's mom you could see in Billy. I can't tell if it's the eyes or smile or what, but he definitely looks more like his mom than his dad.

"Something is off with the ground turkey. I can't use it. I don't want any of us getting sick. Do you and Zach mind running to the market to grab something else?"

"Sure thing, Mom," he says, as he reaches for his keys on the end table beside him. "Let's go," he says to me.

Within minutes we are walking around Joey's Fresh Market looking at the selection at the butcher's counter. Billy decides to get ground beef instead and is looking for the package with the best date on it when I feel someone stop short beside us and draw in a deep, uncomfortable sounding breath.

I turn slightly to the right and see Cammie standing there, arms crossed, staring daggers at us both.

"Excuse me," she says quietly and points to the case in front of us all.

"Sure. Sorry," I say, and step back, giving her space.

I wonder if Addison told her everything. Then I think about her face when she saw me a minute ago. *Yep, she knows we broke up. She's her best friend.*

She reaches over and grabs a package of chicken wings and then turns to leave.

"Hey, Cammie?" I say before I can even stop myself.

Billy cuts a look at me. I shrug and focus back on Cammie.

"What's up?" she replies sounding like she didn't just give me the deadliest look ever.

Then I chicken out. *How could I ask her about Addison? What would I even ask?* "How's it going?" I say, finally spitting it out.

"Good."

We all stand there awkwardly. Billy is rifling through the pre-packaged meats, pretending not to listen or care. Cammie and I just stand there staring at each other.

"Look," she says a beat later. "I don't know what happened with you guys. Addie still won't tell me anything. But whatever it is, let me tell you, it's stupid and pointless and you both need to get over it. She's miserable, okay, Zach? She'll kill me later for telling you that, but it's the truth." She stood up a little taller and stepped closer to me. "So swallow your pride and go talk to her, alright?"

Then she turns, gives an awkward wave to Billy, and walks out of the store.

She didn't tell Cammie what happened?

"Chicks," Billy mutters, shaking his head. Although the look in his eyes shows how much he is missing his girl, too.

Breakups suck, I think.

* * *

Later that week I can't get what Cammie said out of my head. "Swallow your pride," she had said. *What pride?* I think. This isn't me being prideful and not going to make things better just for the sake of looking better. I don't care about any of that. I just want Addison to be happy. And if she needs space to figure out what happy means now for her, then I'd give her that. I don't want to give her space, but I would. *So, no, Cammie, this isn't about my pride or what I want.*

What was I supposed to do? She won't answer my calls or texts. She hasn't been at any of the places we usually go or I usually see her.

I'm still not sure what makes me do it, but I pick up my phone and call a number she added in my phone months back in case of an emergency.

Two rings later, she answers, "Hiya!" It's so like her to answer the phone that way, so chipper and happy.

"Carrie?"

"This is she! Who am I speaking with?"

"It's Zach. Zach Walker," I say praying she won't hang up as soon as my name registers with her.

"Well, I'm really glad you called, dreamer boy."

I draw my head back from my phone for a second and my brow furrows. *Dreamer boy?* I shake it off and think about the other part of that statement. "You are?" I ask.

"Yes, sir! I'm glad you finally got around to callin' me!"

"Finally?" I ask.

I hear her laughing on the other end of the phone. "Boy, I thought you'd call last week!"

I am not understanding the humor she seems to be finding in this right now. Being honest, Ad's Aunt Carrie is a very interesting person who I can't quite figure out.

And yet she's the one I call for advice.

I decide to shrug off the comments about my calling her and just cut to the chase, "How do I get Addison back? What did I do wrong?"

"Listen," she says. "I've done my fair share of stupid things when it comes to relationships. I was much different in high school than I am now, or even how I was by the end of high school." She laughs to herself. "Just ask your uncle."

After a minute she adds, "No, wait. Don't actually ask him. Okay? Promise?"

"Promise."

"Anyway, I don't know that I'm the best person to give anyone on this planet dating or relationship advice. But, I think I can tell you what not to do and also how to try to repair something once you've broken it."

"I broke it? I never wanted to hurt her," I tell Carrie.

"Don't worry, dreamer boy, I know that. Believe me, I know that. And I think deep down she knows that too. She's a young, teenage girl just about to start college. She's confused. Not to mention that girl is wise beyond her years. That trip and the experience she had there was something most eighteen-year-olds don't do. If anything, they're studying abroad in France to find themselves, not traveling there for healing. The trip changed her."

There's a bit of silence before I say, "I know it did."

"Now," she starts. "That is not to say she's changed so much that you're out of the picture. I think she needs to find a way to make all the puzzle pieces fit. Right now you're a center piece, something she's always had but has to figure out a way to get it to fit after she gets all the corner pieces in place. Without you the puzzle picture will look empty, but she also can't start with just you. She's gotta figure it out on her own."

A puzzle piece?

"Well, what can I do to fit better?" I ask.

"I think you need to look at your own life a bit, too, and evaluate where she fits in for you."

"Oh," is all I say. It's silent for a minute on the other side of the phone. I fill the silence by saying what I know is true, "She fits. She definitely fits in my life. I don't really want to know what it's like if she doesn't fit."

"I figured you'd say that," she tells me.

Why does she keep talking like that? Saying things like "I figured you'd say that" without having a follow up. I need answers. I feel like Carrie's the only one who can help me at this point. "Carrie, what should I do? Please, I'm begging here."

"Meet me tomorrow in the town square before 8."

"P.M?" I ask.

"Nope. Morning, silly. Dress nice. See ya then!"

Click!

I look at my phone, the screen going blank after the call has ended. *What? What's tomorrow? What's going on?*

* * *

The next morning I get up early, my alarm blaring to make sure I get up on time. I toss on some khaki pants and a button down shirt and get in my car, driving to the town square.

It is really sunny outside and already hot and humid, even though it's still very early in the morning.

I pull into one of the many open spaces along the gazebo. There are maybe two cars in the whole three block vicinity.

I can see Addison's aunt standing on the steps of the gazebo, waving her arms wildly with a big smile.

"Don't you clean up nice!" she says as I walk up to her.

"Where are we going?" I ask, not really one for surprises.

"I think you need to see things from Addie's perspective. I don't think it's your fault you don't see things this way. God knows I never used to. I just think you need someone to explain some of this stuff to you so you can understand where she's coming from better."

"Alright," I agree, still wondering why khakis were necessary for her to explain Ad's side to me from the gazebo.

"Let's go!" she exclaims, somewhat skipping down the steps of the wooden gazebo.

"Where are we going?" I ask again. She just shakes her head and chuckles.

A few minutes later, after walking through town, we come up to a building I had seen many times in my years here at Madison. I always thought the building was really cool, with interesting architecture and tall towers in the front. I guess I hadn't ever really stopped to consider what the building was or read the sign out front. Today I do.

It reads: **St. Peter's Church.**

"Come on in," Carrie says. "Everyone's welcome." She winks and begins walking through the double wooden doors as others file in behind us. I think to myself that it's crazy so many people get up this early. I see a ton of people from our town filling in the wooden benches and talking amongst themselves.

A little while later a piano starts to play. Carrie hands me a folded piece of yellow paper with words printed on it. I realize they're the words everyone around me is singing. It strikes me that all these people seem so awake and happy, even at eight in the morning. They're all singing, some with incredible voices and some not so great, but either way it's kind of cool how they're all coming together, not caring about anything else, just happy to be there.

I had seen some church services on television or in movies in the past, scenes depicting what it's like. I thought I knew what it would be like, figured I had pieced together enough to get a rough idea of what the idea of church was.

But being honest, all those ideas were nothing like what it was. In today's day and age, it was just neat to see all different people coming together for the same purpose. I recognized some people from our town sitting with others who I never thought they got along with or really knew. The man who owns the market, Mr. Don, was smiling and talking with the florist, Gwyneth. I've never seen them talk before out and about. I am not sure why I find that so interesting, but I do.

Part way through, Carrie leans over and whispers, "I brought you here at eight because Addison has been coming at ten."

Music began playing again, and it sounded really cool. Carrie continues in a low whisper, "So if you want to know more about what she believes in -- besides you, because I know deep down she still believes you two will make it -- but if you want to know, it is up to you. You can come at ten and she'll know you're here and see you. Or...you can keep coming at eight, learn about her world a bit more, and when you're ready, you can talk to her about it."

I smile and nod at Carrie, finally understanding what this morning was all about.

For the next two weeks I go to the eight a.m. mass, sitting in the back, taking it all in. I also spend a while researching the place she went in France and reading up about the history of the girl from the place who found the water.

I realize late that night, I am doing this for Addison. I want to know what she knows and understand better what happened to her on her trip. But I realize that I'm also doing this for myself.

I think I need something bigger than myself and bigger than the dream world to believe in.

I think maybe everyone does.

21

- Addison -
Friday, September 2nd, 2022

We were still waiting for answers what seemed like hours later. I don't even know how long it had really been. I just know it seemed like forever.

"I'm going to grab us all some coffees," Mitch offered.

"I'll go with him," my dad suggested, picking up his phone from the table it was resting on and snapping it into place on his belt.

My parents eventually got around the traffic and made it here a little bit ago. The first thing my mom did when she got here was wrap me in a hug and tell me everything was going to be alright.

At first, as she hugged me, I was just so grateful to have her there, comforting me and helping me.

But then, I felt a pang of guilt. Zach's mom couldn't be here to comfort her son, let alone grasp the fact that she's his mom, and he's the one in the hospital.

What right did I have to be saying I needed my mommy when it wasn't even me that all of this was happening to?

As if my mom could sense I was thinking this, she said, "Sweetheart, it's okay to be nervous and worried. It's normal to cry or yell or whatever you need, okay?"

I let out a deep breath and hugged her tighter. "Thank you for coming."

"Of course, Addison!" my mother replied, as if even insinuating it was a choice or chore to come was ridiculous. "Come sit with me out here for a second."

I turned and looked back at Zach lying in the bed sound asleep. "But--" I started.

"It's okay. We'll just be a minute."

"Okay..." I slowly followed her out into the hallway. She gently placed her hand around my back as we walked through the door frame and into the bright fluorescent lights of the white hallway.

"Talk to me. What are you thinking?" she said, holding my shoulders with both her hands and staring into my eyes.

I really thought I could hold it together. I really thought I was handling this all relatively well.

But there's just something that happens within you when your mom asks you what's going on and how you're feeling. It's like the wall that was up preventing the rest of the world -- and sometimes yourself -- from acknowledging your feelings begins to crumble. There's something so therapeutic about that wall crumbling down when you're with your mother.

The tears flowed, steady and hot down my cheeks. I reached up to brush them away with the back of my hand, feeling the cool metal of my ring on my cheek, the diamond catching a tear, the water's glint against the gem.

"What am I going to do, Mom?" I asked, finally completely and utterly breaking down.

She wrapped her arms around me again, comforting and strong. "I don't know, Addie. I don't know what's going to happen. But I do know that it will all work out. You and Zach have been through a lot, but I know your story won't end anytime soon. It's going to be okay. You will get your happily ever after."

"How do you know?" I asked between sobs.

"I just know," she replied, the classic "mom" response; and yet right then, it was exactly what I needed to hear. "I'm sorry we couldn't turn around for the box."

"Charlie went to get it," I told her.

"Did you tell him there was an accident on sixty-five? Things are moving pretty slowly. He may be a while."

I nodded. "He went all back roads," I told her, knowing once he got back with that box everything would work out. That was all I needed.

"Why don't you try to get some rest? Or at least sit down for a little while? I'll let you know if anything changes."

I don't know what Mitch said to the staff here at the hospital, but suddenly they were allowing all of us to be back in the room with Zach, at least until the results came in.

My mom and I both walked back into the room. I settled into the uncomfortable chair next to Zach's bed, reaching out to lace his fingers through mine.

I looked up at my mom. She had a look on her face I had only seen a couple of times in my life. It was a face that seemed to be full of love, but also full of worry. I remember seeing that same face when I was thirteen and had the flu so bad I had to go to the hospital for dehydration. I saw that face again when I had been explaining my dreams to her and my dad.

Now she had that look on her face again and forced the sides of her mouth to turn up into a small smile. "Get some sleep," she whispered. "I'll let you know when Charlie gets here."

I nodded and tucked my head into the side of Zach's arm. It was both incredibly uncomfortable and incredibly comfortable at the same time.

I concentrated hard on what I wanted to dream of in that moment. *Whatever he's dreaming of,* I thought, and let my mind soar off through the crossing between worlds, finally landing where his mind was, in his dream.

* * *

The room is full of a heavy grey fog, coating everything in sight and weighing down on my body and my heart.

"Hey, beautiful," he says with a grin.

"Hey," I swoon.

He looks even more handsome in my dreams. His smile is wider and brighter. His eyes are bluer and happier. His voice is like velvet, smoothly saying everything. His laugh is richer and heartier, like he laughs without care as he throws his head back. In my dreams and in my mind, Zachary Walker is perfection, clear and shining amidst the grey.

"What memory are you trying to find?" I ask him as I float closer to him.

He takes hold of my hand, squeezing it tight. "I want to finish the dream I was having earlier. This whole time I've been going back and forth," he says. "From dreams that don't make any sense to dreams of the past. Dreams of me and you."

"I've got a good one," I tell him, smiling.

Suddenly, a giant film strip appears in front of us, floating in the air. Each little space depicts a different scene. I walk along the strip, looking for the right one.

I find it, right in the middle, just like the memory is right in the middle of our story together, the turning point.

"This one," I tell him, reaching out my hand and pulling the box holding the memory down from the film strip. An empty space now where the box had just been, dividing the film strip into two parts.

He smiles and steps into the box, and I follow him, the two of us stepping into the past, into the memory.

22

- Addison -
Sunday, September 2nd, 2018

I'm sitting on a metal chair across from her as she sits, upright and tall, in her bed. I just look at the room she's in. It needs more color I think. It needs more life in here. A bed should have pillows and blankets, not just a sheet. This room really does need some livening up. Maybe some flowers would help.

I smile at her. "Can you tell me another story about your son?" I ask her. "What was he like when he was little?"

Her face lights up. She loves talking about him. That's one thing I have noticed in the past few weeks: she is not much of a talker, but if you ask her about her son, she has so much to say.

"Well," she starts, brushing a stray piece of her long hair behind her ear. "He was such a sweetheart. He always wanted to be with his mama. I swear he was the only thing that got me through my nightmares."

"Nightmares?" I ask her, pretending not to know how her life used to be, and maybe still was.

"Yes, darling. Not all dreams are good dreams."

"Believe me," I tell her, leaning in closer, "I know."

"Don't we all?" she laughs and flicks her wrists.

I have been stopping by The Haven every two days these past few weeks. I realized recently that just because I was no longer with Zach didn't mean I should stop visiting Meg. That wouldn't be fair to her. Plus, my aunt had encouraged me to keep going. She said visiting his mom might help me to better understand where he's coming from. I think she was right.

Suddenly the door to Meg's room swings open.

"More visitors!" Meg coos. "I love visitors!"

I just stare up at him, standing in the doorway, not moving. He's wearing one of his baseball style shirts. He always looks so good in those. His hair is pushed back a different way than usual. And of course -- because this is the way the world works-- he is holding a vase of flowers, very brightly colored flowers to brighten up Meg's room.

"Ad?" he chokes out, looking shocked to see me.

"Hi, Zach," I say, not moving my gaze away from him.

"You've got a good girl here, son. Quite a young woman."

Zach blinks, turning his attention to his mom. I know what he's thinking, of course I do. For starters, Meg said "son" to him. But the look on her face and the tone when she had said that tells me it was just an expression, the way she's always calling me "darling" or "sweetheart", not that she actually knows or believes that he is in fact her son. Also, I know he's thinking about the rest of what she said, too. Either the part about me being good or the part that said "you've got," because at the moment, the use of the present tense didn't match our situation.

I realize as he stands there in front of me that I have not seen him in weeks. I figured I would have seen him around by now, at the store or around town. But I have not run into him at all.

"I know," he tells Meg. "She is quite a woman."

Meg scoots over a bit. "It's so wonderful to have you both here together today! Please sit," she directs and gestures to the bed. "I really need more than one chair in here."

Zach sits down beside his mom, and again I'm struck by how much they look alike. It's the eyes, mostly.

The way he is sitting makes it so that he has nowhere else to look besides right at me. I feel bad instantly. This was a bad idea. This is his mother, not mine. I shouldn't be here, in his space, like this.

I start to stand up, "I should get going. Let you two chat for a bit."

Meg turns her head slightly, looking at the clock hanging on the wall. "You always stay for at least an hour. You can't leave so soon. It's only been twenty minutes."

Zach tilts his head, looking at me with a question written all over his face. "Always?" he mouths to me, questioning.

I look back at Meg. "I don't want to impose, Mrs. Walker."

"Nonsense! No imposition. Please stay. I never get to see you both together anymore," she says, tugging on my arm to make me sit back down. I do.

Meg continues, turning to Zach, "Addison here says you've been really busy, that that's why you aren't with her when she comes every other day. I'm glad you could come today."

Zach turns back to look at me. The look on his face as the realization sets in is almost heartbreaking.

"You've been coming to visit her?" he asks.

"Of course," I say to him.

"Zach, dear," Meg says, tapping his arm. "Tell me another story about your new friend."

Zach looks nervous, like he doesn't quite know what to say.

My heart drops. *He met someone new. Of course he did. I should have guessed...*

"Well," he says, clearly thinking of how to break this news to me. I think about getting up and leaving. I don't really want to stick around and hear him tell his mom about his new girl. I don't think my heart could take it.

"Father Jameson said he'd love to meet you sometime," Zach says to Meg.

"Sure! I love visitors!" Meg repeats again.

Wait...did he just say Father Jameson?

I picture the old pastor at my family's church, with his gray hair and glasses. *New friend? Why would Zach be talking to Father Jameson? And why would he want to meet Zach's mom?*

What's going on?

Zach turns back to look at me and gives a small shrug.

"You know Father Jameson?" I ask him, my voice coming out barely above a whisper.

This time he is the one to simply say, "Of course."

I have no clue what is going on or what to expect right now.

Zach grabs his mom's hand and says, "It was so nice to see you today, but we have to get going now, okay?"

Meg nods. "Come back together next time?"

"We will," Zach answers.

He stands up and walks to the door, holding it open.

"See you later, dear," Meg says to me as I stand to leave.

"Goodbye, Mrs. Walker."

I step out the door and take a few steps down the hall. Zach closes the door behind us and walks behind me. I stop and turn around.

"Can we go somewhere and talk?" I ask him.

He smiles. "Of course."

We both drive our cars over to the town square, parking in the spaces right by the gazebo. I put my car in park and sit there for a second. *What am I doing?* I ask myself, wondering if I can really take sitting there and talking with him without my heart breaking any more than it already has.

I decide I should at least hear him out, see what he has to say, talk with him a bit.

I take a deep breath and step out of the car. Zach walks over from where his car is parked and nods to the coffee shop across the street from where we stand.

"Can I get you an iced tea?" he asks. Today is probably the hottest day yet this summer. An iced tea sounds like a good idea.

"Sure," I say, and follow him to the little shop.

A bell chimes as we step inside, the air conditioning wrapping around us, nice and cool.

Luckily there is not a line, so he orders for us right away, paying for the both of us.

"Thank you," I say sheepishly.

"No problem," he answers, putting his wallet back into his pocket.

The barista finishes up our teas and hands them to us and says, "Have a wonderful day! Enjoy the sunshine!"

We thank her and start walking across the street and up the steps of the gazebo.

It's so weird to me, walking with him without our arms brushing against each other, his hand not holding mine. We aren't walking that far apart from one another, but the distance feels like miles.

"So you've been visiting my mom? A lot?" The way he says it isn't an accusation. It is filled with hope.

"Yes," I tell him. "I'm sorry. I probably shouldn't have. I should have asked you. I'm sorry."

"Sorry?" he almost laughs. "Are you kidding me, Addison? That's crazy. You shouldn't be sorry."

"Oh, all right."

"My mom's right."

"About what?"

"You're really something," he says, locking his eyes with mine. It is still there, that spark and that feeling I get when he looks at me.

"Well, thank you, but I'm not that great." I look away from him. "Look, Zach, I'm sorry. I was rash, and the things I said to you were hurtful. I didn't mean it."

He took a sip of his iced tea. "I'm the one who should apologize."

"What? Why?" I ask. The wind blows and my skirt flips up at the bottom, so I reach my hand over, smoothing it down.

"I didn't even try to see things your way. I was so afraid of things changing, of you changing on that trip, or your dreams going away, that I panicked."

"Really?" I ask him. "What did you think would happen?"

He looks at me funny, like I'm missing something. "Exactly what happened, Addison. You came back. Things felt different. You were acting different. Then you told me to leave."

"Oh..."

"Yeah, exactly what I was worried would happen happened. Although I think I'm the one who caused it to happen."

"Zach, it wasn't you." I try to sift through the words in my head, unjumble everything so I can say things right. "I had to figure things out for myself."

"Sort through the puzzle pieces and see how it all fits together," he says almost absentmindedly.

"What?"

"Oh, nothing," he says, shaking his head.

Someone just said that recently, about the puzzle pieces. *Who just said that?* I rack my brain for where I heard that before.

It clicks. "Did my aunt tell you that?"

He looks away sheepishly. "Yeah."

"You talked to my aunt?"

His gaze finds mine again, this time looking more sure of himself. "Ad," he starts, and I'm happy just to hear him call me that. "In case you couldn't tell, these past few weeks have sucked, okay? You wouldn't answer, so I thought you needed space. But then space wasn't doing anything for me and I wanted to try to piece together what even happened to us, how I screwed things up. So I've been talking to Carrie to try to find a way to talk to you."

Of course, I think. "I've been talking to my aunt a lot lately, too. She's been helping me to figure all of this out. She kept saying I needed to--"

Zach cuts in, saying, "--see things from the other perspective?"

"Yes," I breathe. "I'm sorry I was so hard on you. I shouldn't have expected you to understand everything about the trip when you weren't even there and--"

"--I want to go!" he says.

"What?"

"I want to go. With you. Maybe not just yet, you just got back. But someday. I want to go there with you. I want to see it all. I've been reading all these stories online, and it sounds incredible. If it means that much to you, I want to see it, firsthand."

"You've been reading about it?"

"Of course," he grinned.

I bite my lip, thinking about what he just said. "I'd like that. You'd love it there. I know you would."

"I'm sure I would. I would also just love travelling with you."

We stare at each other for a minute or so.

Oh, Aunt Carrie, I think, looking back at this wonderful boy sitting on the bench across from mine, *only you could pull off something like this. How could I not have guessed she would do what she could to help fix our relationship?* Here she'd been telling both of us to see things from the other person's point of view, and somehow, here we were, meeting somewhere in the middle, while we sat exactly in the middle of town.

Could we really get back to the way things were? Could we really have that happily ever after?

Just then I hear someone call out Zach's name. I turn and see Father Jameson standing by the steps of the gazebo. "Same time tomorrow?" he asks Zach. "Hello, Addison," he says to me.

"Hi, Father," I reply, looking back at Zach incredulous.

"Yes, sir. See you then."

Father Jameson smiles and then turns to leave, heading down the path towards St. Peter's.

"What was that?" I ask Zach.

"Well... I've been going to church lately. Your aunt actually got me to start going with her. She introduced me to Father Jameson a little while ago, and he's been meeting with me to explain different things about your church and also the place you visited and the history there. It's insanely cool, actually! He knows so much. Talking to him is amazing. I see why you guys like his talks; they're really inspiring."

I stare at him, my mouth hanging open.

"Did you do this for me?" I ask.

His eyes have a twinkle to them as he says, "No."

"No?" I repeat.

"I did it for us."

A tear spills over the corner of my eye. "Us? Can there even still be an us?" I ask him.

He stands up, takes a few steps toward me and says simply, "Of course."

I stand up, taking a step closer to him. "I still dream," I tell him.

"You're still my dream," he responds.

I throw my arms around him, knowing there's no turning back now. He kisses me and wraps his arms around me. I kiss him back and stand on my tiptoes, deciding that this gazebo might just be the most magical place in town.

I decide right then and there that I don't care. I don't care if I only get to be with him for another month or another year or another lifetime.

All that matters is being with him, having him back in my life. I want what he said. I want the travelling the world together.

It's like a dream, standing there in his arms again. A very sweet dream. *The* sweetest dream.

23

- Zach -

Saturday, September 3rd, 2022

Everything hurt. I felt like I had been hit by a bus. I had heard people use that expression before and always thought it was overly dramatic. *How could you feel like you've been hit by a bus without being hit by a bus?* I always wondered. But today I understood.

It was like every part of my body hurt. Every nerve. Every joint. Every bone.

How is this possible to feel this horrible?

"It'll be okay," Addison said, rubbing her thumb in circles on the back of my hand-- the hand without an IV in it, of course.

I gave her a weak smile. "Yeah," I said.

The two of us sat there in the hospital room, waiting for answers. Her parents and my Uncle Mitch were all sitting out in the waiting room, giving us some space. I wondered what they were all talking about or what it was like for them all to be sitting out there together. They used to be good friends back in high school. I wondered if it was weird for them now, or if it felt just like old times.

"He said he'd be back in a minute," I said, getting tired of waiting. "Where is he?"

"I'm sure he'll be back in soon, Zach," Ad said, a calmness radiating from her, even though I knew there was no way she was calm right now. I was grateful for her faking it for me though. It helped.

I wanted the doctor to come back in because I wanted answers. But I also didn't want the doctor to come back in just yet. I didn't think I was ready to hear anything bad. It felt bad. Something inside me just felt...bad.

Suddenly, the door handle jiggled and then twisted, opening. *Here we go,* I thought.

I could hear Addison holding her breath beside me. *I'm not ready,* I thought.

But when the door opened fully, I didn't see a doctor in a white lab coat. I saw Charlie.

He gave me a weak smile and said, "Hey, bud. How are ya?"

"Been better," I said.

"Well, in case you were wondering, I got her number."

I laughed out loud. "You would..."

Addison shot him a look and said, "Not the time, Charlie."

Charlie and I both laughed. Then Addison sprang up from her chair and rushed over to Charlie. She grabbed a box from his hands and rushed over to the edge of my bed, dumping the contents of the box on the white cotton sheet by my feet.

"Thank you so much for getting this," she told Charlie. "You're a lifesaver!"

"Ad, what is that?" I asked.

But it was like she didn't even hear me. Addison Smith was on a mission, looking for something. You could just see the focus on her face.

"Where is it?" she asked to no one in particular.

"Where is what?" Charlie asked. "I thought you just wanted the box. Oh, dang, did I get the wrong one? Can't be. You only had one blue box in your room."

When was Charlie in Ad's room? When did he even leave here? I was so confused. I didn't even know what day it was. It felt like it was years ago that I was at dinner with Charlie.

"No, this is it. It should be here! Where is it?" she yelled, tearing through the box. There were what looked like scarves and pieces of paper. There were two empty bottles, the kind you get at the store in the dollar section before you go on a trip to fill with liquids before you fly on a plane so it's less than a certain number of ounces.

"Did I forget something?" Charlie asked, sounding very concerned. "I had one job. Gosh, I'm sorry, Addison."

"No, no. It's not you. I just don't know where it is."

"Where what is?" I asked her.

She didn't answer. Instead she ran out the door.

"What's she looking for, man?" I asked Charlie.

"Beats me. She just said she needed that box. I didn't look what was in it, just grabbed it and came back."

"Hmm," I said, considering what could be in the box. I didn't remember seeing it before.

"So, how are you, really?" Charlie asked. "You seemed fine all night."

"I don't know... I just--"

Addison came back in the room then with her mom following close behind her.

"Honey, I'm sure we still have some. Even a little bit would help him," her mom said, soothingly. She started rifling through the little trinkets sitting on the end of the bed with Addison.

"A little bit of what?" I asked.

"It's not here, Mom," Addison said, sounding worried.

What could they be looking for that's so important?

"Oh no."

Addison gasped and they looked at each other. "The Morrisons."

"What is going on? Ad, what does this have to do with the Morrisons?"

Ad looked like she was about to cry. "How could I have used up so much of the water so soon? It hasn't been that long. Why did I keep just giving it all away?"

"Addie, sweetie," her mom said, wrapping her arms around Addison. "You were being helpful. You were trying to help other people and being caring and compassionate as always. There's no way you could have predicted this would happen or that you would need to save some of it for Zach. None of us could have predicted this happening."

"But I need to give him the water. He never took it."

Charlie motioned to me that he was going to step outside and give us all some space. I nodded, and he left the room quietly, leaving me with Addison, her mom, and a pile of trinkets and papers at the foot of the bed.

"What didn't I take?" I asked Mrs. Smith.

"The water she brought back. She said you never actually drank any. So she had Charlie go get the box of things from France to have you drink some now, hoping this would help. We've actually given it to many people since we've returned from the trip, and it has helped many people with many different things. I guess we both assumed we had more of it. We're all out. We gave the last bit to the Morrisons just last week..."

Then everything clicked into place. *That's* what Ad was freaking out about. It wasn't just *any* box she had Charlie go get. It was her box of things from her trip.

Now Ad was crying and saying, "This is all my fault. This is all my fault."

I knew how much this stuff meant to her. Quite honestly, over the past few years it had become pretty important to me, too. I may not have believed her when she came home back then and told me to just have faith and trust her. But now I did. I definitely did.

"Let's go then," I said.

She looked up at me through her dark eyelashes, tears still forming at the corners of her eyes. "What?" she asked.

"Let's go. Today. Tomorrow. As soon as we get out of here."

"Zach, come on. We can't just go."

"Why not?"

"Can we?" she asked.

"Come here," I said, and she walked back over next to me, placing her hands in mine. "Please. Ad, I want to go. I told you back then that I want to see this place that changed your life. I want to be there, with you. Now, I don't know what happened tonight or what's going on with me, but I know that the only thing I really care about is you, and this place changed you. It helped you. So I want to go and see this place. And while we're there maybe I can find some healing, too, for whatever this is that's going on. And while we're there we can get more of the water and bring it home so you have more to give to anyone you meet who needs a miracle."

"Really?" she asked, smiling through her tears.

"Really," I told her. "Let's go."

"I love you," she told me.

"I love you, too," I told her.

I looked up and saw the door open again, and this time the doctor did walk in.

This time I was the one holding my breath.

Addison's mom stepped out and Addison turned to face the doctor.

"So the MRI came back..." he started.

My stomach dropped, and I didn't hear anything else after he said the words "could be cancerous" and "tumor."

I don't really remember anything else. I blacked it all out.

All I remember is the doctor saying he was sorry and that he'd do everything he could, and then he left the room.

A minute or so later Addison stood up and reached for her phone. "I'm booking us a flight. We're going to France."

"Okay," I said. I would go anywhere with her. I would try anything to fix this.

24

- Addison -
Tuesday, September 6th, 2022

*a*s soon as Zach was released from the hospital, we packed our bags and waited until Tuesday, which was the first flight we could get to Paris. Then from Paris, we had a short flight down to Lourdes the next morning. I was happy that it worked out that way, so I got to spend a night showing him all the places in Paris that I could possibly fit into one day.

The doctors wanted him to come back in two weeks for some more testing and some form of treatment. We had two weeks. So I booked us flights and hotels and got everything in order so we could go there for a few days.

This has to work, I prayed. *Please let this work.*

The past few days have been a blur, every moment running into the next, but also seeming to drag on and on.

The only thing from the past few days that stuck out was yesterday, when Zach came back to our house, because my mom didn't want him staying in his apartment alone. His friends still lived with him, but they worked all day, and we didn't want Zach to be alone if he needed anything. So Zach came home with us, and not even a few minutes after he settled in on the couch, the doorbell rang.

"Who could that be?" my mom asked, walking over to get the door. I sat on the floor next to the couch and crossed my legs.

Zach pointed to the couch and said, "You can sit here. I'll move over."

"No," I said. "You look comfy there. I'm good on the floor here." I leaned my head back, and he ran his hand through my hair. I closed my eyes and prayed things would be okay.

"Mitch?" I heard my mom say by the door. "Come on in."

"Thank you, Annie." Mitch's deep voice came into the living room. "This is Diane, an associate of mine."

"Hi, Diane. It's nice to meet you," my mom replied.

"Hello," a woman's voice said.

"Zach's right in here," my mother said, leading Mitch into the family room.

Mitch walked in, an unreadable look covering his face, and a woman followed him in. She had auburn hair that was cut in a clean bob that framed her round face and fiercely blue eyes that seemed to pierce through the room and look right into your soul.

"Hey, kid. How are you feeling?" Mitch asked. Mitch was there the other day when we got the news. He said he had some ideas, a plan maybe. But then he left the hospital, and we hadn't seen or heard from him since. I figured he skipped town or something. But I guess I should give him more credit than that. He was here, wasn't he?

"Great!" Zach said, a sarcastic tone coating his voice.

Mitch turned back to my mom and smiled. She took the hint, "I'll give you all some time. I have a batch of cookies in the oven."

"Chocolate chip?" Zach asked, perking up.

"Of course!"

"You're the best, Mrs. S!" he called as she left, and I leaned into him.

"So," Mitch started, he and Diane both settling into the grey sitting chairs across from the couch. "We have some things to discuss with you both. I've been working with Diane for a while now. We think we have a plan, or at least a start. We would like you two to be involved."

"Involved with what, exactly?" Zach asked.

"Well, if I may?" Diane asked, cutting in. Mitch nodded and gestured for her to take the floor. "Let me begin with this, I know what you both are."

What we both are? I repeated in my head. *That makes it sound like we're vampires or some mythical creature.*

"And," she continued, her blue eyes still boring into my soul, "I want to begin by assuring you that I am just like the both of you. I am a dreamer."

"Cool," I muttered, a little too annoyed. "Sorry," I said a second later, looking away from her eyes.

"It is very *cool*," she said. The way she spoke reminded me of an elementary school teacher, very precise and formal. "This is a gift, Addison. A very important one, might I add. First and foremost, you and Zachary must understand this. You both are more gifted than others."

"Oh, no, Diane," Zach said. "I must interject here. I am just a regular ol' dreamer. But Addison over here, now she's special." He winked at me as he said this, and I fought back a smile.

"In any event," she pressed on, "we are assembling a group. We would like for you to join us."

"A group?" I repeated.

"A dream team, if you will."

Zach chuckled. "Dream team? How long did it take you guys to come up with that clever name?"

Diane ignored this comment completely and continued on with their pre-planned speech. "I'm sure by now you've heard the rumors."

"What rumors?" I asked.

"We believe there is another group, another force, at work. There are ties to this group and your town here. Not only is their presence strongly felt in your small town, but also imposed on many others around the world."

"What is the group called?" I asked.

"We don't know," Mitch said. "Although," he turned to Zach. "I'm sure you've heard your mother go on and on about *them* in the past."

"Who?" Zach questioned. I could tell by the look on his face that he was trying his best to think back and find the group his mother had apparently talked about.

As we all sat there, it sank in. A certain word Mitch had just said, with slightly more emphasis on it than the other words in his statement. *Them.*

"Them?" I asked, wondering how a pronoun could have such a terrifying connotation to it. But I guess I should've known, because after all, I used to be terrified of a man I referred to as It. "So this other group that has ties to Madison is not a good group then. This is the 'they' Meg freaks out about."

"Yes," Diane admitted somberly.

"So you're telling me this group has no name? Everyone just refers to them as 'them' or 'they' or 'those bad people' like my mother has said before?" Zach said incredulously.

"I wish we had a name for Them," Diane told us. "It would make things much easier."

"So how do you know who They are?" I asked.

"We don't."

"So what does the dream team do?"

"Well," Mitch started, standing up and pacing a bit. "This is where the two of you come in. We need to gather the other dreamers. There are more out there. There are millions of us. We just need to find them. We need to assemble the dreamers out there who are like you, Addison; naturally talented and gifted. Not that we can't use the other dreamers to our advantage...there's a certain skill the trained dreamers have. But dreamers like yourself have so much untapped potential. They also are the most likely to be targets for Them to find and haunt."

"But what could They possibly do?" I asked.

Zach looked sad. "Have you seen my mom?"

"But she's just in The Haven," I pointed out. "She's alive. She seems to be doing better."

"Addison," Mitch interjected. "What you said the other day--about the pills? I think you're onto something. Diane and I discussed it, and we think there's more to that story. We think this shows that there could be something medically that we could do."

"So what do we do?" Zach asked.

"For starters, we need you to find other dreamers around the world. We are starting an online group of sorts. We need them to connect with the rest of us here in Madison. The more our group grows, the greater chance we have of tracking down this group and stopping them once and for all," Diane explained.

"And since the two of you are heading to France tomorrow --" Mitch said, raising his eyebrows.

"You want us to find dreamers there?" I filled in.

"Bingo."

"Mitch, we are not going there for anything dream related, okay?" I said, growing angry. This trip wasn't about that. It was about helping Zach.

"That's just it, though, little Addie."

"What's just it?"

Then Zach spoke up, his voice sounding angry. "It is dream related."

"What is?" I asked him.

"What's happening to me. It's my brain, Ad. It's my mind. They're the reason this is happening. My mom went crazy; Sandy prescribed herself one-too-many pills; my grandmother got sick and was also crazy; and now, there's something wrong with my mind."

"No, it can't be."

"There's no other explanation, Ad! I've been thinking about this a lot. This isn't just a normal thing. I mean, it's never a normal thing. But my point is, what is happening right now... I just know it has to be because I'm a dreamer. There's something off about all of this." He turned to face Mitch. "Mitch, tell me I'm wrong."

"I don't know that I can, kid. I happen to think the same thing."

"Well, well...what do we do then?" I asked, suddenly more worried about everything happening with Zach-- and I was already extremely worried.

"We find the others. We assemble a team. And we finally, after years of their mind-control and torture, we finally put a stop to Them," Diane said, her voice rising with a certainty and power often heard in politicians and leaders. "We will end this. *I will end this.*"

"Okay," Zach and I said together. He reached down and grabbed my hand, squeezing it tight.

No, I thought staring right back into Diane's fiery eyes. I *will end this. If it's the only thing I ever do on this earth, I will end this.*

* * *

Zach and I stood in airport security, waiting for the agents to check our luggage and let us through, on our way to the place that changed my life once.

I just needed it to change it one more time.

25

- Zach -

Tuesday, September 6th, 2022

The flight over really did me in. I was exhausted, and the time difference sure didn't help. But the minute the flight touched down, I could just see the excitement sparkling in Addison's eyes.

She squeezed my arm and said, "We're here, Z! It'll all get better now. Just wait."

I smiled at her and kissed her forehead, right in front of a bright colored headband she was wearing.

She looked so happy as we sat there waiting for the plane to taxi to the gate. She was almost bouncing in her seat. It was so cute to see her so excited.

"It'll work, Zach. I know it will," she said.

"I know it will," I repeated, hoping she could tell I really and truly meant it now. I believed in this stuff now. All of it. I believed that if she believed this would work, that it would.

About a half hour later we were off the plane and in a taxi cab, pulling up to a very tall building with this amazing old architecture. Ad and I tipped the driver and got our bags from the trunk of the car.

There was a revolving door in the corner of the building, the entrance, and we walked through it into the hotel lobby.

Addison was looking all around, mouth gaping open, at all the decorations and design in the lobby. Meanwhile, I was just watching her taking it all in. This girl literally just travelled to another country for me. She dropped everything and spur of the moment hopped a flight to France. Just for me. Addison doesn't do anything spur of the moment.

* * *

"So...I've been thinking...about the wedding..." Ad started, stirring a tiny spoon around in her espresso cup around and around, not looking at me.

What has she been thinking about? I started thinking maybe this was all too much for her. Maybe she's rethinking everything. Maybe she wants to postpone it.

"Yeah?" I asked, trying to catch her eye. She wouldn't quite look at me.

"I know we already talked about it, briefly. I know we had said a Spring wedding might be nice. May or June or so. But...why wait that long?"

"What are you saying?" I asked her.

"Well, I think we should get back home. See how treatment and all that goes, and then maybe speed up the timeline a little bit. I just don't want to wait until May in case...in case--"

"Hey," I said, cutting off that thought quickly. "You said yourself this thing is going to work, right? This trip. The water. So no worries. Really. Let's keep things planned as they are."

Finally, she looked at me. "You really think so?"

I grinned at her. "I mean, I'd marry you tonight, here in Paris. But I want our family and friends there, so I'll just have to wait. Plus, I want you to have your dream wedding."

She laughed at this. "My dream wedding, huh? So will we be getting married within a dream then?"

"You know what I mean," I said. "So which do you prefer?"

"Which what?"

"May or June?"

She smiled and pushed her hair behind her ear. "May. I would like to get married in May."

"May it is then."

I had realized then that in the whirlwind of things that have happened since we got engaged just a week ago, we really hadn't talked about too much.

"Anything else?" I asked her, not sure what else there was to discuss.

"Well...I was talking with Jess a bit a few weeks ago."

The waiter came back to the table to refill my coffee cup. I have to say, we had only been here for a few hours and already I loved this place. It was like everyone in this city just stops during the afternoon. They all just take a break, sit down at a little restaurant -- outside, of course-- and drink coffee while talking. I kind of wish people took the time to do that back home.

Addison continued once the waiter left, "You know sometimes how she tells me to picture a specific scene and then see if I can dream myself there once I fall asleep?"

I nodded. I had seen Jess test this many times with Addison. It seems to be another one of those things that Jess spent months training on and Addison is able to do without thinking about. For a while it really frustrated Jess, but now I think she is fascinated by Ad's natural abilities and comes up with all these tests and trials so she can learn more through Addison.

"Well, we realized something recently."

"What is that?" I asked.

"It's always the same scene. I'm running through or just standing in these fields of lavender. It's like the purple flowers go on for miles and miles. It's beautiful. I didn't think a place that beautiful could really exist, but Jess did some digging, and it turns out it does. It's actually here in France, in the Provence region."

I started reaching for the little map book she had on the table in front of her. "Where is it? How far is it? We should go!"

She took another sip of her espresso, finishing it off. "I'd love to go, but, first, it isn't super close and we have to get you down to Lourdes. And, second, Jess actually texted me yesterday suggesting the same thing, but we looked it up and the lavender is harvested in August. We just missed it."

"We'll come next year!"

She smiled, "Okay, Zach. We can come back. I actually think it would be really cool to see it someday. I've been dreaming of this one place for years. I never knew it really existed. I had honestly never even seen a photo of this place before. It was completely my mind dreaming this up."

"That's so neat that it's a real place!" I commented.

"So Jess reminded me of this the other day, and I've been thinking, I'd really love to do the wedding stuff all in purple. I think it would be really pretty to have lavender, soft purples and greens. What do you think?"

"That sounds great!" I said. Honestly, I would be okay with anything.

"Oh, yay! Jess said she'll help, and we'll make it all look just like that scene."

"And I agree with you," I said. "We need to get that chocolate cake for the wedding."

"Oh, of course!" she said. "Oh! Let's get chocolate cake now! We have to get something here. My mom got an 'eclair here, and she was in absolute heaven!"

"I'm always down for chocolate cake," I told her, just as the waiter happened to come back to our table.

"Can we please have some of the chocolate cake?" Addison asked the waiter in surprisingly pretty decent French.

"Oui," he replied, heading back inside the restaurant to get it for us.

As soon as he was out of earshot, Addison grabbed my hand from across the little table and said, "Well, that was easy."

"I know! Look at you. Who knew you could speak French so well?"

"Not that, silly."

"Then what? Basically planning our wedding over coffee in Paris?"

"No. We already found a dreamer," she said, with a look on her face like 'how-can-you-not-be-following?'.

"What are you talking about?" I asked her. "We haven't even talked to anyone yet except the taxi driver and the concierge at the hotel."

"You really didn't notice?"

I sighed. "Notice what, Ad?"

"The waiter."

"The waiter?" I repeated.

"Yes!" she exclaimed, exasperated. "His eyes. I can tell."

Wow, I thought, *how did I miss that?*

I sat up a little straighter and finished off the rest of my coffee. "Well, what do you think we should do?" I asked her.

She rested her chin on her hand, thinking. "Let's just talk with him. See what we can find out."

"All right," I agreed just as the waiter was returning with a piece of chocolate cake that honestly looked so good. "Pardon," Ad said.

"Oui?" The waiter set down the cake, right in front of Addison and then looked up at her, then at me.

It felt like the second he actually looked at us --maybe he looked at our eyes-- but the second he looked at us, he stood up a little straighter and took a step closer to our table.

"Parlez vous anglaise?" I asked, a phrase Addison had taught me before we left.

"A little," he replied back to us in English.

"Oh, great!" Addison said. "Do you have any recommendations for dinner?"

The restaurant we sat at now was geared more for breakfast, lunch, and this mid-afternoon coffee time. We had noticed on the door when we got here that they close at four or five each day.

"Oh, yes! I do!" the waiter-- Jacques, his name tag read-- said. He began in pretty good English explaining how to get to a restaurant near the Eiffel Tower that he said has great steak dishes.

"That sounds perfect! Thank you," Addison told him, shrugging at me and asking, "Want to go there tonight?"

"Yeah! Sounds great," I agreed, wondering how this girl was going to bring up the subject of dreams to our waiter right now. To me it seemed so strange. *How was she going to broach a subject like that? Especially with all these people around? Also, he was working right now. What would he even say?*

But I have to give Ad more credit. She's pretty sly.

As she reached for the bill the waiter was handing us, she ever so slightly touched his hand. Most people, if they even noticed, would have thought nothing of it. It happens all the time, you reach for something and accidentally bump into someone. Spies use moves like this all the time to swiftly and secretly pass things off. But I knew better. Addison was passing off a dream.

If he was a dreamer, he would see and understand it all instantly. If he wasn't, he probably wouldn't even notice.

The surprised look that crossed his face just then led me to believe he was a dreamer, just like us, just like Addison had guessed.

The waiter said he would be right back with our change and left.

I stared at her, surprised but also not surprised that she came up with something so clever and simple to test if he was really a dreamer.

"What did you show him?" I whispered to her.

She didn't say a word. She just reached across the table and took my hand in hers, squeezing it tight as an image flooded into my mind.

It was a dream of my mother. She was standing right in front of Addison's view in the dream, like in the movies when they're trying to show someone is right in the main character's face so they stand directly in front of the camera, really close, and their head fills up the screen.

In the dream my mother screams, "Hurry! Get out while you can! They're coming for you!"

"Who is?" Addison's soft voice questions.

"You know who!" my mother yells with a new sense of urgency. "Them! They, the bad people! They are coming!"

"Who are they?" Addison asks.

"Oh, honey, don't you know? All dreamers have heard of Them. They are coming, soon, to get rid of us all. You're a dreamer, aren't you?" my mother asks in a hurried, anxious voice, her face close and looking pained.

Addison let go of my hand and suddenly my mind was back at the little bistro table on the streets of Paris.

"Wow," I said. "That dream was the perfect pick!"

How she dreamt up something that simple and clear was beyond me. If he really was a dreamer, and if he in fact had heard of Them, there was no misinterpreting the meaning of that vision.

The way the dream was set up felt like my mother was talking directly to me, asking me that question. You are a dreamer, aren't you?

I'm sure the waiter felt the same.

The waiter came back just then, pulled the little black leather book from his white apron, and handed it quickly to us. He left not even a second after handing us the change and receipt.

"Must not have been what I thought..." Addison said when he left, her voice trailing off, clearly frustrated and wondering how we would find at least five new dreamers for Mitch and Diane.

"Well, maybe he is a dreamer, but maybe he just hasn't heard of Them. Or maybe he doesn't care," I whispered.

I looked down at the receipt.

"Hey, Ad?"

"Yeah?" she asked, slinging her purse over her shoulder.

"Read this."

I turned the receipt around and pointed to the very small, handwritten words at the bottom of the bill.

I reread it and reread it as Addison just stared at the paper. It read:

Champs-Elysees
South end
17h15
Aidez-moi, s'il vous plait

"What does that mean?" I asked.
"It means we may have just found our first dreamer."

26

- Addison -
Thursday, September 8th, 2022

Today was our second day in Lourdes. Honestly, this place was more incredible than I could have ever remembered it. There was just something so peaceful and calming about this whole town. It's as if the second I set foot here every other concern just floats away. I wasn't quite as worried about everything else going on in our lives right now; not Mitch's plan, not Zach's news, not the feeling like everything in my life was falling apart around me. Instead, it was like the sun was shining down from a cloudless sky, washing everything around me in a golden glow, as if God was saying, "Everything will be all right."

We had planned to go to the baths later today. Yesterday, when we arrived, we got settled into our hotel rooms and then came straight over to the sanctuary. The very first thing Zach said was, "Where's the water?"

We walked around the corner of the mountainside, passing a beautiful church with stained glass and gold and an overall picture of the beauty that people can create with the gifts they were given. We came up to the side of the hill where a notch was formed in the rocky surface and a statue stands today commemorating what had happened there many years ago.

"Wow," Zach said under his breath as he stared up at the immense magnificence of the view in front of us. I swear, even the grass looks greener here, more full of life.

"Isn't it incredible?" I asked him, holding his hand in mine.

"It is, Ad. You were right." He looked down at me and smiled. "This place is even cooler than I pictured it, even cooler than the pictures you showed me."

"Pictures can't do a sight like this justice," I told him.

So I walked him over to the place where the water comes out of a spigot on the side of the mountain. This time he didn't even question it, just cupped his hands, let the water flow into them, and then brought his hands to his lips to drink the water.

As he did I whispered, too quietly for anyone to hear, *Please, please let this work. Please heal him.*

He stepped aside and motioned for me to take a turn drinking the water. I did.

As I drank, I felt a tingly feeling on my lips and on my tongue and down my throat. *What does that mean? Am I just thinking things?* I wondered.

"Can I ask something?" Zach whispered close to my ear.

"Of course," I said, stepping back, out of the way so another lady could go up and fill her tiny bottle.

"Is it supposed to do that?"

I looked up at him, surprised. "Do what?"

"Feel all weird and warm and... I don't know, fuzzy?"

"Fuzzy?" I asked. "Like tingly?"

"Yeah!" he said, enthusiastically. "Does that mean it worked?"

"I'm not sure. But I felt it, too."

"Interesting," was all Zach said.

Now, today, we sat at a little cafe sipping coffee while the sun shined around us. We knew we should probably head back to the baths soon, but we still had a couple minutes to just sit and breathe.

"So," Zach started, adding another packet of sugar to his coffee. He was always adding more sugar or milk to his coffee.

"So," I repeated, smiling at him with his coffee.

"Jacques."

"Yes, Jacques," I agreed, knowing we needed to talk about the situation sooner rather than later.

The other night, Zach and I decided we had to meet with the waiter from the restaurant and see what he had to say. So we made dinner reservations at the place he had suggested for later in the evening and then headed to Champs-Elysees to do some shopping and see if he showed up at the time his note had said.

More than once, Zach, ever the protector, said, "Maybe we shouldn't go. Maybe this guy is pulling one over on us, thinking we are just stupid tourists or something."

"Zach, he needs our help. He saw what I was trying to show him and understood it. He has to be a dreamer."

"But what if he is one of the bad ones?" Zach proposed. I had to admit that I hadn't even considered that possibility.

"I think we will be able to figure it out pretty quickly," I told Zach that afternoon. "We have to do something though. Mitch is counting on us."

"Never thought I'd hear you say those words," Zach commented, rolling his eyes. But nevertheless, he agreed and said we would go at the time written on the bill and wait for only five minutes. If he didn't show up or if we saw anything or anyone who seemed "shady" or like "one of the bad ones," we would leave. I agreed.

So we stood at the south end of the famous street around 5:15, waiting. We were looking in the window of a very big name designer's store. The clothing in the window was beautiful! The fashion and the style here was just so incredible.

I think both of us were looking for the waiter, still in his white apron and black button down shirt. So when someone came up beside us, in khaki pants and a blue sweater, also looking in the window of the shop, and said, "Bonjour, dreamers," we both jumped a bit, startled. And after a minute we realized it was him.

"Bonjour, Jacques," we had greeted him.

He cut right to the point, no dilly-dallying or dancing around the subject. "How did you know?" he asked, directing the question to Zach.

"Your eyes," I spoke up.

"Ah..." he sat down on a bench and motioned for us to sit as well. "How did you do that earlier?"

"Do what?" I asked.

Zach, knowing what he meant, said, "She's a dream sharer. She passed that dream to you when you handed her the bill."

The waiter scoffed. "Those don't exist. Just a rumor. What kind of joke is this?"

"It's no joke!" I rushed to say. "It's true."

"Then how do you do that? Explain to me," he said, sounding doubtful.

"I-I can't," I stammered.

Zach stepped in, explaining, "It's just one of her natural abilities, Jacques. We don't know how she does it, she just does. She doesn't have to think about it either. It just comes to her naturally."

Jacques considered this. "I don't believe you."

"Well, it's true," I said, probably not helping.

"Listen, Jacques," Zach started, "Whether you believe she's a natural dream sharer or not is completely up to you. But either way, she shared a dream to you. You saw it, or we wouldn't be having this conversation right now. And, clearly, what she showed you in that dream concerned you or you wouldn't have asked to meet us here. So I'm just going to cut to the chase: we are looking for dreamers, much like us, much like yourself, who can help us."

"Do you even know who They are?" Jacques asked Zach.

"We know They are a threat. However, we can't put a name to it besides They or Them as we have heard the group referred to before."

"My mother," Jacques whispered.

"Your mother was involved?" I asked, shocked.

"No!" Jacques looked mortified that I had even come to such a conclusion. "She is a saint, my mother. But They changed her. Took her spirit. Then her mind."

It sounded eerily close to what happened with Meg.

Now, sitting and sipping coffee with Zach in Lourdes, we discussed how we would get Jacques involved. After talking to him for close to an hour the night before, we had established that he wished to help us in the assembling of the team. However, Jacques was terrified They would come after him as well. He gave some contact information (a mailing address only) to Zach and said his only rule was that his name not be given to Mitch or Diane. Only Zach and I could know who he was or how to reach him.

"We have one so far. One dreamer. That's it," I complained to Zach.

"Ad, seriously?" he gaped, shaking his head. "We found one dreamer in our *first day* here! Not even twenty-four hours in another country, and you manage to find a dreamer. Mitch will be thrilled."

"I hope so."

* * *

A little while later, I sat on the cold bench, watching Zach walk confidently into the room for the baths. He looked so strong, so sure of himself, even despite everything going on. Or maybe it was because of everything going on, where we were, his belief that this might just work, that gave him the confidence just then.

As he disappeared behind the door, more people settled in on the benches, and others moved forward in line awaiting their turn. Again, for the second time in this very spot, I was struck by how every single person who comes here or is here right now has a story. I will never know all of them, or even any of them besides Zach's and mine. But just the idea of millions of people flocking to this very spot for years and years before me and will continue to come for years and years after I'm long gone. This place is rich in miracles, believers, healings, and most importantly, hope. Everyone here has a story. Everyone here is here because they have hope. They hope this place will help them in some way.

"It is so lovely to see you," a quiet voice whispered behind me. I turned, very slowly, around.

The face I saw staring back at me was one I never expected I would ever see in my life again. Her kind, very bright eyes stared into mine, and her smile seemed to spread across her entire face.

"I want to thank you for what you did for me. I just never thought I would get the chance to thank you in person. What a miracle!"

"Becky?" I asked, recalling the name I kept tucked away in my heart and mind.

"Bonjour," she replied, nodding her head. "Addison, yes?"

"Yes," I said, still shocked to see her. After a few seconds, I remembered the biggest thing about Becky. She was a dreamer like me!

"I use the rosary you gave me every day," she told me. I was so touched by that, I had no words. She continued on, "I must tell you,

Miss. Your kindness that day forever changed my life. I came here that day because I was in a very dark place in my life, the darkest I had ever been. This was my last resort, my only hope. I felt so alone. My life was a nightmare. Then you sat down beside me, and you smiled at me and showed me kindness and love when you didn't even know me. I left that day so much brighter. You gave me hope that even living a life like ours, we can have a beautiful life. You showed me that not all dreamers' lives are nightmares. Some of them live very sweet dreams."

I just stared back at this woman, my mouth probably hanging wide open. *What?* I wondered. I couldn't believe that the time I spent with this woman -- less than five minutes, over five years ago-- had such an impact on her life. I hadn't even known how dark things were for her. How could I have known?

I just thought she looked like she could use a smile.

I didn't even realize she was a dreamer at first.

"So thank you for that, Miss Addison," Becky said to me, clutching my hands in hers.

"Oh, Becky, you don't have to thank me. I can't believe you're here!"

"Well, wouldn't you know...someone told me in a dream last night that I should come back here. That something important was here, and I needed to come right away."

"Are you serious?" I asked, shocked that all of this was happening.

"Yes! I can't believe you are here either! I'm so happy to be seeing you again." Then a look of concern crossed her face. "Did a dream tell you to come here as well? What brought you back here?"

I looked back at the doorway to the baths. "Well... my fiancé, actually. He wanted to see the place I've been talking about all these years."

"Oh, I hope he loves it! Is he here? May I meet him?" she asked excitedly.

"He is in there right now," I told her pointing over my shoulder to the entrance. "Actually, we could use a miracle right about now. A big one."

She lowered her voice, "Is he a dreamer also?"

"Yes, he is. There's something wrong with his brain. The doctors aren't sure what it is. I mean, how could they be? It probably has something to do with his dreaming-- at least, that's what Mitch and I think." I paused, unsure why I was telling this woman from my past everything going on right now. But it felt good to talk about it, tell someone who maybe understood. So I continued, "He's sick. That's all we know. I just... we just need help. We need answers. Maybe someone before has had this happen?"

"It's possible," she said, sighing. "I am very sorry. But you have come to the right place," she told me, smiling again.

"I hope so."

"Maybe if we knew other people like us we could find someone who has dealt with all he has?" she suggested.

"Do you know any other dreamers?" I asked Becky.

"There are two in my town who I believe are like us, yes."

"Do you think you could find out for sure?" I questioned.

"I suppose I could."

"Well, I know quite a few," I admitted to her. "In fact, many people in my town of Madison back in the states are dreamers like us. We are trying to find others around the world as well."

"Madison, you say?" she asked.

"Yes. Have you heard of it?" I would be surprised if she had. It's a very small town.

"I have read about it."

"Read about it?" I was so surprised to hear her say that.

"Yes," she said. "Shortly after I met you, I decided that I was in fact not alone in this. At the time, I thought you were the only other one. I began researching dreamers and found there are in fact many of us living all around the world right now. All dreamers stem back to one small town... yours. Or so the books say."

"Books? What books?" I asked her.

"I can write them down for you." she suggested. I immediately handed her my phone, and she began typing in the titles of books. There had to be at least five.

"How did you find these?" I asked, my eyes wide, as she handed me back my phone.

"Well, I started reading old folk tales. Many talk about people who dream or have long slumbers of hundreds of years. I kept digging. There is truth behind every old tale, you know? Some books called them the 'people of the night' or the 'sleeping beauties' or even the 'dreamers.'"

I knew Jess had some type of book that Mitch had given her, saying it had been passed down through his family for years. I don't know why I just assumed that was the only one. *Why had I never thought to look for more?*

"Becky?"

"Yes," she answered.

"Could you do me a favor?"

"Anything for you. You have done me the greatest favor. I owe you my life, truthfully," she told me wholeheartedly.

"We could really use your help."

Then I held her hand and passed the same dream I had shown Jacques to her.

After the dream had gone away, she opened her eyes and stared deep into mine. "I have read about Them as well. I have a feeling that They were the darkness I was feeling. They are who killed my family one by one, leaving me all alone. They put the dark, hopeless thoughts in my mind."

She sat for a minute, thinking. "What can I do?" she asked a few minutes later.

I explained how everyone seems to know that the group (Them/They/the bad people) exists, but no one has ever seen or met someone in the group. We all have no clue who is involved. They could be living in our small town with us, for all we know.

I explained how the more people we get together on our side, the better our chances are of stopping this group. Becky also chuckled at Mitch's term of "The Dream Team," just like I had when I heard it the first time.

"Well, as I said before, I owe you my life. I will do whatever I can to help. I have a vast collection of research I've compiled over the past five years. I would be more than happy to share it all with you, Addison."

"Wow, thank you so much, Becky! That would be so helpful!"

The line was moving up, and it was getting closer to the two of us. I had figured I would go in the baths again. *Who knew when or if I would ever be back?*

"It's almost your turn, dear," Becky pointed out.

"Yes, thank you." Then we exchanged email addresses so we could keep in contact in the future. She said she would send me some information she has found, and I told her I would share her information with Mitch and Diane and let them know she was willing to help. Then Becky agreed to speak with the others in her town who she suspected were also dreamers. She will pass along the information and invite them to join in our venture as well.

Becky nodded for me to take my turn and said, "Thank you again, Miss Addison. Thank you for showing me there is more to this life."

I just smiled back at her, a wholehearted smile, because I didn't know quite what else I could say. I don't think the woman realized how much she had also impacted my life.

As I was walking in to the women's room before the baths, along with the two girls in front of me, I saw Zach leaving.

He walked up to me and said very quietly, "I'll wait for you over there." He pointed over to a railing across from us with a bench beside it.

"So, how was it? How do you feel?" I whispered back.

"Oddly, better." Even he seemed surprised by this.

"Really?"

"Yeah. I can't explain it. It's weird. But I feel... I don't know...different."

"That's great, Zach."

The line was moving forward. It was my turn.

"Zach," I hurried up and said to him, "Look over at the women's benches. Do you see the woman with the braided hair sitting there in the row by herself? That's Becky. I talked with her and she's going to join us. She wants to fight Them too."

"Who?" he asked, looking around.

I turned back toward the benches to look where she had been sitting.

There was no one there.

27

- Zach -

Friday, September 16th, 2022

"Lie very still, all right, Zach? I need you, once you're in there, to be as still as you possibly can. Quite honestly," the nurse said, "we often suggest that patients just take a nap, that way you can relax and not be fidgeting around." She checked her clipboard. "Dr. Summers is requesting a pretty extensive look, so this scan could take upwards of an hour."

"Okay," I told her, even though all of this was anything but okay.

I'm on a gurney being wheeled back for my MRI scan. The MRI scan is extensive, as the nurse said. They're confirming what the other scans said back around Labor Day. "That word that starts with a 'c', " as Addison and her mom have been referring to it for the past few days when they think I'm not in earshot.

But I am. I hear them talking.

But every single thing they say, I have already thought myself. I've already worried about it. Already guessed what would happen if this is all true.

I thought I knew what the word 'nightmare' meant. I really, honestly, thought I did. *I mean, who would know better than someone like me?*

But, man, I had no freaking idea. Until now.

"Just take a nap," she said, as if it were as simple as that. But you see, Nurse, I'm not like your other patients. Which means that if I were to actually "take a nap" while in the MRI, my mind would be going so haywire, your machines and scanners wouldn't know what to do. My mind doesn't work like your other patients, to begin with. Try adding some tricked-out nightmare into that equation, and then we can all watch the doctors scratch their heads and say "What is going on here?" or "Well, this is new!"

I just can't believe I'm getting an MRI, I thought.

Being honest, I thought this was all some horrible dream, similar to the one Addison had years ago. I really thought I would just wake up one morning and all of this would be over. But I know I'm not dreaming.

This is real.

This really sucks.

They said they'll get the results within twenty-four hours. Dr. Summer has set up an appointment with me first thing tomorrow morning. Ad is coming with me to the appointment. I didn't want to ask her. I've asked enough of her recently. But I didn't have to ask her because she just offered before I even could ask.

When I said she didn't have to, she said, "Zachary Walker, I love you, and I'm with you. I'll be there." And that was that.

The nurses began to walk me through what would happen in the next few minutes, reminding me to stay still and again suggesting to take a nap. They said the CD that Addison had brought for me would be playing through speakers, so I would be able to at least listen to my favorite band while I laid there.

I also thought I knew what the word "claustrophobic" meant.

Again, I had no clue until now.

This *tube* thing felt like it was swallowing me whole. This white, cold metal surrounded me. Everywhere I looked was the same thing.

I hear some beeping, then some whirring sounds. The scan is starting.

It was strange. I felt vibrations. Just slightly, but there was definitely some strange feeling there.

I felt myself starting to get antsy and just wanted to move around. *Stay still, stay still,* I warned myself.

Have you ever noticed how when someone tells you not to do something, it makes you want to do that thing more? Or when someone says to stay still, it suddenly becomes *impossible* to sit still?

I tried to think of something else, anything else, than staying still. Maybe then I could actually stay still.

I pictured just a few days ago, standing at the mountainside while Ad was drinking some of the water.

As she did, I whispered, too quietly for anyone to hear, *Please, please let this work. Please heal her.*

I know she said the water already did help. Her dreams have definitely gotten better. But she deserves better than that.

I feel so selfish now for wanting her to always keep her dreaming abilities. That's why I took that moment to try to reverse what I had been wishing for all those years ago. This time I really did wish for her dreams to just go away.

She shouldn't have to deal with something like this. If there's any possibility of Them going after her next, I'm going to do everything I can to make that possibility go away. If there's a chance for her to be in the position I am in right now, I will do anything to make sure that doesn't happen. If there's a likelihood at all that she winds up in The Haven, or a place remotely like it, I will do my best to make sure that doesn't happen.

That's the only reason I'm even agreeing to help Mitch and Diane.

I want Addison as far away from Them as humanly possible.

I want to be the warrior for her. I want to fight away all the nightmares for her.

* * *

The next morning we sat in the doctor's office. The results from the scan were in. We were just waiting to hear what they found.

"Mr. Walker," the doctor started, nodding at me, his grey-green eyes looking anywhere but at us. "Ms. Smith," he acknowledged, turning to Addison, as she wrung her hands.

"Yes, Dr. Summers," I said, my tone prodding for more information.

"You two might want to sit down for this..."

He pulled one of those blue leather office chairs with the wheels over, closer to us, and took his good old time sitting down. Addison and I both sat in the grey chairs across from him-- the ones up against the solid white wall of the oncologist's office.

Oh no... I thought, realizing the troubled and confused look on the doctor's face as he tried to come up with the right words could only mean something was very wrong.

He sighed, cracked a knuckle, looked up at us finally, and said, "The test results came back. We have some news..."

28

- Meg -

Friday, September 16th, 2022

She feels different lately. Lighter.

She smiles more. She sings to herself less and less with each passing day.

She no longer cries herself to sleep, mourning the loss of her baby.

Instead, she sleeps soundly, instantly falling into a blissful slumber the moment her head hits the pillow.

Now she knows the truth.

Now she can start really living.

All these years she has been cooped up within these cold, sterile walls that suffocate any inkling of hope, any breath of fresh air or new life, any dreams for a brighter future.

These walls close in, quickly, quickly. These so-called medicines take over, quickly, quickly.

She sits up straight, in her small, uncomfortable bed. She smiles at the vase of brightly colored flowers-- the only things flooding this room with life. Isn't it funny how something so simple as a yellow daisy can change so much? she wonders, looking on.

They have a plan. Things will change.

She knows now that this place she called a home for so long is no such thing. It is a prison, not a haven. It is a place that rather than offering healing, helps to bring about new dilemmas, illnesses, and irrational thoughts.

This place killed her without ever truly killing her.

This place will haunt her, years after escaping its ghost-filled halls.

This place itself is an illusion. It masquerades as a place meant only to help. But in reality, this place is full of heartbreak, tears, cries, screams, whispers, and empty promises that echo through the thin walls. This place is home to no sweet dreams.

No.

This place is a living nightmare.

And finally, finally, she looks at the yellow daisies that her visitors have been bringing for her lately, and when she sees the flowers, she sees love. She sees hope. She finally, finally sees a reason to fight, a reason to fight the nightmares that lie before her and live in her past.

That's all the poor woman ever needed.

She just needed the will to live. The will to fight. The will to dream.

Part Two

Bringing Sweet Dreams

29

- Meg -
Friday, May 12th, 2023

She sat up in her bed, too excited for sleep, too happy to focus.

But she tried her best, flipping the pages of her book. She read silently, her lips moving slightly, making the shapes of the words as she said them in her mind.

The book had no pictures. The book was not meant for a child. The book was a classic novel written by a classic Russian author. Oh, how things have changed, she thought to herself.

She had become a voracious reader in the months that had passed. She read every book in The Haven's library at least three times, cover to cover.

She always used to love to read, you know. She read hundreds of books as a child and spent many of her nights as a teen up late into the night reading. Honestly, the worlds of books were more comfort to her than the world of her own dreams and nightmares. She found great comfort in reading about the lives of others rather than focusing on the horrid nightmare that was her own life.

Her father enjoyed reading. In fact, he was a big fan of the author and book she read now in her little room at The Haven. Reading and books were the only topics that she and her father could seem to discuss without approaching an argument. He always said she was too much like her mother, always dreaming and escaping reality. But the one escape from reality he approved of was reading. Mitch was never one for reading, so it was a subject she could share with just her father. Something they could talk about. So, she read all the time.

She sat, reading her book, fighting to keep her eyes open. She didn't want to dream right now. Not yet.

A few months back, Nancy, her main nurse, was relocated to another facility in North Dakota. Nancy had always been very strict about taking the pills. Four o'clock on the dot. No sooner, no later. Toward the end, Nancy felt Meg was becoming unruly, unable to be controlled, so Nancy made the call to double her dosage.

What Nancy never found out, however, was that Zachary, Addison, Mitch, and others had been popping in for a "visit" slightly before four o'clock. Each opportunity they could, they would swap out one of the pills with something else or some type of sugar-pill. They never figured out what type of pills Nancy had been bringing to Meg's room each day. All they knew is that it was meant to keep her sedated, foggy, out-of-it.

The longer the pills stayed out of her system, the more and more she remembered from her past, the more she could understand about the present times. For years she lived in a child-like state here at The Haven, but now her mind was back where it ought to be.

When Nancy got relocated, a new nurse had Meg placed on her caseload. This nurse's name was Gracie. She was very kind, very sweet.

The first thing Gracie did was consult with the new, head doctor about taking Meg off the pills. She said-- and the doctor agreed-- if Meg was not feeling ill or was not in any way a danger to herself or others, then there was no reason to keep her on such a strong prescription. In time, the only pills Meg was taking were vitamins and supplements to keep her bones and immune system strong.

One day, a couple of months ago, the boy who had visited her the past many years came in. His name was Zachary. He was tall and kind and had dark hair and dazzling blue eyes. He usually brought a lovely young lady with him. Her name was Addison. She was small and sweet and blonde and had striking blue eyes. They had come to tell her they were engaged. The ring was lovely. They looked happy.

On that visit, in the middle of a conversation in which she was explaining some things she knew about the dream world to the two of them, Zach asked her a peculiar question.

"When did you know I was a dreamer like you, Mom?"

As soon as he said it, he looked embarrassed, like he had slipped up somehow. *Why does he look so confused?* she had wondered then. *That's a very understandable and good question.*

"Right away," she told him. "I knew you were a dreamer right away. It took a while though to see your dreamer personality and abilities come through."

"Wait, a second," he said, standing up. Addison reached up, lightly touching his arm. She looked like she was holding her breath, too. "Do you know who I am?" he asked, skeptically.

Meg scoffed. "I think I would know my own son."

His eyes filled with a couple of tears. None of them spilled over, but they were there.

"Mrs. Walker?" Addison said to her. "I thought you said your son was dead?"

She thought back to years ago, when Zach had come for a visit. He told her everything. How Mitch and Adam had tricked her with that horrible, horrible plan. They lied to her. They told her that her son was dead. They broke her heart-- no, they shattered her heart. That day she had screamed at her brother, yelling at Mitch for his involvement in this.

But then, as always, nurse Nancy had perfect timing and came swooping in, calming Meg and giving her her pills. "She just needs her medicine," Nancy had told Mitch and Zach, ushering them out of the room.

After that day, after the pills, that memory had somehow sunk to the very depths of Meg's mind, just out of reach. She had forgotten all about it.

Until just then, when Zach asked who he was.

It was like years and years came slipping perfectly into place. It was like a puzzle. She finally had that very last piece, and it seemed to click perfectly into place, completing the picture.

"They lied to me," she told Addison. "It was all a big scheme. He is not dead. He is right here. This is my son."

"Are you sure?" Addison asked, staring very deeply into Meg's blue eyes.

"Of course I am sure! He is my son! I gave birth to him. I think I would know who he was. Look, he has my eyes!" she pointed out.

"Yes," Addison agreed, looking at Zach and not Meg. "Yes, he does."

Now, back in the present, reading her Russian novel in her room, she sat, excited, waiting.

Only a few more hours now.

Soon.

* * *

She sat there, hair freshly brushed. A new, crisp outfit pressed and on. She felt lovely, for the first time in a long time.

A card sat, waiting, on her nightstand table. She wrote it all herself.

Next to it rested a box wrapped in shiny silver paper with silver bells printed on it and the word "Congratulations!" was all over the wrap as well.

Inside the box was a silver frame with pearls. She had Gracie pick it up for her. There was also a painting on a small canvas. Meg made the painting herself. It was clouds in a sky, a dreamlike scene. That day's date was painted in the clouds. Along with a quote about love being patient and kind and many other things love ought to be.

A knock came at the door.

"They've just arrived," nurse Gracie announced. "You look beautiful, Miss Meg. Let's go!"

"I just love weddings!" she cooed.

Gracie walked her out the door, and down the hall. This sort of thing usually wasn't allowed. But Gracie convinced them to make an exception. Just this once. Meg had been doing so well, her behavior impeccable in recent months. So the big-wigs agreed, saying this was permitted. Just this once.

Gracie opened the door to the rec room, gesturing for Meg to walk in first.

She did.

Standing there, by the nice new fireplace someone had just donated, was her little boy, now all grown up, standing in a tux.

Next to him was a girl dressed all in white, like a vision straight out of a dream.

"Hi, Mom," Zach said.

She smiled at her boy, tears brimming over her eyes.

"We're so happy you could be here for this," Zach told her.

30

- Addison -
Thursday, May 11th, 2023

I was pacing around in my room, making sure everything was in order for tomorrow, going over all of the little details in my head.

Tomorrow was the most important day of my life.

Tomorrow I would marry Zach.

May 12th would be a day I would remember forever.

As I thought back on everything that has lead us to this point, I thought about another very important day in mine and Zach's love story.

It was a day I would always remember clearly. God knows I will never be able to forget it.

* * *

September 16th, 2022.

They called it a miracle.

They had no idea how true that statement was.

Nine months ago, on that very hot September day, the doctor came in the room and sat down in front of Zach and me.

"We have some news," the doctor said. When he said those four little words, my stomach dropped. We expected the worst. No one wants to hear those words. No one.

But in our case -- our miracle case-- those four words were followed by two more words that were equally as life-changing as the first.

"It's gone," Dr. Summers had said.

"What? What's gone?" Zach stammered, standing up.

Dr. Summers looked puzzled, like he himself could not figure all of this out. "The tumor. All signs of cancer. Everything we saw two weeks ago is no longer showing up."

"What does that mean?" I asked.

"It means that it's gone." The doctor still looked confused. "Honestly, I have never seen anything like it. Not in my thirty years here. I can't figure it out. We've run dozens of tests and scans, and everything is negative. It's quite remarkable."

"Can't there be false negatives?" Zach asked.

"There can be. But typically another test will show us that is the case. Here, everything is showing signs of being cancer free. In fact, it appears as though nothing was ever wrong."

"What does this mean?" I asked again.

"It means it's a miracle. Whatever happened. I've had a whole team of professionals looking at this case with me, and that's all we can say. Now, I'll want to schedule a follow-up with you in about six months, Zach. And if anything should come up, be sure to come right in." Finally, Dr. Summers smiled at us, "Congratulations, Zachary."

"Thank you, Dr. Summers," he said, shaking the doctor's hand.

I remember I just stood there, staring blankly as the doctor told Zach a few more details, and then he smiled and left the room.

The door closed behind the doctor, and it was just the two of us in the room. I looked at Zach, standing there, with my mouth wide open. I didn't know when I started crying, but sure enough there were tears streaming down my cheeks.

Zach continued to stand there.

"Did you hear that? Zach! This is incredible!" I exclaimed through my tears.

He continued standing there, not saying a word, not looking at me.

For a split second, I wondered if I was dreaming. I worried that any second I would wake up and the news we just got would not have been true. Maybe I was just dreaming.

But then something brought my mind back to the present, which was not a dream, but real life.

That something was the sight of Zach falling to the ground on his knees in front of me. I jumped up from the chair and rushed over next to him.

"Are you okay?" I asked, fretting the doctors were wrong. He was passing out again. He needed help.

"Addison," he said. He started to cry. I realized then that I hadn't seen Zach break down like this before. He was sobbing and his shoulders were shaking. He covered his face with his hands leaning over.

"Yes?" I asked, wrapping my arms around him.

"Can you believe it? It worked! The water worked!" he said, lifting his face up to look at me.

His eyes were shining through the tears.

I smiled at him, and my tears began to flow more steadily.

He took my face in both his hands, pulling me closer to him. He kissed my forehead. "Thank you. *Thank you,*" he told me and pressed his lips against mine.

"I love you," I whispered to him.

He's okay. He's okay. He's okay, I repeated over and over again in my mind.

We both sat there on the floor of the doctor's room, holding each other tight as we both cried tears of immense joy and happiness.

On the way home from the doctor's office, I drove the whole way home with one hand on the steering wheel and the other hand in Zach's. Every few minutes I would steal a glance over at him just to make sure I wasn't dreaming, just to make sure he was really there and really okay. Every time I looked up he was already looking at me.

"Wait, pull over," Zach said, pointing to a side road about a hundred feet away. I turned onto the side road, asking him what was wrong.

"I just want to make a quick stop, real quick. I've got somebody I need to thank. Give me a minute?" he asked.

I looked up and saw the sign, realizing why he wanted me to pull over on this road.

Zach got out of the car, flashed me one of his signature grins, and then walked confidently across the street, up the many steps, and into the church.

I gave him his time in there and sat in the car thanking God for the miracle myself.

* * *

That September day was truly the best day of my life.

Until tomorrow of course. Tomorrow would be the best day of my life.

Now, on the night before my wedding, I sat up in my bed and looked at the clock. It was 11:11 at night, a magical time when I would typically hold onto something blue and make a wish. But tonight, instead, I sat there with a big smile on my face, wondering what I could possibly wish for that I didn't already have.

31

- Zach -
Thursday, May 11th, 2023

Addison has this thing when she sees a clock read 11:11. She stops whatever she is doing, closes her eyes real tight, and makes a wish. She told me once there's this thing about holding onto something blue when you make the wish. I guess it helps your chances of the wish coming true.

All I know is right now it is exactly 11:11. I know she is probably sitting in her room right now, curled up in her bed, holding onto her blue comforter, and making a wish. I wonder what she's wishing for.

She swears it works. I don't know if it works or not. I think her "wish" is moreso a "prayer." And I know her prayers work.

They worked for me.

All I know is because of her I don't have anything else I need to wish for.

I looked around my apartment. Everything was neatly tucked away in boxes that were clearly labeled. <u>Zach's Clothes.</u> <u>Office.</u> <u>Kitchen.</u>

Ad came over earlier this week to help me go through all of my things. I didn't have too much here. It was just a bunch of us guys living in an apartment, and we pretty much had the necessities. Couch. TV. Gaming system. Pots and pans that were rarely used. Stuff like that.

She and I went through it all and figured out what we should keep. She had a whole bunch of stuff at their house still from the shower. I remember when I went, at the end of the shower, and when I walked into the restaurant where they were having it, there was so much stuff! Towels, blankets, cooking utensils, pots, pans, and other things we put on our registry.

I remembered the day Ad and I went to go register. We walked into the one department store in Madison-- and when I say *one*, I mean it. They had literally everything you could ever think you would need. They gave us one of those scanner guns and told us to walk around and scan anything we wanted to add to the list.

When the lady handed over the scanner, Addison got the cutest look on her face. She looked crazy with power. "We can pick *anything*!" she squealed. "Anything!"

We walked up and down the aisles of stuff. I would stop from time to time and mess around with some gadget. Meanwhile, Ad was just having the best time.

"Let's get these dishes! They're red. Your favorite." She held up a plate that was bright red. There was a whole line of matching bowls and mugs lined up behind the plate.

"Do you like them for our house?" I asked, wanting to make sure she actually liked them. There was a blue set right by the red. I knew blue was her favorite. I really didn't care what color the dishes were.

"*Our house*," she swooned, kissing me right there in the middle of the dishes aisle. "I love that!"

"By the way," I told her then, "Randy called back, he said if we like that last townhouse we saw, we just need first and last month's rent plus a security deposit and we're good to go. The current owner is moving in April, so it works perfectly for us to move in early May."

"Oh, yay! I loved that one!" she cheered. Then she held up the dish and wiggled it in front of my face. "Zach! These plates would look PERFECT in that townhouse!"

I laughed. "Really? How?"

"Because, silly, the brick on the front of the house is red! And all the countertops were gray! It's meant to be."

"Sure is!" I agreed with her. I remembered months ago, looking at the book her mom had given me, a composition notebook with pictures taped all through. There was a page where she wrote Dream Home on the top, and the page was full of photos of blue houses. All of them had darker blue shutters and picket fences.

As if she could read my mind, she set down the dishes, scanned them, and said, "Zach, I love the townhouse we found. Really! It is perfect for us. The perfect first home."

"I'll get you your blue house someday," I promised her.

"I know you will," she said with a smile. "But for now, this will be great. It's perfect."

I looked up and saw a shiny silver waffle iron.

I grinned. "I know what this registry needs!"

"What?" she asked, looking all around, wondering what on earth we had missed from her list.

I took the scanner from her hands and dramatically ran over to the shelf with the waffle iron and scanned it.

She was laughing as she walked over to me. "How could I have walked by that before?" she asked sarcastically.

"You were too focused on the plates," I told her.

"I was," she admitted. "I'm so glad you scanned that!"

"You are?"

"Yes!" she said. "I love *eating* waffles! And you love *making* waffles! So you can make me breakfast in bed, and we can have our waffles on our fancy red plates."

"That sounds like a plan."

We walked around the store for another hour or so, scanning this and that, checking things off her list and talking about all the things we could ever need or want for our home. Emphasis on "our."

* * *

Billy was back in town for the wedding tomorrow. He was my best man. But he told us the other day that he had actually been applying for a few months for positions back here in Madison and was finally offered a job at a great company not far from the town square. It would be cool to have him around more.

He was planning to come back and crash here tonight. Tomorrow morning, me, my groomsmen, my uncle and Ad's dad were all going to go golfing. Billy was going to just stay here for the night, but that was before everything went down at the rehearsal dinner tonight.

It was crazy.

Addison was flipping out.

We had been practicing walking up and down the aisle (as if we couldn't walk in a straight line without first rehearsing it), and I could tell Ad was on edge.

"Where the heck is he?" she kept muttering under her breath.

"He said he's on his way," I told her, showing her the text he had sent me just minutes before.

"I swear, if he's late tomorrow..."

"He won't be late tomorrow. He's coming with me, remember?"

She looked up at me. "You better not be late tomorrow!"

"I won't! I promise."

"Let's try that one more time," the wedding coordinator said with her lips in a tight line as if she was anything but pleased with how Addison's little cousins were walking. I think one was three and the other was five. They both looked so bored.

"Let's get this party started! My boy's gettin' hitched!" someone called from the back of the church as the doors swung open dramatically. In walked Billy, who slowly and casually walked down the aisle as if he weren't holding anything up.

The wedding coordinator looked ready to flip a table.

Ad was trying so hard to keep a straight face. As mad as she would ever say she was with Billy, even when he and Cam broke up back in high school, she would always end up laughing at something he said minutes later.

He walked up to the two of us, clapping me on the shoulder. "Hey, brother! How crazy is this?" He lowered his voice and leaned over to whisper to me, "You, uh, sure about this? There's a side door over there. I could sneak ya out."

He turned his head to the side, smiling a big, cheesy smile at Addison, and she swatted his arm, just as he pulled her in for a hug. "Oh, Addie, I'm just kidding! You're the best thing that's ever happened to my best friend right here."

He stepped back, turned to look over Addison's shoulder, where her maid of honor was currently standing, acting like she was retying a bow on the side of a church pew. "Hey, CamCam!"

Cammie rolled her eyes. "Ad, how does this bow look?"

"It looks gr-"

Before Ad could finish her sentence, Billy cut in, saying, "Great. You look great, CamCam. Really."

Cammie turned abruptly, facing Billy. "Hello, William."

Ouch.

"Brrr. It's like Antarctica in here!" Billy said, still smiling, while he rubbed his arms pretending to be cold.

"Are you the best man?" the wedding coordinator asked, walking up quickly, high heels clacking against the floor loudly.

"Yes, ma'am! Best Man Billy reporting for duty!" Billy stuck his hand out to shake her hand, but she just looked at him and then began giving him instructions on where to stand.

"He's such a child. So immature," Cammie huffed, walking by us to go readjust another bow.

"Zach," Addison said in a whisper. "I thought you were going to talk to him about this? About Cammie?"

"I did. I even told him how she was talking to some doctor."

"Well, clearly he didn't get the message," she said.

"He said, 'Persistence is key.'" And as if to prove that what I just told Addison was true, Billy picked that moment to catch Cammie's eye and wink at her, very dramatically.

"Oh, gosh!" Addison fought back a smile, holding her ribbon bouquet in front of her face to hide her smile.

"I give it until the end of the wedding," I told Addison.

"Don't encourage him, Zach!"

"Why not? Everyone always said how great they were together before. *You* always said how great they were together," I pointed out.

"Yeah, but that was before they broke up."

"Well...if it's right, it's right. They'll figure it out. Besides, if she really liked this doctor dude, why isn't he coming tomorrow with her? She isn't bringing anyone as a plus one."

"They aren't *there* yet," Addison replied, using air quotes.

"Or...she's still hung up on Billy."

As I said that, Billy was playing an air guitar every time the wedding coordinator turned around or wasn't looking at him.

"Right. She's still hung up on Billy," Addison said, raising an eyebrow at me. "Because he is just so grown up and mature now."

A few minutes later, I was standing next to Billy at the front of the altar. Cammie was practicing walking down the aisle right before Addison would. Billy winked at her. She stuck her tongue out at him. He leaned forward and whispered, "She still digs me."

I just laughed.

* * *

Later that night, we were loading some last minute things into Mr. Smith's truck bed. I was lifting a cardboard box up and putting it in his truck when Billy came up, holding a box, and said, "So, I think things are going well."

"Do you?" I asked, skeptically, knowing that Cammie had barely given him the time of day that night.

"I mean, I don't know why we can't just pick up where we left off a few weeks ago."

"Where who left off?" Addison asked, walking over and carrying a couple bags of things.

Cammie must have overheard and rushed over. "Oh, Addie! Let's go grab that thing inside."

"Cammie?" Ad asked, looking at her best friend with a very confused look on her face. "What's Billy talking about?"

Cammie's face got so red. I don't think I have ever seen that girl look embarrassed. It was so strange.

"Cammie?" Addison asked again.

"Let me fill in the blanks for ya, Addie!" Billy interjected, stepping into place between Ad and Cammie, putting his arms around the both. Cammie shrugged away from him, but still couldn't shrug off her red face.

"A few weeks ago," Billy started. "I had an interview for the job I was just telling you guys about. After the interview, I stopped for a cup of coffee -- it was early in the morning, and I hate mornings. Anyway, just as I'm opening the door to walk in, wouldn't you know Cammie here was pulling on the door to walk out. I crash into her, she crashes into me. Her latte spilled *all over* the one nice suit I had. I jokingly told her that she just had to sit and have a coffee with me because I had clearly made her spill her coffee. She must have been distracted from seeing my good looks again after pining for me all those years. We had coffee then walked around town. We talked. She admitted she still loves me. We kissed a little. And we've been texting all day, everyday since then."

"We have NOT been texting all day, everyday since then!" Cammie interjected.

"It's okay to admit it."

"Okay," Cammie said. "I will admit that YOU have been texting me all day, everyday since then."

"Persistence is key," Billy said simply.

"And I did not admit I still love you!" Cammie yelled.

"You broke things off with that other guy after we hung out though, didn't you?"

"That had nothing to do with us," Cammie said flatly.

"Us?" Billy asked with a grin.

"I did NOT say *us*," Cammie protested.

"Actually," Billy turned to Cammie. "I was just thinking about that."

Cammie looked up at Billy, arms crossed, and simply asked, "What?"

"Well, I was thinking," he started, but Cammie was pretending not to care and went back to counting the little cards with table numbers to make sure she had them all in the box she was holding. "Could you look at me, please?" She tilted her chin up. "Thank you. Anyway, I was thinking... I don't even remember why we broke up. I just remember being miserable without you. And we did have a fun time that day a few weeks ago. And we are both going to this wedding tomorrow. Solo."

"Yeah?" Cammie asked, setting the box of table cards on the ground.

"You drive me crazy, Cam. Always have. But I kinda like it. I still like you, too. And it's obvious everyone else thinks we should still be together, so why not?"

Addison's mouth dropped, and she grabbed my arm, squeezing it and whispering to me, "Oh, my gosh, it's happening! I dreamt this! But it was Fall Ball! Junior Year. This is crazy. I bet he's gonna kiss her!"

I looked at Addison, "No way."

Cammie crossed her arms and stood a little taller, clearly looking upset.

"You're mad," he said when she didn't answer. "I'm sorry. I know you're probably busy and crazy helping Addison plan this wedding, but... you know what? No. I'm not sorry."

Cammie's face changed then. She looked worried.

"I waited for TEN years for you, Cammie. Then we spent about a year together and it was the best year of my life. Then we split with college coming up and different lives and all that junk. I've waited FIVE more years for you, Cammie. I'm done waiting. Do you want to go out with me--again -- or not?"

I whispered to Addison, "She's gonna kill him."

Cammie just stared at Billy for a while.

"Wait for it," Addison said, smiling.

"Okay then...If that's not what you want, if all those years of how we felt for each other before meant nothing, then forget I said anything."

He closed up the hatch on the truck bed and turned to leave, but Cammie reached out and grabbed his elbow.

"WAIT!" she yelled, even though he was right there.

"What?" He looked straight at her.

"I'm done waiting around, too. I miss you, Billy."

And then, the two of them were literally standing in the middle of the parking lot -- kissing.

I turned to Addison. She looked so happy. "They're perfect together, aren't they?"

"So does this mean you'll be my date for the wedding tomorrow?" Billy asked when they finally stopped.

"I mean..." Cammie looked at Addison, who was nodding and smiling with great enthusiasm. "I guess it would only make sense for the Best Man and the Maid of Honor to dance a couple of times and maybe--"

"--I'm taking that as a yes!" Billy said, planting another one on her.

He turned back to me. "Told you. Persistence is key. Told you I'd wait forever for her."

32

- Addison -
Friday, May 12th, 2023

*M*y eyes fluttered open, after a dreamless night, to find the sun shining through my window. The light slanted in the room and washed over the window seat I have always loved.

I crawled out of my bed and walked, barefoot, across my shaggy rug to my window seat. I settled in, tucking my knees up to my chest. I took a deep breath and looked out the window, watching the sun rise higher in the sky and the shades of pink in the sky fading into the blue of morning.

I'm getting married today! I thought, unable to control the smile that was crossing my face then.

"Good morning, sweetheart." I turned to see my mom tiptoeing into my room. She had a mug in each hand with little swirls of steam coming off the top of each mug.

"Hi, mom," I smiled, leaning in to her side as she kissed my head and handed me a piping hot mug of tea. The mug she handed me said "bride" in glittery letters. Her's was one I had painted for her birthday many years ago. She drank her tea from that mug all the time. I remember when I made it. I accidentally swirled my brush all around in the light pink paint after having forgotten to clean it off in the water. Dark purple ran all through the nice pink paint. The mug turned out all messed up with swirls of all different colors, all blending into a dark black in the center. But I'll never forget how happy my mom looked when she unwrapped it on her birthday. She said it was the best present anyone had ever given her and that she would have her tea in it the next morning. She did. Then she kept drinking her tea from it almost every morning for the past fifteen years.

"How are you feeling?" she asked, settling in on the other side of the window seat.

That was something I always loved about my window seat. It could fit two people all curled up on it. My mom and I. Cammie and me. It was the perfect size.

"Good," I told her, as I fiddled with my engagement ring on my finger.

"Nervous?" she questioned, sipping her tea.

I shook my head. I actually hadn't been feeling nervous at all. I felt really happy and at peace. I was excited, but not nervous. It all felt right.

I saw my mom's eyes settle on a few of the other boxes of my things in the corner of my room.

"You know," she started, still looking on at the boxes, "I remember the day you left for kindergarten. You were so excited! You got a big girl backpack. It was purple. And you had your light-up tennis shoes on and a red shirt you picked out yourself. You looked so cute. So grown up already. I wasn't ready for you to leave, but you were happy. You were so excited for school." She swallowed.

"Mom..." I said, not wanting to see her cry already today. I knew that would make me cry.

She looked away from the boxes and looked right at me. She reached out, holding my hand. "You know," she said again. "I also remember the day Zach came over and your dad and I got to meet him for the first time. You were so excited! You looked so happy. He was talking to your dad, answering all of his many questions. But I just watched you, watching him. You looked so cute. So happy. And I knew he was right for you. The way you smiled around him...well, that's all I ever wanted for you, Addie, that happiness. But the way he smiles around *you*. My, my, my. *That* is what I always hoped for for you, prayed for for you. I've always dreamed you'd find that boy who saw you for the beautiful, wonderful girl you are and looked at you like you were the most amazing thing he had ever seen. Zach does. I wasn't ready for you to leave, I'm still not, but you are so happy. You're so excited for your future, and I am so excited for your future. Just remember, I'll only be fifteen minutes away if you want someone to drink tea with in the mornings, and you will always be my little Addie."

The tears were flowing steadily now; there was no stopping it. I set my tea down on my desk and hugged my mom. "I love you, Mom," I told her.

It was weird thinking today was the last morning I'd wake up in my own room. The last morning we'd drink tea sitting in my window seat together while I lived here. The last few hours that I would be a *Smith*.

In just a few hours, everything would change.

I would be *Mrs. Walker*. New last name, new life, new future path.

"Well," my mom said, wiping under her eyes and sitting up straight, "We have five more minutes for tea time, then we've got to get started getting ready. Also, I know you have your something old and borrowed; but I realized you didn't have your something blue or new."

I realized then that I had planned to get blue shoes, but forgot about that idea and found a silver pair instead.

My mom pulled a small jewelry box from her robe pocket and handed it to me. "This is from your father and me."

Something New & Something Blue

It had written on it.

I opened the lid, revealing a silver necklace with a simple, square blue topaz gemstone pendant. It was beautiful! It was so me.

"Mom, I love it! Thank you!" I gushed. I played with the necklace for a few seconds.

My mom stood up to leave, but I held her arm and said, "Five more minutes?"

She smiled and sat down beside me, smoothing back my hair and sitting with me in my little window seat one last time before the day got started.

* * *

I sat on a chair in the basement of St. Peter's. The baby pink and blue walls and blue carpet down here looked exactly the same as they did when all the little girls and boys were getting lined up for our First Communion back in the second grade. I guessed this room would still look the same in ten years, too.

I sat in the chair looking at the reflection in the mirror. It was just me and my closest friends in the room right then.

I looked in the mirror at each one of them, smiling as I thought back on all of our memories together. I never thought I'd be the first one of this group to get married though. But I guess I also never thought I'd meet Zach.

My eyes fell on Sophie in the back corner of the room. She was wearing the lavender colored silk robe I got for each of them as we got ready this morning, and her light hair curled in tiny little ringlets and piled into an updo at the top of her head. She was bent at an odd angle trying to look in a very tiny mirror on the wall in the corner as she gently lined her brown eyes with dark eyeliner. She caught my eye in the reflection of both of our mirrors and winked.

She put down her makeup and walked over, standing behind me and putting a hand on the sleeve of my white robe. "Hello, Bride, can I get you anything?" she asked.

"Nah, I'm good. Thanks, Soph."

"Of course. You look absolutely stunning by the way!" she whispered and hugged me from the side.

"Oh, wait!" Cammie squealed. "That's so cute! Stay just like that! Don't move!" She ran over, with her phone at the ready, and snapped a photo in the reflection of the mirror of Sophie with her arms around me, both of us smiling.

"Perfect!" Cammie told us, handing her phone to Sophie, who gushed over how adorable the photo was.

"Send me that, will you?" Sophie asked.

"Of course," Cammie told her, then smiled and went back to straightening her dark brown hair next to me.

As Sophie walked away and went back to applying her makeup, I looked at Cammie. Cammie was my Maid of Honor. I could remember the two of us as little girls talking about our weddings someday, promising we'd be each other's Maid of Honors. There really was no question though, all these years later. We are still just as close, if not even closer. She's like a sister to me. Cam was there for the engagement, the first one to see the ring and see me standing there with my fiance'. She'd be standing there next to me today, too, when I get the second ring and Zach becomes my husband.

Last night, before the rehearsal, she gave me a gift bag that said "Mr. & Mrs." on it in really pretty lettering. It was a pretty big gift bag.

I tilted my head, looking surprised at her. "Cam, you have already gotten us so many things. What is this?"

"Just a little something I've been working on." She smiled and gestured for me to open it and told Zach to walk over and see it, too. "I wanted to give it to you guys tonight so I could see you open it."

I pulled out the white tissue paper and reached into the bag. There was a box-type thing inside. I pulled it out to find that it wasn't a box, it was a canvas.

I turned it over, and stared at the beautiful painting on it as I felt Zach's arm wrap around my waist.

The canvas was painted to look like there were wooden planks all over it, they were distressed and had a grey-ish color to them. Across the planks, it said, "Addison & Zachary 05.12.23" in Cammie's precise and beautiful script. Coming up from the bottom of the canvas were painted lavender flowers, tons of them. It looked like a field of lavender.

"Oh, Cammie! This is incredible!" I said, pulling her in for a hug. "It's beautiful!"

"This is great, Cammie. Thank you," Zach told her, giving her a hug, too.

"Good! I'm glad you like it," she said.

"I love it, Cam. You're the sweetest!" I turned to Zach, holding it up so we could both look at it again. "We'll put it in the family room," I told her. She smiled.

"Hey, Cam?" I said to her, now in the church basement getting ready for the wedding.

"What's up, girlfriend?" she asked, running her straightener over a strand of hair.

"You didn't tell me about last night, yet," I pointed out. "Are you happy?" I asked.

"Happy?" she repeated. "For you? Oh my goodness, my darling, I am ecstatic! I have been waiting for this day for you for so long."

"Well, thank you. But I mean are you happy? With last night? You haven't said anything."

She set down the straightener, bit her lip, and turned to face me.

She looked upset.

What did Billy do? Geez, how could he have already screwed this up? I thought. *Those two are perfect together. They always have been.*

Then her face lit up and you could tell she was trying to not let the smile flood her face like it was right then. Her cheeks flushed, bright red. She stared right in my eyes, and I could tell instantly how happy she really was.

"I didn't say anything because today's your day. I didn't want to take away from it," she explained.

I pointed next to me at the chair right behind her. "Oh, please! This is big! I want to hear about it! Besides, Jess went to go find the hairspray. Sit. Spill!"

She smiled and sat down in the chair beside me, leaning close to whisper.

"Okay, so, after the dinner--"

"You kissed him!" I interrupted.

She blushed and her eyes went wide. "Yes! And oh, my goodness, Addie," she lowered her voice even more, "I forgot how good of a kisser he was!"

We both laughed, and then she continued dishing on the night before, "Anyway, after the dinner, and, yes, after we kissed, we decided to go out to grab a drink. So we went to that little bar off of 85, you know the one we went to when I turned twenty-one?"

I nodded.

"So, we pretty much sat there drinking wine. Who knew Billy's super into wine?"

"He is?"

"Yes! He's into wine tastings and all that stuff! He picked one out for me to try, and it was so good! I loved it! Okay, anyway, we just sat at one of those little tables by the fireplace they have there, and we talked. For hours. We talked about everything that's been going on with us since graduation and what our plans are now that college is over. He accepted that job offer, you know? He's going to be moving back here to Madison. He seemed really happy when I said I was teaching at Madison High now. He said he always knew I'd be doing something great like that. He said it was perfect for me. He said I was still so beautiful, but that I'd gotten even more beautiful than he remembered. Everything felt...I don't know... like it just fit. And I'm sorry I didn't tell you about that time he came back a few weeks ago. I didn't think anything would come of it. But I've got to be honest with you, Addie, seeing him again that night was crazy. I couldn't think about anything but him for days. Then, I knew he'd be at the wedding and everything, I mean, he's Zach's best man. But I figured that night before didn't mean anything. I didn't think he'd be moving back for good or that he actually still had feelings for me. But he is back and he does and...we said last night that we're going to give it another shot. Am I crazy?"

"No," I told her. "Cam, I saw you guys grow up together. You were both in love with each other but neither of you said anything for years. The rest of us knew it was only a matter of time. I think if it feels right and if he makes you happy, then you should go for it. See how things go."

She smiled and squeezed my hand. "Well, this hair won't straighten itself! Better get back to it!"

I leaned forward and was inspecting my eyeshadow, making sure it didn't crease already. *Still good!*

I looked behind me and saw Lily getting ready behind me, unzipping her garment bag to show the lavender colored chiffon bridesmaid dresses all my bridesmaids had. Her's was a halter neckline and was belted at the waist. Her hair, now more of a burgundy color than a fiery red, was curled and fell loosely down her back. She's been growing her hair out much longer since high school, too.

She was someone from Madison High that I was friends with all through high school, but she had gone to school out in California, so I didn't think we'd really be able to keep in touch all that much. But we did. All four years of college we would hang out through the summers, go to dinner every Christmas break, and we talked on the phone often, too. She and Brad broke up pretty soon after graduating from Madison High. If you ask me, he was always a player. Now she's dating a new guy named Conrad. He seems really sweet; he would be coming to the wedding later today. She laughs constantly around him. It makes me really happy to see her that way.

My fourth bridesmaid was a good friend from my psychology classes in college, Amanda, but she's always had me call her Mandy. I met her sophomore year on the first day of the new semester. It was snowing horribly outside, inches and inches of snow. The roads were a thousand times worse than they had predicted they would be. It took me forever to get to class that day. It wasn't held on the main campus, it was held at the little annex around the block. I got there late. I was never late. I rushed into the lecture hall, so worried because of how tough the upperclassmen had told me this professor was. There was an empty seat on the end next to a girl with a straight, blonde bob and a bright pink sweater. I slipped in there and sat down. I was flipping through the syllabus trying to find what page they were on, clearly flustered.

The girl reached out and pointed with her pen to the line the professor had just spoke about. Then she angled her notebook on her desk so I could read it. "I'll catch you up after class! Don't worry!" she whispered.

"Thank you!" I whispered back.

"I'm Mandy, by the way," she said giving me a little wave.

"Hi. I'm Addison."

"Oh, I love that name!" she said, then went back to writing more notes.

She stayed a bit after that class to catch me up and even invited me to join in a study group she was making for that class. She had had that professor before and said he was, in fact, a super tough grader. Soon we were great friends, sitting next to each other in every class we had, staying up late studying, or watching movies when we should have been studying, and painting our nails.

My fifth bridesmaid was none other than Jessica Clark.

Honestly, if you would have told me back in high school early on that Jess and I would become best friends again and that she would someday be in my wedding, I would have told you you were crazy!

It's sad sometimes to think of how the jealousy between us and darkness of the dreamworld kept us apart for so many years. The saddest part is that we were both going through the same thing. We just didn't know the other was suffering. We thought the other could never understand how our life was. But I also think those years apart made our friendship stronger. Now we see each other more clearly and have found a common ground. I found that she was actually incredibly sweet and thoughtful and that the girl she was back when we were little was still inside of her, just buried beneath the nightmares life brought her way. It took me a while to let my guard down around her, but now I know in my heart that she is there for me always, and I will always be there for her.

Just then Jess came back in with three cans of hairspray.

"Geez, Jess! How much of that are we going to use?"

"All of it!" she teased.

She held up a small box wrapped in silver paper. "I saw Mr. Dreamboat out there, and he asked me to give you this," she said handing me the box, "and this."

She handed me a folded up piece of paper.

Addison was written across the top in Zach's handwriting.

"Leave it to dreamboat to write a romantic letter on your wedding day," Jess commented. "My cousin better not have written anything that's going to make you cry, because your makeup is perfect exactly how it is." She turned the dial on the curling iron. "I'll keep curling your hair and you just sit there and read his letter, okay?"

"Okay," I agreed, unfolding the note.

Jess was right. Leave it to Zach to write me a letter.

He really was perfect, wasn't he? I thought as I smoothed out the page and began to read.

Dear Addison/ Tour Guide/ Beautiful/ Dreamer Girl,

33

- Zach -

Friday, May 12th, 2023

"I'm marrying Addison today," I said.

Mitch grinned, clapping me on the back. "I know, bud."

I turned and looked at him. "Can you believe it?"

Mitch chuckled, then reached out to straighten my black bow tie. "Here," he said, untying it and starting over. "You have to go this way first."

I stood there for a second, thinking about the fact that Mitch was basically my dad growing up. He was the one showing me how to tie a tie (not a bow-tie though, which was why I was clearly struggling now). He was the one who helped me learn lacrosse and practiced with me in the backyard of whatever house we were living in at the time.

"I'm glad you're here today," I told him as he finished up the tie.

"There," he said, stepping back to make sure it looked alright. He waved his hand and brushed my comment away. He was never one for anything like that. "Ah, well...where else would I be?"

In the past few months, ever since that day at the hospital, Mitch has been around way more. You can tell he's really trying to make amends. I think he really has changed. Although from the stories I've heard of how he was when he was younger, I think maybe he was always more kind hearted than he was letting on the time I've known him.

"Well," I said, "thanks. It means a lot."

"Sure, kid."

"I just wish mom was here, too..."

Mitch's face twisted up all strange. He cleared his throat and said, "Yeah, well...I'm going to go see where Billy went. Don't want that boy running off and losing the rings."

I watched as Mitch walked out the door and headed down the hall the way Billy went a few minutes before. He gets so weird anytime I say anything about my mom lately. I thought he wanted to help her get better as much as I did.

She's not one-hundred percent better. Not yet though. And it sucks.

I always knew growing up that my mother wouldn't be at my wedding, that there would be no mother-son dance. But when I found out she was still alive and I got engaged to Addison, I thought that maybe...

It was stupid anyway, to think she'd be able to be here today.

No one ever leaves The Haven they all say.

I was happy to at least have Mitch there with me though. It was like I had at least a little piece of my family represented. I think it means a lot, too, that after all that has happened, Mitch and I have been able to find common ground.

I wasn't sure originally if I should invite him.

But after how much of a help he was that day and all he has done to help Addison and I since, I started wondering if I should have him at the wedding. I had no clue how I could ever bring that up to Addison though. He put her through so much pain. I still hate him for that.

But one day, when we were talking about guest lists, she handed me a slip of paper that said "Must Invites," and his name was at the top of the list, right beneath her immediate family.

"Are you sure, Ad?" I had asked her that day.

"Zach, he basically raised you. For as much wrong as he's done, that's one thing he managed to do right. We can't not invite him. You wouldn't be you if it weren't for him. I'm thankful for that," she had said as if it were a simple answer in her book.

As I remembered that moment, I thought to myself, *That girl never stops amazing me.* And all over again I was just blown away that someone like her was seriously marrying someone like me today.

I walked over and leaned on the edge of the table, trying to balance as I tied my black shiny shoes. I shook my head, knowing she was downstairs, probably already ready and getting her pictures taken. I smiled, knowing she picked me. I got nervous, knowing she was going to look the definition of stunning, because she always did, even when we were just having a night in watching movies and eating Sal's fries take-out. But today, I haven't even seen her yet, and I know she looks amazing.

Billy came back in the room then.

"Hey, where's Mitch?" I asked when I saw Mitch wasn't with him.

"He was talking to Addie's aunt, I think?"

"He was?"

"Yeah," Billy shrugged, like this was no big deal. "Anyway, I left this in my car by mistake. Sorry it's a bit late. But Addison told me to give this to you. I was supposed to give it to you first thing this morning." He stuck out his hand, passing me a small box that was wrapped the way Addison always wraps her presents. It had a little card tied to it that said *Don't be late! XOXO*.

I unwrapped it and opened the box. There was a watch inside.

Ever since our first Christmas dating, when she got me a watch and said that "Time stands still when we're together," she has gotten me a watch for big events like graduation and some holidays. I have a sort of watch collection now. All of them from Ad.

This one was really slick. It had a dark face with a dark gray leather strap. I figured she wanted me to wear it today, so I took it out of the box and set it on the table in the room my groomsmen and I were all getting ready in. I was unfastening the watch I currently had on, the original Christmas gift watch, when I noticed something on the back of the watch. It was the way the light was hitting the back, making the metal shine, that I realized there was something else on the back.

I picked it up and looked closer. She had it engraved. It said:

Ad + Zach ... Time stands still 05.12.23 3:00

I smiled at the watch. Ad was always super thoughtful with her gifts like this. I hoped she liked the bracelet I got for her today. I thought it would look nice next to my mom's.

Anyway, like I've been saying, I just can't believe she's going to be my wife today.

I glanced down at the watch.

Two hours.

34

- Addison -
Friday, May 12th, 2023

     I have never written a love letter before. To be honest, I thought it would be hard, seeing as I'm not one for letter writing in general, let alone a love letter. But the instant I sat down with this pen and paper, all these thoughts and memories of you filled my head, and now I'm not sure any amount of paper or ink would ever be enough to tell you everything that I love about you.

     First of all, I want you to know how happy I am that this day is finally here! Those awful two weeks last year had me worried this day might never happen. But here we are. The first day of the rest of our lives! I'm sure that sounds cheesy, but it's true-- plus, I know how much you love cheesy things! I am just so thankful and excited to go on this journey with you, wifey.

You really are the girl of my dreams, Ad! *wink, wink*

You are perfect in every way that I need you to be. You are there for me. Always. Your smile lights up a room. You are crazy beautiful and insanely kind-hearted.

And yet I think the thing that I love the most about you is that you don't even seem to know or understand how amazing you are -- not only to me, but to everyone around you. Your natural abilities as a dreamer, or your eyes, or everything else that makes you you-- it's like you don't even realize how great you are at those things. And you are SO GREAT at them. Believe me, Ad, I know I'm marrying up. But I promise to spend my whole life trying to be better, trying to be the kind of man you deserve and can depend on, trying to be even a fraction of how giving you are.

Thank you for everything you are to me. I love you and can't wait to see you soon and start our life together in our little townhouse with our red dishes.

Love your (almost) husband,
-Zach

* * *

I stretched out my hand and my mom took it gently in hers. She wrapped the first bracelet, my something borrowed, around my wrist and fastened it in place. It was silver, and had a bunch of little pave beads, so it looked like it sparkled when the light hit it. The bracelet was Meg's. She had a few things in a trunk that Mitch had kept each time he and Zach moved over the years. It was a small trunk and had mostly old photographs, a few pieces of jewelry, some baby clothes of Zach's, and a bouquet of pressed flowers. There were also a couple of old journals that I hoped to read someday soon. When we told her we were engaged and when the wedding date was, she said I just had to have the bracelet and told Mitch he had to find that bracelet. Mitch found it in the trunk and gave it to Zach to give to me. I've saved it in my dresser all these months to wear today. It was beautiful. It was nice to have a small piece of her here today for the ceremony.

Then, my mom wrapped my new bracelet around my wrist right behind Meg's bracelet. It was what had been in the box from Zach this morning. It had the same type of pave beads, and every other bead was a light purple pearl. It matched my flowers and the bridesmaids' dresses perfectly.

Once my dress was on and everything was pretty much ready to go, I had asked my bridesmaids to leave the room for a bit so that it could just be my mom and me. She had helped me do some touch-ups to my makeup and was now helping me with my jewelry.

I had my "something blue and new" necklace on. We had asked the florist to fix an old sparkly broach my grandmother had to the front of my bouquet for my "something old." Satin ribbons in lavender and gray criss-crossed down the stems of the flowers, and the broach secured them in place.

The flowers were beautiful! All different shades of purples, grays, and greens. There were sprigs of lavender and eucalyptus spraying out from the bouquet. It smelled heavenly, too!

My mom stepped back and spun me to face the one full-length mirror in the room.

I took it all in, staring at my reflection as my mom fluffed out my veil, making it lay just so.

I look like a bride! I thought.

I am *a bride*, I reminded myself.

Oh my gosh! I'm about to marry Zach! It's finally happening!

I looked at myself in my dress, hair, makeup, veil, and holding my bouquet. I felt the same as I did the day I found my dress. I felt happy, loved, beautiful, and ready to marry the man of my dreams!

"You are stunning," my mom told me with her hands squeezing my shoulders and tears threatening to spill over the brim of her darkly-lined eyes.

"Thank you, Mom," I told her, looking into her eyes in the reflection, hoping that she could see I meant it for more than just her compliment then. I meant thank you for everything.

My dress, *the* dress, was all white lace from top to bottom. It was simple, but the simplicity is what made it elegant. It had a sweetheart neckline and flared out at my knees, trumpet style. The same lace that was in the dress lined my veil. I had added a belt made of pearls and rhinestones at my waist.

It was...me.

It was my *dream* dress.

A knock came at the door. It was my dad.

"Bob, look at our little girl!" my mom cooed.

"Addie, honey," my dad started, hugging me tight, "You are the most beautiful bride." He looked at my mom and added, "She's all grown up, Annie."

The three of us stood there talking for a few minutes. My mom tearing up every once in awhile. My dad looking at me and shaking his head, amazed, like his little girl had grown up right before his eyes.

"Are you ready?" he asked, looking at the time on his watch.

I thought back to Zach's letter.

"How could I not be?" I replied.

* * *

I heard the music start to play, an instrumental piece I've always dreamt of walking down the aisle to.

"I love you, little girl," my dad told me as I slipped my arm through his.

Deep breath, I told myself.

The doors opened. Everyone stood and stared.

For the slightest of seconds, I got nervous. There were so many people. Looking at me.

But then I looked straight ahead and my eyes locked with his and everything faded away. All I thought about was how much I loved him and how perfect he looked, standing up there, staring back at me.

35

- Zach -

Friday, May 12ᵗʰ, 2023

The wedding was starting. The wedding coordinator got my groomsmen and me all in line standing at the side door of the main part of the church. Soft music was playing as we walked out and across the front of the altar to where our places were.

We all stood there for a couple of minutes before the music Addison had picked began playing.

Billy tapped me on the shoulder. "You ready, man?" he whispered.

"Been ready," I told him and straightened my jacket.

"You nervous?" he asked.

"Nope," I told him. But I guessed that was a lie because I was. "A bit," I added.

He chuckled and then stepped back into his place.

Ad's bridesmaids walked down one by one.

Cammie was the last to walk down because she was Ad's maid of honor. As she walked, I heard Billy whistle quietly. "Daaannnnggg," Billy muttered under his breath behind me while he stared at Cammie.

She was looking right at us, shaking her head and trying not to laugh at Billy as she kept walking down the aisle.

She got to the front and took her place to the side of the altar.

The little flower girls came down next, one of them getting distracted halfway down the aisle by their mom sitting on the edge of the pew.

"Hi, Mommy!" she called out, waving. "Lookie! I'm a flower girl!"

"I know, sweetie. Keep going!" the mom was whispering back, looking embarrassed and pointing to the front of the church. The girls kept walking then and soon made it to the front of the church, little rose petals scattered on the floor where they had thrown them.

Here goes...

The double doors at the back of the church swung open as the music got louder and more dramatic. As they opened, I could see Mr. Smith in his suit and tie standing proudly with someone's arm draped through his holding on tight.

The doors continued to open and suddenly...

There she was.

It was like I forgot how to breathe in that moment, and it was the best feeling in the world.

She had her veil pulled down; white, flowy fabric covering her face. But through the veil I could see her eyes, bright and blue, looking right back at me. A smile filled her whole face. She winked.

I swear, no one on this whole earth has ever, *ever*, looked as beautiful as she did right then. Ever.

A couple hundred people were in the room filling the pews of the church, all craning their necks to get a look at Addison. Luckily, I had a crystal clear, straight-on view. In some churches the groom can't see the bride for half her walk down the aisle. But I really lucked out with this one, because I got to see my girl the whole walk down. And despite the hundreds of other people trying to see her or wave hello to her, she wasn't looking at a single one of them. I guess I had thought she'd be waving back or saying little greetings to the people as she passed them. But, nope. My girl was staring right back at me the entire time.

She was still feet away, but I wished the aisle was shorter. I wished she could just get here sooner. But at the same time, this was literally the best thing I had ever seen in my life, so she could take her time.

It was like every step she took closer to me, she got more and more beautiful. She was wearing this dress that looked like it was made just for her. It was tight, but in an awesome way, and the bottom of the dress floated behind her as she walked closer to me. Her hair was down and curly, the way she had worn it to our prom. I loved when her hair looked like that.

Her smile though, *that* was worth a million bucks.

Finally, finally, she got to the end of the aisle.

I reminded myself to walk down the couple steps and meet her at the bottom of the altar.

Her dad lifted her veil up and over her face, and I could see her face clearly now. Her beautiful face. Then he gave her a hug and kissed her cheek. He turned, placing Addison's hand in mine, and then he walked to his seat, leaving just me and Addison standing there.

"Hi," she whispered. She squeezed my hand, and her smile widened, if that was even possible. Her eyes were shining.

I tried to say "hi" back. I really wanted to, but no words came out. I just stood there, staring at her and smiling. *Real smoothe, Zach. Real smoothe.*

Her cheeks got all red, and she looked down at our hands, peering up at me through her lashes.

"You look..." I started, but honestly couldn't think of a word good enough to finish that statement.

She lifted her head, looking straight at me again and laughed one of her little, quiet laughs. She just got me. I didn't have to finish the sentence, she just knew. "You look...too."

Then we walked the couple of steps up to the altar where we stood with our close friends and Father Jameson, the man whose advice all those years ago helped me to get Ad back and figure myself out better.

Father Jameson cleared his throat and began to speak, "We are gathered here today to witness the love and union of Zachary David and Addison Grace..."

Addison faced me, and I took both of her hands in mine.

"I love you," she mouthed to me as the priest was talking about marriage.

"I love you," I said back.

Yep, I thought to myself then, *I'm definitely marrying up. No doubt about that.*

36

- Addison & Zach -
Friday, May 12th, 2023

Sunlight flooded in through the stained-glass windows above us and sent twinkling beams of color dancing all around the both of us. It was like heaven. Everything was perfect. I couldn't stop smiling at him.

I took his hands in mine and began to speak with my whole heart the words that I think my whole life had been leading me to say to the man standing in front of me:

"I, Addison,"

"I, Zachary,"

"Take you, Zachary David Walker,"

"Take you, Addison Grace Smith,"

"To be my lawfully wedded husband,"

"To be my lawfully wedded wife,"

"To have,"

"And to hold,"

"From this day forward,"

"From this day forward,"

"For better,"

"For worse,"

"For richer,"

"For poorer,"

"In sickness,"

"And in health,"

"Until death do we part,"

"Until death do we part."

"I do."

"I do."

I was staring into his beautiful blue eyes, smiling like a fool. I was his and he was mine.

"Zach," the priest started, pausing for effect and what seemed like eternity.

Hurry up and kiss me already! I was thinking and could tell by Zach's face he was thinking the same thing.

"You may kiss your bride."

Yay! I thought just as Zach put his arms around me and pulled me to him, kissing me for the first time as my husband.

I think people were clapping, but in that moment, there was nothing else, no one else in that big church besides Zach and me.

Zach was my husband now! Oh. My. Gosh.

It was the best day of my life.

I was staring right at her, waiting, but hating the waiting, until finally, finally, Father Jameson said, "Zach."

Yes...

"You may kiss your bride."

Thank God! I thought, and pulled her to me, kissing my wife, Addison Walker, for the first time.

I could vaguely hear people clapping and cheering all around us, but I honestly could care less.

Addison was my wife now! Wow.

It was the best day of my life.

37

- Addison -
Friday, May 12th, 2023

"**A**ddison, look a little to the right. Yes. Tilt your chin down a bit. Perfect! Right like that, don't move. Okay, now, Zach, move around behind Addison and look over this way at me. Great! Oh, this is a good one!"

Jenny, the photographer, pulled back to look at the screen of her camera, shielding the screen with her hand to block out the bright sun. We really did luck out with the weather today! It was absolutely beautiful. It was raining when I woke up this morning, so for a while I was worried, but the skies cleared, the sun came out, and the day was just perfect.

"Wonderful! These are great, guys," Jenny said. "Absolutely beautiful!"

"You can say that again," Zach whispered in my ear, hugging me.

I twisted to look up at him, smiling even bigger than I had before, which I didn't even think was possible.

"You look beautiful, Ad," he said.

"Thanks, Z. You clean up pretty well yourself!"

I just looked at him, and he just looked at me; both of us happier than we ever thought we'd be.

I faintly heard the shutter of the camera and just barely saw the flashes.

I knew whatever photo Jenny just took would no doubt be my favorite. We'd get it printed, big and beautiful, and hang it above the mantle of the fireplace in the townhouse we'd go home to tonight.

I want to fill that whole house with pictures of us.

Pictures everywhere.

"Alright, can I have Addison and the bridesmaids one more time?" Jenny asked.

"That's my cue," Zach said, as he kissed my cheek and walked away, out of the scene for the photos.

"How perfect is this day?" Cam asked as she came up in place beside me, looking all around and gesturing to the clear skies and nice weather.

"So perfect," I agreed.   Because it was. It was perfect.

* * *

After all the pictures had been taken, it was time to head to the reception. There was still about forty-five minutes of the cocktail hour remaining, so we had enough time for one more thing. I had planned it this way. I wanted to make sure she was a part of today.

Zach and I rode in the back of a black limo, sitting close and holding hands. We were talking softly, almost a whisper, even though we were the only ones in this limo, so we really didn't have to.

The limo came to a stop, after only driving for five minutes. The venue for the wedding was ten minutes at least from the church.

Zach looked around. "Why did we stop?"

"Well, I thought we'd make a quick stop. Don't worry, we have plenty of time."

"Okay..." Zach said, looking at me skeptically.

The driver came around and opened the door. Zach got out first and then helped me out, carefully lifting the back of my dress so it wouldn't get stuck.

Another car pulled up behind us. My parents, my Aunt Carrie, and Zach's Uncle Mitch all got out and walked over toward us.

He handed me the train of my dress so it wouldn't drag and then turned around, finally realizing where we were.

"Ad?"

"Yeah, babe?"

He remained facing the entrance of the building we had walked into together so many times. He was just staring.

"Why are we at The Haven?" he asked.

I replied as simply as I could while still trying to convey through my voice how important this moment was, "Every mother deserves to see her son get married."

"But..."

I explained, "Well, I thought we could have our own little wedding ceremony here, with your mom, after the main one. I just thought she deserved to see this moment, to be here with you. She is so important to me, because she gave me you. Believe me, I have called this place and come in to speak with management for *months*, but they all said there was just no way she could safely be allowed to come to the ceremony. That it was against all protocol. So, I figured, why not bring the ceremony to her? They said because of her recent good behavior, they would allow more than two guests at a time. They're letting us use the rec room! It'll be great. Father Jameson should be here in a minute. He's just giving us an extra blessing."

Zach shook his head, staring at the crooked sign above us that read "The Haven". "You always surprise me, Ad. Thank you."

"Of course," I told him, taking his hand in mine.

"Are you ready to get married?" my dad asked, a joking tone to his voice, as if he hadn't already asked me that question today.

"I would marry him again and again and again," I replied.

"Ah, young love," my aunt sighed.

There was a split second-- so slight you could have blinked and missed the whole thing-- but there was a split second that as Carrie said those words, her eyes locked with Mitch's and there was a moment there. I would never know what it was they said in that instant without ever saying a word to each other, but the look they shared spoke volumes. They used to be young and in love, too.

I don't think anyone else noticed that moment.

But I did.

Then, all of us were escorted into the rec room where the new fireplace, coincidentally donated by an old friend of Mitch, was on and burning bright, warming the whole room. The Haven had a way of feeling cold, even on the hottest of days.

But today the room was glowing, and there was a sense of warmness over everything.

It was a couple of minutes before the new nurse, Gracie, returned with Meg. In those minutes, Zach looked very nervous. He kept turning to me, asking question after question, like, "What if she forgets who I am again?" or "What if this is too much for her?"

I just held his hand tighter and told him I would be there for him either way, but that today was a good day so everything would be okay.

The side door opened, and Meg walked in, Gracie following close behind in her nurse's uniform.

Meg's whole face lit up, full of joy and love and hope.

"Hi, Mom," Zach said.

Meg smiled at her son, tears brimming over her eyes.

"We're so happy you could be here for this," Zach told her.

"So happy," I echoed.

Meg looked so different today. A good different. She didn't have the typical Haven pajamas and robe on. Her slippers were nowhere in sight. She had on a nice sundress, ballet flats, and her hair looked like it had been done just for the occasion. I'm sure Gracie had helped her out. But more importantly than the hair or the new clothes was that Meg was smiling. My new mother-in-law seemed genuinely happy and excited for the first time in decades of living in this place. The greatest thing about seeing her walk into the rec room then, ready to see her son get married, was just how present she was. She was there, all there. She got to be in that moment, not just physically watching a wedding take place, but mentally there.

Then everyone gathered around the two of us.

Father Jameson gave Zach and I a marriage blessing. We said the traditional vows to each other again and then both took turns and spoke from our hearts, our own personal vows.

"This is just a dream come true!" Meg squealed, pulling me in for a hug after the mini-ceremony was over. "This day has just been a dream!"

"Yes," I agreed. "A real dream come true!"

38

- Zach -
Friday, May 12ᵗʰ, 2023

After we said our vows again, we made our way to the wedding venue. We had picked a ballroom at the fancy hotel in town. It was where most of the weddings took place here in Madison. Ad said that it felt like tradition, getting married in the church her parents did, having the reception in the same place her parents did.

Sitting there, in the limo, now married, was crazy. We were *married* now. This girl, this amazing girl who would go to so much trouble to make sure my mom was involved today, was mine.

I really was not expecting that! I had been trying to get it in my head for months that my mom simply wouldn't be at my wedding. I didn't think there was any way it could work.

Then Addison goes and figures out a way to make my mom feel special, feel a part of it. My mom looked so happy. My mom's new nurse said my mom had talked of nothing but the wedding for the past few weeks, ever since Addison figured out the loophole of bringing the wedding to her. She even had been using her recreational time the past few days to work on a painting for Ad and me. She said she wanted to paint a "dream scene" for us. It was actually really great. I didn't even know my mom could paint like that.

I just didn't even know how to put into words how great it was to have my mom there. Having Addison plan something like that... it was just one more reason to prove she was the perfect girl.

* * *

We arrived at the venue and made our big entrance into the room as husband and wife.

The bartender for the wedding, a tall guy named Jeremy who also bartended at Sal's, came over and greeted us, handing me a tall glass of cold beer and Addison a glass of that fizzy pink wine she likes. Madison was a pretty small town. The kind of town where you know the bartender and he remembers basically everyone's favorite drinks.

"Congratulations, guys!" he said.

"Thanks, man! And congratulations to you, too!" I told him.

"Oh!" Addison said. "That's right! You just got married, too! Congratulations! Kristin is the sweetest girl! Tell her we said congrats, too."

"Thank you! I will tell her." He looked at me, "Well, I'll let you and the ol' ball and chain go make the rounds! Let me know if I can get you guys anything, okay?"

"We will," we both told him.

Then the two of us walked around and visited as many of the tables as we could-- talking with our family and friends and thanking them for being there-- before Addison squeezed my hand, which had yet to leave hers, and told Mary and Will, her neighbors, "Thank you both so much for coming! It means the world!"

Then, two steps away from the table, she said, "Mr. Walker, can I have this dance?"

"Always," I told her, and we made our way toward the patch of hardwood-looking tiles that was the dance floor.

We had picked a song that meant a lot to the two of us. It was a song we danced to at Fall Ball (first in her dream, then later in real life).

The song had some lyrics in it about dreams and feeling safe around someone. To anyone else listening to it, it would probably just seem like a typical song, but for us, all the lyrics had a second meaning, a meaning that applied only to us and our lives in the dream realm. It was like our secret song, holding even more meaning than just two people in love. Then, before we knew it, it kind of became our song. We listened to it a lot.

Two years ago, the singer who sings the song was actually coming for a concert less than an hour's drive from Madison, so Ad and I went to the concert. Being on college budgets and all, we couldn't afford the nice seats, so we got tickets for the lawn section, where everyone just piles in and sits on blankets, stands, or dances. We sang along to the songs we knew, listened to the ones we didn't, and waited, hoping she would sing this song, even though it was a few years old and not from her most recent album. Toward the end of the night, the second to last song, the guitarist switched out his electric guitar for his acoustic one, and began plucking the strings and playing the cords of the song we had been waiting all night for. I remembered Addison looking up at me, smiling, saying, "It's our song!"

So, a few months ago, Addison said, "Okay, now we need to decide on our first dance song."

We listened to a couple songs that were popular right then, songs that the bridal magazines she was reading said would be THE first dance song of this wedding season. But after five or six songs, she hit pause on her phone, stopping the music.

"What's up?" I asked. "You didn't think that was the BEST love song ever?"

"What are we even doing?"

I had been flipping through some paperwork but stopped and looked up at her. "What do you mean, Ad?" I asked.

"I mean...this isn't even a question, right? It's obviously this one." Then she switched the song, and a new one began to play, one we both knew very well. "Our song. It's perfect. It was our first dance, all those years ago, so it only makes sense that it's our first dance song as a married couple!"

I wondered how we could have forgotten it and not suggested it earlier that day. I agreed that the song would be perfect and stood up from the kitchen table, pushing back my chair. "Mrs. Almost Walker, can I have this dance?"

She took my outstretched hand and stood, turning up the volume of the song. "Always," she promised.

And we danced in the middle of her kitchen, knowing it was the best choice for our first dance song someday.

And now that someday was today.

The DJ's voice came through the speakers, "If everyone could turn their attention to the dance floor. It is time for Mr. and Mrs. Zachary Walker's first dance."

The music started.

And so, like so many other times before, I took her hand in mine, pulled her close, and we danced to our song.

39

- Addison -
Friday, May 12ᵗʰ, 2023

*T*he sound of knives tapping the sides of glasses filled the room for the hundredth time that evening. *But I was most certainly NOT complaining!*

Zach leaned closer, his elbows resting on the gray tablecloths, his eyes pulling me in like a magnet. He flicked his eyes toward all our family and friends looking at us, as the clinking sounds continued.

He smirked. "I guess we've got to give the people what they want. I think we have to kiss? Again?" he joked.

I playfully rolled my eyes, "Fine. If we must."

"Oh, we must," he said with a laugh and closed the gap between us.

A minute later, as the salad plates were being taken away and dinner plates replacing them, Billy stood up from his seat beside Zach and was handed a microphone.

"Check, one, two? Check, one, two?" he teased, tapping his finger on the top of the microphone and making fuzzy, loud noises come from it.

"It's on, Billy. We hear you," Cammie whisper-yelled across the table at him.

"Well, hi, everyone! I'm Billy, the best man."

One of Zach's friends from college, Tim, called out, "Hi, Billy," trying to get others to echo it with him.

Billy, clearly pleased to have interaction in his speech, smiled and then continued, "I have known Zach since junior year at Madison High when he showed up and sent all the girls in school into a tizzy. Seriously, they were all flipping out because this quote 'dreamboat' shows up *just* in time for Fall Ball date-finding time. We weren't exactly friends at first...probably because all of us guys thought the new kid was going to swoop in and steal our girl. But, anyway, from the get-go, this kid's got his eye on this one girl. It was obvious, too, dude," he said, turning to Zach and clapping him on the back. "I mean, I once overheard him trying to ask for her number. Cheesy bro. So cheesy. And what's sad is that it took her a few minutes to catch on to the fact that he was asking for her number." He turned and shook his head at me, whispering *tsk tsk.* "Now," he continued, "Addison had been a friend of mine for years. More accurately, she was best friends in the 'whole wide world' with my neighbor, Cammie, a girl I have always been in love with. So essentially wherever Cammie was, I was. And wherever Cammie was, Addison also was. Before I knew it, Addie and I were pretty good friends, too. So, at first, when I saw the new kid giving my good friend Addie so much attention, I was skeptical. What if he hurt her? What if he broke her heart? But soon enough, Zach and I became great friends, too, and I saw that he was a pretty cool guy. There was just something about him and something about Addison that just...fit. I know people say a lot, 'they were made for each other,' but those people have clearly never met Zach and Addison, or as Cammie refers to them, 'Zaddison,' because I have never seen two people so happy as them."

Wow, I thought. *That was really sweet.*

"Here's to the happy couple, the dream team, the dynamic duo, Zaddison!"

People clapped. Zach stood, and Billy and he did this weird handshake thing that I'm sure they made up junior year before some lacrosse game and still do. Then they had one of those "bro-hug" moments. And when Billy was clapping Zach on the back, he looked at me and said, "Congrats!"

And in that moment, I realized something I should have seen a very, very long time ago.

How could I have missed it? How could I have been so stupid all these years? We were so close. We were always together. How could I not have seen it sooner?

This really and truly changed everything.

Does Zach know? Could he tell all this time? Why would he never bring it up to me? Why have we never talked about this? How do I even tell Zach if he doesn't know, hasn't figured it out yet?

Billy-- funny, light-hearted, always the jokester, Billy-- had bright blue eyes.

I had always known this. I had seen his eyes many times. Many times.

But maybe I was too naive to see it before, maybe I never paid enough attention until Mitch asked me to.

There was a darkness there, clouding the brightness in his eyes, like he had seen so much, at only twenty-two.

I knew now what that darkness means.

I saw the same darkness in my eyes when I looked in the mirror. I also saw the same brightness shining through the cloudiness.

His eyes had the same hallmark trait that I see in Jess. The same I've seen in all of the people we've met in recent months.

Billy was just like me, and Zach, and Jess.

Billy was a dreamer.

40

- Addison -
Friday, May 12ᵗʰ, 2023

I never knew I could feel this happy.

I felt this immense and overwhelming feeling of joy and happiness, and so many things that I didn't even know how to express.

The wedding was over. Family and friends were gathering centerpieces, sneaking another cookie, and saying goodbye, all making their way out the front door where they would be waiting as Zach and I left to start our new life together.

We walked over to where we would say some more goodbyes and then leave for the night. Cammie stood waiting there with my bouquet. She handed it to me and then started to cry. "I'm just so happy for you!"

I wrapped my arms around her. "Thank you for everything, Cam!"

"I love you, Addie!" Cammie sobbed into my shoulder, hugging me tight. "Okay, time to go," she said, straightening up, and she pulled on the glass doors to open them.

Zach and I came out, Zach helping me down the front steps. When my feet-- no longer in my heels and very tired from dancing-- hit the pavement of the sidewalk, I saw all of our family and friends in two columns, lining the walkway to the car that would take Zach and I to our new home.

"Alright!" Jess called out. "One! Two! Three!"

Everyone raised their hands in the air and tossed something.

And suddenly there I was, back in the field of flowing lavender. I could picture that dream scene clear as day in my mind.

But I snapped my eyes open and took in the amazing sight that was happening right before me.

Everyone we loved was showering us with little flowers of lavender as we made our way to the car. Everyone we loved was here with us today. Everyone we loved helped us to both get to where we were today, to become the people we both were today. Everyone we loved helped to make this the very sweetest dream.

I inhaled the sweet scent of the flowers cascading all around us as I ran hand-in-hand with my new husband through the path of our closest family and friends.

It felt like a dream, or maybe even better than any dream I had ever had.

Except I wasn't dreaming. No. This was real.

Today was better than any dream I had ever dreamt in that field.

Today was the start of our forever.

A Few Months Later...

41

- Addison -
Friday, September 15th, 2023

*T*he timer was going off like crazy.

"Okay, okay, I hear you! I'm coming!" I said, even though the oven could not hear me.

I stopped twisting the thing on the top of the salad spinner, a gift from my cousin. Then I rushed over to the oven, not wanting the potatoes to be burnt rather than roasted.

I threw open the oven door and waved my hand in front of the smoking pan. I slipped on my red pot holders and removed the pan from the oven. The potatoes were fine! Not burnt. Roasted to perfection.

What was smoking then? I wondered. But as soon as I thought that, I looked at the other pan.

Oh no! The carrots...

I pulled those out, too. And those, in fact, were burnt to a crisp.

"No, no, no, no, no!" I yelled, waving my hands back and forth and then opening the little window above the sink.

"What's wrong, babe?"

I turned to find Zach sliding the slider door closed behind him with his foot, his arms full of his fancy tools to clean the grill.

"The carrots are ruined!" I complained.

"They look fine," he protested.

"Zachary. The carrots are black. Burnt. They do not look fine."

He set down his things and reached out, grabbing a burnt, shriveled up carrot and popping it in his mouth. It was clearly very hot; I had just taken it out of the oven. He looked like he was in pain and tried to breathe out the sides of his mouth while faking a smile. "Amazing. Really, Ad! Great!" he choked out.

I swatted his arm with my potholder. "You are a horrible liar!"

"I'm sure they won't mind."

"Zach! Those are inedible!" I walked over to the fridge, rifling through the vegetable crisper. *What else could I make quickly?* I wondered.

"Ad," Zach said, walking up behind me and wrapping his arms around my stomach. "Chill. Please," he said, and kissed my neck.

I twisted around in his arms to face him. "Zach, it's our first big dinner party!"

"It's a cookout, Addison. Two different things."

"Neither of them usually involve burnt food!"

"It is okay! Just make a salad or something, and no one will even care there's no carrots."

"You're sure?"

"I'm positive," he told me and kissed the tip of my nose. He reached behind me, pulling the packages of steaks out from the fridge.

Tonight Cammie and Billy, Sophie and Todd, and Jess and her new boyfriend Landon were all coming over to our townhouse for a cookout.

After the wedding, Zach and I had actually been away traveling a fair amount. So far we have been to (and found dreamers to join our team) Pittsburgh, Johnstown, Akron, Cleveland, Portland, Kennebunkport, and Hartford.

There were so many dreamers in the northeast region. It blew me away.

I didn't have any classes through the summer, so I've been working with Jess, Mitch, and Diane on "dream team" stuff. Two days a week I work as the receptionist at a psychiatry office ten minutes outside of Madison. On the weekends, Zach and I are either traveling all around the country or don't even leave the house and order takeout all weekend.

I could tell Zach was getting frustrated. He hates travelling this much. Every time a new city was suggested for our search he asked what the point of going to all of these cities is.

"The point," I told him every time this came up, "is to find more dreamers."

"But why?" he would ask, time and time again. "What does it matter how many dreamers we find, Ad?"

"There's power in numbers, Zach. Someone, somewhere has to have more answers for us. If we keep searching, at some point we have to find something big, right?"

And every time, Zach would sigh and say, "But to what end, Ad? When will this stop? I'm tired of this. Why can't someone else go?"

"Don't you want answers?" I would ask him. "Don't you want to know why all of this happens to us?"

"Of course I want answers, Ad. I just don't know how this is working."

"Maybe not *yet*," I would tell him, emphasizing the word "yet".

"Fine. One more trip. But then that's it, Addison. I'm sick of never being home," he would say. And that's the way that conversation went. Every. Single. Time.

For our little Dream Team, Mitch found a place to rent. It's a lease on a unit in a big office complex. There are two rooms in the unit. One is a smaller room, where we have private consultations with other dreamers one on one. It is also where Jess has been conducting some study on the sleep cycle. The other room has a very long, oval table in the center with many chairs around it. This is where the dreamers have been meeting. We have yet to meet with everyone. It's usually three dreamers here, five there, but never have all seventeen of us sat down together.

That will all change tomorrow though. We have been planning a convention of sorts. All seventeen dreamers we have assembled will be there somehow. We have a decent amount of them able to make it in person, but for those who live in other areas of the world, we were able to set up a video conference so that their voices can be heard as well. We also invited some trusted psychologists and neurosurgeons to attend, too. It will be great!

The doorbell rang. I untied my blue gingham apron and set it neatly over the back of the barstool.

I went down the hall and swung open the door. Cammie and Billy were standing there. Billy had an arm around Cam's shoulders and the other hand holding a bottle of white wine that he held out to me now. Cammie was holding a white ceramic platter with tons of vegetables and crackers and cheese. "I know you said not to bring anything, but I wanted to!" she said.

"Come on in," I told them, stepping out of the way so they could come in. "And, oh, my goodness, Cam! You're a lifesaver! I just burnt the carrots."

"Nice," Billy mumbled teasingly.

"Oh, Billy, shush!" she told him, then turned to me and added, "I'm sure they're wonderful!"

"They're not," I confirmed. "But thank you for bringing this! Here, let me take that."

I took the dish out of their hands and they followed me back into the kitchen.

Zach came back inside just then from putting the steaks on the grill.

"Hey, brother, want some help out there?" Billy asked him.

"Sure!" Zach agreed. He gave Cammie a side-hug thing since his hands were all full. "Hey, Cammie!"

"Hi, Zach! You and *Mrs.* Walker have a nice place here!" she complimented.

"Thank you, but you've seen it before, haven't you, Cam?" he asked.

"Yep!" She nodded. "I was here just the other day. But I wasn't here for your first official dinner party as a married couple."

"See," I told Zach. "It is a dinner party."

"Grill's smoking, bud!" Billy called out, and the two of them grabbed a beer and went out to man the grill.

Cammie sighed.

"What?" I asked her.

"You guys seem happy here. Being married must be great. Is it great?"

I nodded.

"You love it, don't you?"

"I wish we were home more, though. I feel like we are always on the road anymore. I really love it here, so I just wish we were here more," I admitted.

"Well, hey, after the meeting tomorrow things should be better."

"You're right," I agreed. "By the way, please don't bring up anything about tomorrow once Sophie and Todd get here. Okay?"

"Addie, I would never. Don't worry. My lips are sealed!"

"Okay, good!"

And as if on cue, the doorbell rang, and I could see Todd's car through the window, so it must be the two of them.

After the wedding and once we got back from our honeymoon, the first people we made sure we saw were Billy and Cammie. Billy was officially moved back to Madison, staying back at his parents' house until he could find an apartment to rent, and officially, all-in, dating my best friend. They had talked through everything and had decided they'd rather be together than apart. They seemed really, really happy.

But still, once I told Zach my suspicions of Billy being a dreamer, neither of us could shake it.

We had to talk to him.

"I just feel like crap," Zach kept saying a few months ago. "He was going through the same thing we were for all those years and we never even knew."

So when we got home from Hawaii we called Billy and asked him to stop by. He came over, and we decided Zach would bring it up and just lay it all out there, all the facts, and see what he said.

I can remember clear-as-day the way Billy just chuckled when Zach asked if he had ever had weird dreams or felt like something was different when he was dreaming.

"What?" I asked, confused by the sense of ease that was around him during a discussion like this.

"It's just so funny," Billy had said that day.

"What is?" Zach asked, looking at me for clarification or any idea as to what was going on. I was lost.

"What kind of a question is that? Does anyone have a 'normal' dream? That isn't a thing. Dreams are always strange. They're dreams."

"Yes," Zach said, "but we mean more strange than most."

"How the heck would I know what other people's dreams are like?" Billy asked, looking at the two of us like we were insane.

Maybe we were...

Zach continued anyway, "Billy, have you ever had any dreams that happened later in real life?"

"It's called deja vu, buddy. Look it up. Nothing new."

"But it is though, Billy."

I spoke up then, saying, "Listen, what we are wondering is if your dreams have ever seemed very real, or if there's anything or anyone strange you've ever noticed in a dream?"

He chuckled again.

Okay, can he stop doing that?

"Are you guys seriously trying to ask me if I'm a dreamer? Because for starters, you're doing a horrible job, and also, it's about time. I mean, I've known you for, what? Six or so years, Zach? And Addie, come on! Is this a joke? You never knew until now?"

Zach and I both just stared at him, dumbfounded.

"Pick your mouths up off the floor, kids. This is nothing new. This has been my whole life. And I know, and have known, that this has been your whole lives, too. What do you think my speech meant about you two being made for each other?" Billy said, exasperated.

"W-what? How long have you known?" I asked him. "Why didn't you ever say anything?"

"Who talks about the dreams they had last night? That's weird, guys. You just suck it up and deal with it. And, hmm...probably since I first met you," he said.

What? How has he known for years and years and I only figured it out last week at the reception?

We ended up talking with him for hours that night, catching him up to speed on everything we knew. He told us what he had known, too. He didn't know it was as much of a thing as it is to be a dreamer. "I just thought I was special...or cursed," he had told us.

We explained Mitch wanting to assemble the dream team, and Billy agreed to join the efforts, vowing to help in any way he could, and that from this point on he would talk to us more about all of this.

He also told us something that broke my heart in two.

He said that senior year of high school his nightmares hit a whole new level. He said most of them involved Cammie getting hurt somehow or something happening to his family. He told us he had been depressed for quite some time and barely made it to school each day because he was so exhausted from the lack of sleep. His parents had taken him to counseling for a bit. His therapist was none other than Dr. Sandra Hardy. He agreed with me that she was up to something, no help at all, and unstable herself.

So that was the reason he broke things off with Cammie back then. He was worried he could never protect her or keep this other world away from her. He said he had to let her go. He sounded so broken then. It was horrible. He just assumed that it was how life was, nightmares and torture and darkness.

He said he had figured things out better since then, and especially now that he and Cammie were doing so well and back together. He had been honest with her about everything.

So now Cammie knows all about everything dream related. And I mean everything.

She has even been involved in some of the meetings. She really wants to help find an answer. She gets so angry and emotional talking about it now. She wants to find Them and stop Them from hurting anyone else the way They hurt Billy and Zach and me.

Now, months later, I excused myself while Cammie opened the wine they had brought, pouring us both a glass. I walked to the front door to let Sophie and Todd in.

I swung open the door, and Sophie practically tackled me with a hug.

"Addison! Thank you so much for inviting us over! We are so excited!"

"You're welcome," I laughed and hugged her back.

She stepped back and was still smiling a big, toothy smile with her bright pink lipstick.

"What is it?" I asked, knowing there was something she wasn't saying.

"We're engaged!" she blurted out and held up her left hand where a shiny new ring was.

"Oh, my gosh! Congratulations, guys!" I pulled Sophie in for a hug again.

"How'd ya pop the question?" I asked Todd.

Then the two of them, taking turns at various parts, started relaying the story of how Todd proposed. It involved the ring hidden in the dessert.

I was smiling and listening, so excited for them, when I saw another car pull in our driveway then. Jess and Landon got out and began walking up the front steps.

The second I saw her I knew something was wrong. She looked...not totally there, like her mind was off somewhere else. She looked sad.

I looked back at Sophie and Todd and heard the back door sliding open. "Zach will be thrilled, too! He's out back grilling the steaks," I told them.

Sophie must have seen Jess and Landon walking up to the door, too. Sophie did a little dance and said "Okie dokie, Addie! I'm going to go show off my ring!"

I grinned, knowing exactly how she felt. When you get engaged, you want everyone and anyone to know. You are just so happy, and all you want to do is tell people.

"Hi, Jess! Hi, Landon," I greeted.

Jess said hello and handed me a plate of chocolate chip cookies. I said thank you and smiled because she made really good cookies.

She set down her purse in the corner by the door and faked a smile. Landon asked where Zach was, and I pointed him to the back deck.

Then I turned to Jess, who was about to walk into the kitchen as if nothing was wrong. "Jess, what's up? Did you and Landon have a fight? Is everything okay?"

"What makes you ask that?" she asked, not looking me in the eye.

"Jess, seriously. You look really upset. What's wrong?"

For a minute, she looked like she was going to just say things were fine and go in with the rest of our friends. But then her face twisted, and I thought she might cry.

"Jess, please tell me. What's going on?" I pleaded.

"Uhhh..." She kept looking all around the room, and I could tell she was digging her nail into her arm a bit, the way she does when she's trying to bite her tongue or hold back tears. "Do you think we could talk for a minute?" she asked.

Jess never asked for help. From anyone. Ever. She was always the strong one, always putting up a facade that everything was fine. Always.

Something was really wrong.

"Of course," I told her.

I walked back into the kitchen and told Cammie to keep and eye on the guys and make sure they didn't burn the place down and that I'd be right out. Then I went back to grab Jess and took her up the stairs to our bedroom.

I sat down on the little velvet bench we had in front of the bed, motioning for her to come and sit with me.

It took her a minute, but finally she sat down.

She burst into tears.

I wrapped my arms around her shaking shoulders and tried my best to calm her down.

What was going on? I wondered. I had never seen her like this.

"Jess, what is it? What can I do?" I asked.

"Oh, Addie, it's awful."

"What's awful? What happened?"

She wiped under her eyes with the backs of her hands, smudging her mascara across her cheeks. She sniffled and sat up a little straighter.

"I did something really bad, Addie."

"Jess, I'm sure it's not that bad. What did you do?" I asked.

"I ruined my life," she said and broke down again.

42

- Addison -
Friday, September 15ᵗʰ, 2023

I held her tight, letting her cry, and smoothing her hair with my hand.

"Jess, please tell me what's going on," I pleaded.

She just said she ruined her life but wouldn't tell me what happened. She was more shaken up than I had ever seen her, so I wondered what could have possibly happened to make her cry so hard.

Between sobs, she finally started to explain. With each little bit she gave me, I tried to piece together what had happened.

The pieces were:

"I've been working with some other dreamers, searching for answers. I was just looking for...I don't know, s*omething, anything at all* to make this make more sense."

"Mitch is going to kill me. I should've never talked to her."

"The girl I found in Kentucky is a dreamer."

"She already had a group of dreamers she knew."

"All the trips lately have really been back to Kentucky to see them."

"It's all in the brain. I agreed with them on that."

"There had to be a medical, scientific answer here."

"Then the pills."

"I thought it would--"

"They told me there were no side effects, so I took them."

And then she broke down again.

I was trying really hard to piece it together, but some things just kept sticking out to me, and I couldn't get past them.

"Jess, I need you to tell me what pills you are talking about," I said sternly, trying to make eye contact. *What could they have given her? Is it the same thing they have Meg on at The Haven?*

Finally, she seemed to be calming down a bit and seemed able to talk more now. "For the experiment."

I waited, giving her time to finish.

She added,"The group of dreamers in Kentucky was running a study. I reviewed everything thousands of times. It seemed safe. They have been working with pharmaceutical engineers for a few years now. The pill was supposed to suppress the dreams and keep you out of R.E.M. longer."

She looked to me, as if for acceptance of this idea they had concocted.

"Jess, that doesn't sound natural," I pointed out. "What was in the pills to make that happen?

"I know!" she threw her hands in the air and let them fall in her lap. "It wasn't natural. And I don't know, a whole bunch of chemicals I can't pronounce."

"So they made some experimental pills and you've been taking them? For how long?" I asked. *If she had only taken them two or three times it would probably be okay and maybe wasn't even fully in her system yet. Some medications take a week to work, right?*

"Last November."

I gasped. "Jess! Why haven't you said anything about this?"

"I tried." She shook her head. "I guess I didn't try that hard. Addie, I just wanted this all to stop. I wanted answers. It all made sense...I was willing to try anything, risk anything...but now..."

So that's why she's been so distant lately, missing meetings, and when she did show up, not saying a word. I couldn't believe she'd been dealing with all of this on her own for so long.

"Jess, you've got to talk to me when you feel that way."

"It's too late now. I'm in too deep. But their plans are crazy, Addison. I don't think I can go through with them."

"You don't have to. We will figure this out."

"I don't know what I'm going to do," she said pulling a tissue from the box I held out to her now.

Okay, I thought. *So this isn't great, but it also isn't terrible. This is fixable. We just have to help her detach from the other group if their plans are that extreme.*

"It's okay," I told her. "We will figure out how to fix this."

"That's not what I'm upset about," she said.

"Oh. Then what is?"

What else could there be? I wondered.

But then I realized that the words "experimental pills" were still looming there, telling me something was not right. I realized that her tone when she said "they said there would be no side effects" before was a tone that said there were, in fact, side effects.

"Oh, Jess. What happened? Are you okay?"

You could tell then that the hardest words for her to swallow were coming back and she'd need to say them out loud to me now.

"I've been having these horrible pains in my stomach. It hurt so bad. The others who were also on the pills said it was probably just an ulcer, that the same thing happened to them for the first few weeks. Weeks turned into months. It got unbearable. I couldn't move."

Oh, no, I thought. *This wasn't sounding good. What does stomach pains mean?*

"I went to my doctor," she said. "She ran all these tests. Those hurt, too. And then, she said--"

Her breath caught and she was crying again.

"I've always wanted to be a mom!" she wailed.

Wait, what?

She was shaking now from crying so hard. "The doctor said..." Then she choked out four very devastating words, "I can't have kids."

My mouth dropped. I couldn't breathe. I couldn't think. I felt horrible. Those dreamers gave her pills for months that were making her sick.

I hugged her tighter than I think I've ever hugged a friend before. "I am so, so sorry, Jess. I'm so sorry," I kept saying over and over again, letting her cry and cry.

My heart broke for her as I sat there and watched her heart breaking, too, unable to do anything to help her.

She started talking really fast, "Addison, what am I going to do? I stopped taking them a while ago, but what if there's other side affects? No one's ever even heard of the drug I'm taking, so I can't find answers anywhere. The researchers and company that developed the drug in Kentucky stopped calling me back when I called them about this issue. They're suddenly nowhere to be found. I thought I could do it on my own. I thought I could get answers for dreaming. I just screwed up my whole life. I don't even know how to tell Landon! I can tell he knows something is up, but what am I supposed to say to him? I screwed up our chances of ever being a family because I thought I could rework my brain? He always says he wants to be a dad someday, that he's a family man. I can't give him that, Addison! I love him so much, but I can't give him that one thing. I feel like I'm broken...like I can't do the one thing I always saw in my future."

"What if they were wrong?" I asked her, standing up and pacing a bit. "What if there's a way to fix it? Or what about a different test? Did you try that? What about another doctor? Another opinion maybe?"

She looked up at me, pained and sad. "There's nothing else they can do. I mean, she said there's a chance. But it's like one in a million, and even if it did happen for us, there's a high risk something could happen to me or the baby in the process. Trust me, I've been racking my brain for days. I even saw a new doctor, and she said the same thing as the first."

I didn't know what to say. *What could you say in a moment like this? What could I possibly say that would make her feel better?*

"I am so sorry, Jess," I told her, rubbing her back. It was all I could think to say. I know it didn't change anything, couldn't change anything. "But you know what? You are such a good person. You have an incredibly big heart with so much room for love. You could adopt or find a surrogate. Besides, I am sure Landon will understand, Jess. I'm sure he will be there for you. Zach and I are here for you, too, Jess, okay? Don't ever feel like you have to hold something like this in again. We love you. I love you. Please talk to us. Don't worry,

Jess. Things will all work out. Give it some time. Pray, and things will all work out."

"Thank you," Jess whispered.

43

- Zach -

Saturday, September 16th, 2023

I was beginning to get really concerned.

Addison has been going crazy with this search of hers. It was all she ever talked about anymore. She was constantly booking trips all over the place, always reading books about old myths and folktales about dreams, and spending hours analyzing every single dream she and I have had in the past month.

She was constantly calling Diane now. Being honest, Diane is ten times worse than Addison. Diane pretty much eats, sleeps, and breathes all things dreamer. I don't think that woman has thought of anything besides "putting a stop to Them once and for all" since she was our age. She's obsessed.

What scared me was how invested Addison was in all of this. Everything Diane said to do, Addison jumped on it. Every time Diane suggested a new place where more dreamers might (key word here being *might*) be, Addison went and had us visit there.

Diane is *consumed* by her dreams and this fear of Them.

I'm starting to worry it won't be long before Addison is, too.

All I wanted to do was focus on us, *our* dreams, *our* lives. But somehow every conversation turned to the Dream Team and how she could do more to help everyone else but herself.

"Alright, everyone. It's time to begin," Addison said, her voice booming with authority. Mitch and Diane approached her last week to be the official spokesperson at the first dreamer meeting. They said since she had found a record number of dreamers in under a year, that she deserved a bigger role. They also agreed with me that since Addison was the one to invite more than three-quarters of the individuals here to join, that they may feel more comfortable seeing her at the head of the table.

Addison had been nervous all week, especially last night. We had some of our friends over for a cookout and she was worrying about all the little details, wanting it all to be perfect. They were all really good friends of ours, almost all of them were in our wedding party, so I kept telling her they wouldn't care if it was perfect or not. Still, all day she was nervous, prepping food and panicking about some burnt carrots, which Billy ate happily. It took me a little while, but eventually I knew that it wasn't about the cookout at all. It was about the meeting today. She was nervous to speak.

"Hello?" Mitch said, waving his hand in front of the webcam. "Can you hear us?"

"Bonjour," Jacques greeted.

"Bonjour," Becky, who had taken a train up to Paris to meet with Jacques, greeted. It was much more efficient for the two of them to meet in Paris, along with one of Becky's other dreamer friends, and video-conference in for the meeting.

"Go ahead," Mitch told Addison and took his seat.

"Welcome, all of you," she addressed the room, taking a moment to smile in the direction of the webcam. "To the first semi-annual Dream Team meeting. We want to start by thanking all of you for attending, especially seeing as we have many dreamers here with us today who have traveled from all over the world. Thank you for coming."

Addison nodded and my uncle stood up, straightening his tie and clearing his throat. *I can't even remember the last time I saw Mitch in a tie. It was weird for him.*

"Thank you, Addison." He turned to the group present, all gathered around a long executive table, each seated in leather office chairs. "I want to take a moment to speak to you all about why Diane and myself decided to start this organization in the first place."

Mitch spoke briefly about his experience with my mom and my grandmother, both of whom would reference Them or They in a panic. He said both of them were constantly afraid someone was after them, that they were being tortured because of their dreams.

"I myself have never seen or heard from any group of individuals or dreamers such as the people my sister and mother talked about," Mitch said. "However, the more into the dream scene I got, the more I realized that my family members were not the only ones who talked of such a group. It seemed that every dreamer I came across was frightened of being found by this group as well. Every single person I have talked to also would only say They or Them. No names. No location. No other information," Mitch explained.

"So," Addison added, taking the conversation back over for a while. "That brings us to our first point of discussion. You all have connected with us today for a reason. You all have acknowledged such a group and also have shown a certain level of fear and suspicion about this group. I am going to open the floor for a few minutes so that everyone can share a piece of information they have about this group."

Addison adjusted her blazer and sat down in her chair next to me. I put my hand on her knee and whispered, "Good job, Tour Guide!"

"Thank you," she whispered back and then refocused her attention on the dreamers sitting around the table.

She looked so professional today. She seemed so in her element. Everyone was drawn to her, hanging on her every word, looking to her for answers. She was a leader. *That's my girl,* I thought. *Leading all the dreamers in this battle.* If there had to be this massive search to find answers, Ad was definitely the person to have at the front of it.

We all heard a crackling noise as Jacques, the waiter from Paris, must have been adjusting the microphone. "May I?" he asked.

"Of course, Jacques," she told him, seeming happy he was the first to speak up.

Jacques spoke for a minute or two, and then the other dreamers followed suit. Everyone was taking notes furiously at first. Diane was scribbling notes and bullet points on the whiteboard that lined the front wall. But after three people spoke (Jacques, a lawyer from Maine, and a restaurant owner from Pittsburgh), everyone stopped taking notes.

All three people said the same thing.

All of them knew about as much as Mitch. Some had a few bits and pieces we hadn't heard before. But other than that, it seemed like a bust. The first three dreamers giving their testimony seemed to only make the group more wearisome.

"How will we ever find them?" Becky, the woman Addison met in Lourdes, asked, and I could see a concerned look cross her face in the monitor.

This question sparked a commotion. Everyone was talking over each other. People were getting more and more short-tempered, wanting answers now. Dreamers were arguing with the other dreamer sitting next to them. The neurosurgeon and the psychiatrist were going at it, squabbling over practice and their opinions of a brain-related topic of debate.

After a few minutes of the craziness, Addison stood up in her seat and slammed her hands on the table.

Everyone looked at her, startled and shocked. I was too, I had to admit.

"Listen," she yelled. "This, *this bickering*, is not helping anyone. We are falling into whatever Their plan is right now. Don't you see that? Dreamers aren't supposed to all get together. There's power in numbers. They don't want us assembling like this. They want us fighting, not helping each other, not getting to the bottom of this. We *need* to get to the bottom of this."

Everyone sat quietly, listening to her.

I had never seen anything like this before. She was commanding the whole room. It was like they were hypnotized by her, mesmerized by her every word. I was too.

"Now," she continued, sitting back down, but clearly still holding the floor. "I suggest we all take a five minute break. Go get some coffee, grab a snack, stretch your legs. Whatever. But be back in this room in five minutes, ready to continue discussing. While you are taking a break...rack your brain. Think back as far as you can. When we all come back in this room, we will go around the table and all say at least two things we have heard about Them. Someone in here has to know something, and maybe individually we know nothing, but collectively, it will all have to come together at some point."

"Exactly," Carrie spoke up. Addison turned to her, gesturing for her to add more. "This is all one big puzzle. It has been a puzzle for years. There are a lot of missing pieces to find and add to the picture. Right now, we each have a small piece of the puzzle. We need to come together and see how they all fit. They have to fit somehow."

What is with Carrie and her puzzle analogies? I couldn't say they didn't help, but still, she somehow always compared situations to a puzzle.

"Yes! Exactly!" Addison agreed, a smile now back on her face like this could really work. "So, everyone, take the next five minutes to search through that special mind of yours and find the puzzle piece you will share with the group."

With that, everyone in the room pushed out their chairs and went into the main waiting area of the office unit, grabbing coffee or some of the cookies that were put out.

"Call back in five minutes," Addison told Jacques, Becky, and Becky's friend. They all nodded and signed off.

Addison put her head in her hands. "Zach, what are we going to do? Everyone's saying the same thing."

I rubbed my hand on her back in circles. That always seemed to calm her down. "Ad," I started. "It will take some time. It has been years that dreamers have been whispering about Them. We can't 'solve this puzzle' in the first few minutes together. This whole witch hunt is starting to worry me, Ad. We all need to take a step back and reevaluate. But... on a positive note, you are killing it today!"

"You think so?" she asked, twisting to look over at me, her head still propped up by her hands.

"They are all just staring at you, listening to everything you say, looking to you for answers. Not Mitch. Not Diane. You. You're a natural, Addison. Really. I'm kind of jealous. I hate talking in crowds, but you look...like you were made for this job."

"Really?" she asked. I nodded. "Thank you," she told me, leaning her head onto my shoulder.

"Besides," I added. "I'm digging the whole suit thing," I told her, looking at the black skirt, blazer, and heels she had on.

"Oh, you," she said, shaking her head.

Five minutes later, we all gathered back in the conference room and waited as the dreamers in Paris connected online. Addison stood at the front again, waiting as all of the dreamers took their seats.

I looked across the table and noticed the lady from Kennebunkport was here. Addison and I had met her a few months back on a trip to that part of Maine. We were walking down the streets of the little town one night and came across a gift shop.

The sign said: **Dream Vacation!**

"Let's go in," Addison had suggested, always wanting to stop in and look around small shops like that with knick-knacks and souvenirs.

We walked in, and the first thing we both noticed is that the shop wasn't just any gift shop. It was stocked full of handmade dreamcatchers, wind chimes, books on dreaming, books on sleeping, leatherbound copies of fairy tales like the one where the girl is sleeping for hundreds of years, and a case of different crystals and stones with a sign that read "Healing Rocks" above them.

"What is this place?" Addison whispered.

I looked around, noticing even more dream and mind related things in the store. "You don't think--"

"No way," she interrupted. "That would have just been too easy."

We walked over to the case of "Healing Rocks," looking through the glass at them.

"Hello," a breathy voice greeted us.

We both looked up at the same time to see a thin, older woman standing on the inside of the wrap-around case, back where the cash register was. She had crazy, curly hair that was somewhere between blonde and silver. But the more striking feature about this woman was her eyes. They weren't blue like Addison's; they were more of a blue-gray. But still, even with the grayness, they were the most noticeable feature about her. They stood out.

I looked at Addison who gave me a look back like, "Wow, that really was too easy!" I knew I wasn't alone in thinking this woman was a dreamer. She had to be.

"Hello," Addison smiled.

"Can I help you find anything?" the woman asked.

"No, we're just looking," Addison told her, never breaking eye contact. "Is this your store?"

"Yes, ma'am," the woman answered. "Been running this place for seven years now!"

"Wow, that's amazing!" Addison said. "It's a great place. It's so beautiful! Everything looks so interesting!"

"Well, thank you!" The woman leaned against the glass case. "Where are you two lovebirds from?" she asked us.

"Madison," I spoke up. Sure, Madison was a small town, but if we were right about her, she may have heard of it before. The town of Madison seemed to be pretty infamous among dreamers. We didn't know why yet, though.

"Oh!" the woman piped up. "Out past the Kingston exit?"

"Yep, that's the one!" Addison agreed.

The woman smiled. "My mother was from Madison! I used to go there years ago when I was a little girl, to visit my grandparents and my aunts and uncles. Lovely town! Very charming! That's part of why she picked this port to settle down in with my father years ago. She loved the small town feel and the port. What a small world!" the woman said, eyeing us skeptically.

"It is indeed!" Addison replied.

"Now, that's quite a drive from here. Eight hours at least, right?" We nodded.

"What brings you both out this way?" she asked.

"We just got married," Addison said, leaning into my side a bit. Even though it had been a month of being married at that point, she still said that anytime people asked why we were visiting the town.

"Oh, how wonderful! Congratulations!" the woman said with a happy sigh and a far-away look in her eyes. "Marriage is such a gift," she told us.

Then she turned around and reached under the front glass case, pulling out a little bag tied at the top. She walked back over to us and handed it to Addison. "A little wedding present for the newlyweds!" she sang.

"Oh, my goodness! Thank you!" Addison told her, untying the little bag and dumping the contents into her hand.

It was two silver keychains. Separately, they didn't look like much of anything, but when she put them side by side, it was clear they formed a dreamcatcher. Little blue and green beads hung from the bottoms of both sides.

"They're beautiful!" Addison said.

"Yes, thank you," I told the woman.

"My pleasure!" she responded, waving her hand like it was nothing. "Go ahead and have yourself a look around. My name is Debra. Let me know if you need anything!"

"We will. Thank you, Debra!" Addison said, then turned to me as the woman, Debra, walked around the counter to go assist another customer. "Look how cute these are! I love it! We have matching keychains now! How coupley is that?"

"Ad."

"Yeah?" she said, still holding up the keychains and looking at them.

"I love you, but let's put those aside for a second. Okay? Are you thinking what I'm thinking?"

Addison put the keychains back in the little bag, tied it, tucked it in her purse and then looked up at me. "Yes. Definitely a dreamer," she agreed.

So we looked around the store a bit more, waiting for her to be done waiting on the other customer. If we weren't sure if she was a dreamer a few minutes ago, we were positive now. Everything in this store screamed dreamer. Plus, her mother was from Madison? That meant she could be traced back to all the other dreamers in our town.

Soon enough we saw the man thanking Debra for her time and he went back to the bookshelf on the back wall, flipping through a book she must have just suggested.

Addison and I walked over toward her.

"Can I help you with something?" Debra asked, looking at us from the corner of her eye as she unpacked a box of greeting cards.

"Actually, yes," Addison said. "We had a couple questions. We were wondering if you had a minute to talk with us?" As she said this, she gently rested her hand on Debra's arm. Debra slowly turned around to face us with a look in her eyes that proved she had seen whatever it was Ad just showed her.

"Of course," she said slowly. "Right this way."

Now, sitting in the conference room at the dreamer meeting, I looked up to see Debra, biting her lip with her hands shaking slightly.

She wanted to say something.

I caught Ad's eye and nodded my head as inconspicuous as possible toward Debra. Ad looked and must have seen what I saw because she spoke up and said, "Debra, would you like to start us off?"

Debra released a breath she must've been holding for a while.

"Yes! Please," she said, rising from her chair. "My name is Debra. I am from Maine. My mother is from here in Madison. She was a dreamer also. Over the years I have done a lot of research on dreaming in general. I too have heard whispers of this group. I don't think I have ever met anyone associated with them, but have definitely felt the darkness you all speak of in my own life. I have found that the spiritual way works for me. Things like Himalayan salts, gemstones such as agate, lavender under my pillow, and dreamcatchers all seem to help me sleep at night."

There were glances all around the room. Clearly some agreed with Debra and others were clearly skeptical themselves.

"I think the first thing we need to do is find a location. Find a place where dreamers are linked to," Debra suggested.

"Like Madison?" Becky clarified.

Debra thought for a minute. "Well, maybe. I'm not sure. But we need to first establish where we think They are. We have to narrow down the search. I think we need to look down south. Besides Madison, I have met many people who I assume to be dreamers in Florida and Georgia. I hear those states the most. I have also gotten many calls to ship products I carry in my store to addresses in Florida."

"Good point," Addison said as Diane wrote "Florida" and "Georgia" on the board. "That definitely could be something. We will have someone here look into that and then send some dreamers down south to check it out."

Debra nodded, seeming happy her suggestion was taken seriously, and sat down.

"Alright," Diane spoke up. "I'll take names. Who wants to visit Florida?"

Florida? Now that was a trip I could get behind. I raised my hand immediately.

Addison smiled and raised hers, too.

44

- Zach -

Saturday, October 7th, 2023

I didn't really want to encourage Ad to continue on this wild goose chase. I had planned to put my foot down after the meeting and tell her no more trips for a while. But when they suggested Florida, I figured that it might actually be the best location suggested yet. I thought it would be a good place for the two of us to go on what I hoped would be the last trip for a long time. Ad needed to relax for a bit. I was hoping I could convince her to stay an extra day and do nothing but sit on the beach all day. We both needed that.

It was so sunny.

There were palm trees everywhere. Every time Ad saw one she'd point and say, "Ooo, look! A palm tree! How cool?"

After the meeting, we had established different locations where everyone would try to search for more dreamers. We also made an online place where we could all log on and chat or post things we had recently found. Jacques had been sharing links to websites about dreaming almost every day last week. Of course other dreamers volunteered to go to Florida, too, but in the end, Diane sent Addison and me, which we would certainly not complain about. Mitch was heading to Georgia today, and Diane assigned Carrie to go as well. Neither of them seemed too thrilled, but everyone agreed Carrie was the one to bring because of her history with dreaming.

Ad and I had been here for two days now. Diane did a ton of research, trying to find where we thought the most dreamers would be. Ironically, she found a small shop, much like Debra's, in a town in southwest Florida. It just happened to also be a beach town. *Win, win.*

"Can we move here?" Addison asked me, while we sat outside a restaurant on the main street, drinking wine while very fancy cars drove past us. We had just had the best meal we may have ever eaten. She fell in love with this town instantaneously.

"Sure," I teased, knowing full well that Addison had no intention of ever leaving our town.

"I'm serious," she protested. "It's so much sunnier here. It isn't cold. Look at these twinkly lights above us! How cute and romantic is that?"

"I thought you loved Madison?"

"Well, I had never been here! I can't wait to spend tomorrow on the beach," she said.

"I don't know if that's such a good idea," I told her.

"Why not?"

"You might love this place too much and never want to leave."

"I already don't want to leave," she said, sipping her wine.

"We have to find some dreamers first though. It's been two days and we haven't found anyone," I pointed out.

"It isn't our fault that little shop has been closed the past two days. Do you think it's ever actually open? Do you think she's away? On vacation or something?" she asked.

"We only have two more days, so I sure hope not."

* * *

The next morning we got up early and went out to the beach. The hotel we were staying was so nice and classy and was right on the beach. We didn't have an ocean view, but we didn't care because you could take two steps from the hotel and be standing in the sand. Plus, anything close to the beach was better than what we had back home in Madison by far. Our view there was trees, trees, and more trees.

We were sitting in those long lounge chairs nice hotels have with the towels that have their logo embroidered on them, eating chips and salsa because *why not?* Addison was reading a book she brought, and I was listening to music. She wasn't doing much actual reading, though, because every two seconds she would lay the book down across her stomach, look up, and start talking about the meeting recently or trying to find the lady who owns this shop that's always closed. I would pause the music or take out one of my earbuds and listen to what she had to say. But nine out of ten times, she would ask me a question, wait a second, and then answer that question herself. Sometimes she just needed to talk things out out loud.

I wanted her to try to relax though. We had just this long weekend to be here, then it was back to the grind. Classes for her and work for me. I kept telling her to relax and read her book, but she'd just smile at me and say "I am relaxing! I am reading!" even though she wasn't. She was stressed, and I could tell.

I leaned across to her chair, moved her chin toward me and kissed her slowly.

"Break time!" I said. "Come in the ocean!"

"What if there's fish?" she asked, curling her legs up like she was scared they'd jump right out of the ocean into her chair.

"Of course there will be fish. It's the ocean," I pointed out.

"You know what I mean," she said, frowning. "Big fish. Slimy fish. Fish that eat people."

"Babe, I don't think there will be fish that eat people in the shallow part."

"What if there are?" she asked. She sounded like a little kid then, the way she said that.

"Then I will jump in front of you and let the people-eating fish eat me instead."

"My hero," she said, kissing my cheek.

I stood up to head into the water but she stopped me saying, "Wait! I don't want the people-eating fish to get you either!"

"Don't worry," I told her. "They don't like dreamers anyway. We are both safe."

She jumped up and hopped on my back then like she used to do years ago when we walked through the town square late at night. And then we went wading into the water (no people-eating fish in sight).

* * *

From the beach later that afternoon, I decided to call the little shop to see if anyone even answered.

Someone did after quite a few rings.

"Hello?" a woman's voice said.

"Hi, we were wondering what your hours are today?" I asked.

"Here until six!"

Before I could even say much else, she had hung up the phone.

Later that night -- before six -- Ad and I went back to the main street, then went down one of the side roads and found the shop again. This time, sure enough, the lights were on and people were buzzing all about.

We found a woman much like Debra actually. They were so similar in so many ways, even the eyes, that Addison even questioned if they were related. We were able to get this woman, Beth's, attention and convinced her to sit and talk with us.

After the store closed, she lead us to a bench right outside her store, and we all sat. She had graying, curly hair, also like Debra, the other store owner. Her eyes looked happy and sad at the same time, almost as if she was happy with her life now, but had been through a lot in the past. A lot of us dreamers had that look to our eyes. She had lines on her face and wisdom in her eyes that showed that she had experienced a lot. I hoped she could share some of that wisdom with us.

Addison and I decided to just be open with her and ask her questions to find out as much information as possible.

The most shocking thing, however, was her response when we asked Beth about nightmares and if she had ever heard of a group haunting dreamers.

She looked at us like we were crazy.

Then she said, "I have never heard of that. Ever. I have quite a few friends in this town who are like me and none of them have ever said anything about this group you're talking about. What is even the name of the group? Who is involved?"

"That's what we are trying to find out," I explained. "There's a lot of mystery around it. The group is just referred to as They or Them."

"That sounds crazy," Beth said, standing up. "They and Them are not names. They are pronouns. They is not very specific. Them is very general. You *can not* be afraid of something like that."

"But--" I started, but she cut me off.

"Please don't come back here and get me all worked up over something that doesn't exist. I left that life behind a long time ago. I will not get roped back in to something that is a waste of my time. It's a waste of your time, too, so do yourselves a favor and stop looking."

Then she walked away.

"What just happened?" I asked Ad while we watched this woman walk quickly away. *Why did she seem so angry? What did she leave behind a long time ago?*

Addison looked at me with wide, blue eyes. "I-I don't know...but I feel like there's more here. She has to know something that she just isn't saying."

"Ad, we can't *make* someone talk if they don't want to."

"What do you think she knows? What happened to her? What did she leave behind?" Addison asked question after question, all the while pulling out her phone and typing out notes in the notes section.

I reached out and placed my hand on hers, trying to get her to stop typing.

"I don't know, Ad. I don't know," I told her. "Let's just head back to the hotel. We aren't going to get any more answers from her if she won't talk to us."

"That's just it, though!" Addison said. "*Why* won't she talk to us?"

Again, I said, "I don't know, Ad."

"You don't think she's...involved with Them...do you?" Addison asked.

And what was crazy about her question then, is that it was the same question running through my head.

But all I said was, "I don't know, Ad."

45

- Addison -
Monday, October 9th, 2023

We were sitting on the beach on our last day in paradise before the real world set in again.

We had one whole day left to ourselves. We didn't look at the clocks, didn't know what time it was. We didn't worry about the fact that this trip was seeming to be nothing more than a dead end. We didn't think about all the what-if's running through our minds the night before. We didn't think or worry about anything.

Our biggest problem today was when Zach turned to me, his face serious, and said, "Ad, what are we going to do?"

"What do you mean?" I asked, wondering why he would dare break the pact we made this morning when we woke up: nothing dream related would be discussed today. Just us on the beach. It was a good pact. Things were going great, so calm, and now he's asking what we are going to do?

"About dinner," he said, still all seriousness.

I laughed out loud at him. "Zachary, I thought you were going to--"

"Shhhhhhh," he interrupted. "Geez, Ad, no talking about any of that today. I genuinely am worried about dinner. Where do we go? Do we go back to that place with the good burgers? You said you loved watching the sunset while we had dinner. Or, do we find some place new? OR do we try the place we went to for lunch yesterday, but try their dinner? They had that brick oven. I bet their pizza is incredible."

"Wow, this really has been weighing on ya, hasn't it?" I asked with a laugh.

"Yes!" he said, exasperated. "It's a very tough, very pressing decision."

"Yes, it is. Quite pressing," I said, amusing him. "So what are you in the mood for?"

"What are you in the mood for?" he asked, grinning. "I can always eat. I'm down for anything," he said.

So we were in the middle of weighing our pros and cons, making the toughest decision we planned to make all day, when we realized the one place we wanted to go had a special going on. Two dinners and wine for thirty bucks. Since this would be a huge pro, we figured we would call and see what time the special went to. If it was too early, we would pick the other restaurant because there was no way we were leaving this beautiful, sunny day behind too soon.

I pulled out my phone, swiped the screen to unlock it and realized I had a ton of notifications.

"What is it?" he asked.

"I have five missed calls from my aunt and like tons of texts from Mitch and Carrie," I replied wondering what they could have found to keep calling back.

"Oh," was all Zach said.

I looked up at him, we locked eyes, and we asked each other if we should break our pact for this. *What if it was important? Or what if it wasn't and we just get stressed out? We only had one day left.*

"Please, just let this wait, Ad," he begged me. "Don't call back. Not yet. Not now."

"What if they found something?" I asked him.

He sighed.

In the end, we decided to call back, so I dialed Carrie's number. She picked up on the first ring.

"Addie, Sweet Pea! I'm so glad you called! Where are you?" she asked in a tizzy.

"Florida," I answered, even though she knew we were here until tomorrow.

"Still?" she asked suspiciously.

"Yeah, Zach took an extra day. We wanted to make today a beach day."

Zach rolled his eyes. Mitch and Carrie both knew how long we were staying.

"Well, we need to talk to you and Zach. Is there somewhere you guys can go so we can talk? Privately."

I sighed. "Aunt Carrie, what's going on? What happened?"

"I'd prefer to discuss this with Mitch and Zach both in on the call."

"Okay," I agreed. "Give us five minutes to get our stuff together." She said that would be fine and hung up.

Zach forced a smile, "Well, hey, we got a few hours in of just us, no interruptions."

"Yes, we did!"

Then we decided to ask the lady sitting in the beach chairs sitting next to us if she wouldn't mind taking our picture. We wanted to have something to remember our "just us" day, even if it ended sooner than we wanted. She did, and it turned out really cute. It may have been my new favorite picture of us.

Then we went back up to the hotel room and called Carrie, putting the phone on speaker so we could both talk and hear.

"Hi, guys," Mitch greeted.

"Hi, Uncle Mitch. Hi, Carrie," Zach said.

"So, we need to talk to you both," Carrie started.

"Did something happen?" I asked.

"No. Nothing happened. That's just it!" Carrie said.

"What do you mean by that?" Zach asked.

Mitch spoke up, "We haven't found anything. Even people we thought were for-sures, wouldn't talk to us. We've tried everything. We've looked all over this town. Nothing. We even found a blogger online in the area who has posted a lot of articles about dreaming and dream analysis, so we figured she would know about it all. She said she's never heard of the group."

"Actually," I interjected. "We found a dreamer down here, too. I think she said her name was Beth. When we brought it up, it was so weird. It was like she shut down. She made us leave and wouldn't talk to us and said the same thing."

"Yeah," Zach said. "It was so strange. She got really upset."

"So did this blogger," Mitch said.

"We've reached a dead end," Carrie admitted. "We are running out of funds, too. We can't keep sending dreamers out or inviting all these dreamers here internationally. We can't afford it."

"Well, what should we do?" Zach asked.

"When can you guys get back here?" they asked at the same time.

Zach and I looked at each other. He spoke up and said, "Listen, guys, we already have tonight paid for. Our flight is first thing in the morning. Ad and I have been traveling so much lately, and she's had classes and planning this dreamer thing and all the meetings, and I've been working like crazy. One night won't make a difference. We'll be back tomorrow morning like we had planned, and then we can all talk about it."

It was quiet on the other end for a minute.

"That's fine," Mitch told us. "You two kids enjoy yourselves. We will see you tomorrow. It can wait until then."

"Thank you," Zach said to his uncle. "We will stop by Carrie's on our way home from the airport."

"Sounds good," Carrie agreed. "We will keep brainstorming what could be going on or options for the group until you get here."

We hung up and looked at each other.

Zach looked worried, "Ad, what are we going to do?"

I knew this time he really was asking about the dreamer things, not dinner. But we still had a few more hours at this wonderful hotel and beautiful beach. So I smiled at him and said, "I know. Dinner is such a difficult, yet very pressing, decision."

He laughed at me and said, "I love you, Ad!"

46

- Zach -

Friday, October 20th, 2023

After the beach trip was over, we hopped a flight and headed home bright and early in the morning. *Too* early for my liking.

On the way home we had stopped at Addison's aunt's house. We talked with her and Mitch about the future for our dream team. *Could we keep going on like this?* We were doing so well at first, but now we really were at a dead end. *Was there another way?*

We had come to the conclusion (the only one we could come up with) that we would hold another meeting sooner than expected-- the next week. We had to talk to the other dreamers and be open with them about this dead end we seemed to have come to. We had to find out if they were having better luck in the search than Addison, Mitch, Carrie, and me. We had to come up with a different plan. We couldn't keep going like this for months until the next meeting.

So, today, Addison stood at the front of the room, at the head of the table, where she belonged.

Over the past week, I could tell how distraught she was over not finding any concrete answers in Florida. If anything, we left with even more questions. I kept telling her to chalk it up to a much needed beach vacation. She kept shaking her head and telling me something wasn't sitting right, there was more to all of this.

I wanted her to be right, that there was more to this. That there would be answers some day.

I also wanted her to be wrong. I wanted all the traveling to take a break for a bit. I felt like I was never home. I was burning the midnight oil, trying to prove myself to my boss, trying to be home with Addison, and trying to do the right thing and travel almost every weekend to help these other dreamers.

Being honest, I've barely slept in weeks. I'm so tired. I'm so tired of all of this. I just want to go to work and come home to Ad and have the weekends off. Enough is enough.

I also can see how much this is weighing on Ad. She has barely slept, too. But instead of just tossing and turning like I do, I can see a blue light radiating off of her laptop each night and hear her typing away as she tries to search the Internet for answers or plans the next trip.

This needs to end, I thought as the others filed in and took their seats, and Mitch set up the video conference.

I looked up at my wife, standing at the head of the table, and thought about how different she looked from even just a few weeks ago. She looked thinner, her jacket hanging on her shoulders. She got those dark circles under her eyes again-- the ones I hadn't seen since junior year of high school-- the ones her nightmares from my uncle caused. I know she wants to help the other dreamers, but it can't be right if helping dreamers is giving her the same dark circles nightmares did.

I stood up and walked over to where Carrie and Diane had set up some refreshments. I grabbed a cold bottle of water and one of the chocolate chip cookies and put it on one of the napkins there. I walked back in the room, following some of the other dreamers, and then went to the front and set the cookie and water down on the wooden oval table in front of Addison and kissed her cheek.

"Thank you," she whispered, and I sat back down.

* * *

We started by asking Jacques and Becky, video chatting with us again for this meeting, what new information either of them had.

"Nothing," Jacques reported.

"Nothing, sadly," Becky admitted, looking ashamed when it was her turn to answer the same question.

"I don't get it," Diane complained. "How could we be getting so far ahead, getting so many answers, and then suddenly, not *one* of us can gather new information?"

She sounded angry, and it almost sounded pointed at Becky, who was the very last person to speak.

"Hey," I spoke up. "This is no one's fault. Maybe we have exhausted all the information we can from this group of people."

"But that's just it," Diane replied. "We need to find more dreamers. How can no one have met any new dreamers?"

"Maybe this is all there is?" Jacques suggested.

"No way," Diane told him angrily. "I will not believe that the people in this room are all the dreamers left in the world. There's no way."

"How would we know that for a fact, though?" Addison proposed, tapping her pen on the table. She was anxious.

"We don't," I agreed with her.

"Yes, we do," Diane said. "There has to be more! There has to be! There has to be answers! I have to solve this!"

"Diane, please." Mitch cast her a look. "Calm down."

"Where's the next location?" Diane asked Addison, pretty harshly and abrupt. "I'll go. I'll find someone. I'll figure this out myself. God knows I'm not getting any help from any of you."

"Diane, no," Mitch said standing up. "We don't have any funds left."

"I will pay for it myself," Diane protested.

"No," Mitch said. Then he turned to Addison, "If I may?" She nodded, so he turned and addressed the rest of us. "This is something we wanted to discuss with you all today. We are out of funds. We cannot afford to subsidize any more trips. We have decided to continue with research, but only what we all can do from our own cities and homes. We have created an online portal where any new information you all find can be submitted and everyone can comment on and add to it. It will be much more efficient this way, not to mention free for the time being and no travel involved. We will keep you posted when we decide what our next step will be."

"Yes," Addison added, "and not to worry, the portal is incredibly secure. Billy was kind enough to code a very secure site for us. This way we can all be certain the information is only seen by the people in this room, and, of course, our friends in France," she added with a nod at the monitor.

"That sounds good," Jess said, jotting something down in her notebook.

The back, glass door in the room suddenly opened and a woman walked in. She had gray curly hair and eyes that had clearly seen a lot in life. The lines on her face showed her wisdom, and the look in her eyes showed her determination.

"Beth?" Addison asked, walking around the table to greet the mysterious woman we met in Florida.

How did she know about this? I wondered. *We didn't say anything about this meeting because we didn't have it planned yet.*

"How-- What are you doing here?" Addison stammered.

"She called me," Debra said, standing up and shaking Beth's hand. "She was the dreamer who was buying items from my store. She called and asked if I knew you two. She said you came to her store. I told her about today," then Debra looked at Beth. "You said you weren't coming."

"I changed my mind," Beth said. She looked very serious. She turned to Ad and took both of Addison's hands in her own. "I apologize for sending you away that day. I didn't want to deal with any of this anymore. I thought I could just stay out of it. But after you left, I felt horrible. I knew I had to come talk to you."

"This is amazing!" Addison exclaimed. She walked back to the front, pulled a chair out from the corner of the room and moved it to the table, asking two of the dreamers to move a bit so Beth could sit. "Here," she said, pointing to the chair. "This is perfect timing, Beth! Perfect! Please sit and share any information you can with us."

Addison picked up a red marker and walked to the white board, uncapping the marker and raising her arm, holding it there, ready to write down anything this woman said.

Something was off here, I thought.

"No, thank you, Addison," the woman answered, looking sad. "I don't need to sit. I just came to talk with you all for just a minute."

"Oh," Addison told her, clearly not sure what was going on either.

"You can put the marker down, darlin'."

Addison's cheeks flushed red, and she put the cap back on, set down the marker and came to sit next to me. She looked at me as she sat down, her eyes wide, wondering what this woman was going to say.

"May I?" Beth asked, walking to the front.

"Excuse me, but who are you?" Diane demanded, her voice clipped.

"I'll get to that in a minute, dear," Beth replied. "May I?" she asked again, this time turning her attention to Mitch.

"Of course," Mitch told her. "You have the floor. What information do you have about Them?"

Beth took a deep breath and ran her hands through her graying hair. Her many brightly-colored bracelets jingled as she moved her arms.

She thought for a minute, then spoke. "I don't have any information to share about Them."

"Excuse me," Diane interjected, standing up. "But do not just *waltz* into this high-priority meeting twenty minutes late and then say that you have no information. Why are you here?" Diane hissed at Beth.

"Diane, please," Mitch pleaded.

"No, no, it's fine," Beth said to Mitch. Then she turned to Diane, her eyes like fire. "Diane, is it?" Diane nodded. "Well, Diane, that is a wonderful question. Why am I here? I could have easily stayed home in Florida and let you all continue to ruin your lives and waste your youth the way I did. But instead, the picture of this young couple," she said, pointing to Ad and me, "kept gnawing at me. I knew I had to come and stop you all."

"Stop us?" Carrie asked. "Stop us from what?"

"From wasting your time!" Beth said, throwing her hands in the air. "Trust me, you all are barking up the wrong tree."

"What do you mean?" I asked.

"The better question," Diane interrupted. "And I will ask again-- but who are you? Why on earth should we trust you?"

"Let me tell you all a little story," Beth said, twisting her bracelets around and around her wrist.

"I do not care to hear your story if you have no new information to share. You want to talk about a waste of time?" Diane scoffed, and then turned to Addison, a fire in her eyes, "Addison, do you know this woman?"

"Many moons ago, there were two young girls," Beth began, simply brushing off Diane's rudeness and telling her story anyway. "One had blonde, wavy hair. The other had bright red hair that was poker straight. Both, however, had brilliant blue eyes. People would comment on their eyes. They would ask if they were sisters because they had the same eyes. They were not sisters. They felt like it, though. They were the best of friends. The girls met when they were four and just starting school. They had so much in common: favorite music, favorite colors, favorite ice cream.

"But one day, they realized they had much more in common. Right before high school, the dreams started. Both of them would have horrible nightmares. Both would wake up screaming or wake up feeling ill. It was the strangest thing, but both of them were dealing with the same thing. They also had the same dreams most of the time. It even felt at times that they were dreaming together, connected. Things got scary for a while. Neither of the girls could sleep at night. The blonde girl could feel her friend slipping away, no longer wanting to talk about their dreams, no longer showing up in her dreams."

I looked around the room, everyone was hanging on Beth's every word, wondering where this story was going. Diane looked annoyed, but remained quiet anyway.

"The redheaded girl claimed someone was watching her mind, haunting her. The blonde girl said she could help, but her friend didn't want her help. The friend started ignoring her, missing school, and stopped answering the phone when she called. The blonde girl felt so alone and wondering what she could have done to upset her friend. She felt like a piece of her was missing without the friend there. One day, the blonde girl got a call that her friend was no longer with them, that she had passed in a tragic accident where her car's brakes didn't work and she drove into oncoming traffic. The blonde knew better, though. The night of the accident, she had a horrible dream of her friend driving very fast, too fast, in a car with lights blaring in her eyes."

There were small gasps all around the room.

"After that day, the blonde realized that the horrible nightmares and dreams were the reason for what happened to her friend. She actually dreamt of her friend all the time. She thought that maybe seeing her friend in her dreams was her friend's way of saying hi and looking out for her even after her friend was gone."

There were tears escaping Beth's eyes as she told the story, but the look on her face said there was much more to this story to come.

She continued, "The blonde made it her mission in life to find out more about the dreams, find out exactly what had been happening to her friend. She wanted to know why, if they were so connected, the dreams impacted her friend more than they did herself. Both of the girls actually grew up in this very town; the blonde lived right across the street from Linda Moore."

Moore? Like Mrs. Smith's mother? Addison's grandmother?

I turned to Addison, who looked shocked to say the least. Then I glanced at Carrie, who looked as if she was trying to piece together that puzzle in her mind, to connect all these dots.

"However," Beth continued. "After the tragedy that happened to her friend, and the need to find answers, she packed all of her belongings and moved south, trying to get as far away from her hometown and all the horrible memories now associated with it. But she did visit, quite often. Her sister, whom she was very close to, had two young children at the time. Of course the blonde would make the trip to see her niece, Sandy, and her nephew, Bill. She loved them so much. She could also tell, from very early on, that they were dreamers just like she was. Her poor niece seemed to suffer the most, though. Sandy was like a daughter to her; they were very close. She, Sandy, and some other dreamers they had met searched and searched, trying to find any answers to what was going on or who it was that was watching her friend's mind, who was tormenting her own mind, and who was causing Sandy's horrid dreams."

"Was it Them?" Jacques asked, a worried look on his face.

Beth responded, "Or so they all told her. She found other dreamers. One of them said something about this other group and only said 'them' or 'they.' There was no better name for these people, no concrete location. She then went to other dreamers, and they all said they had heard whispers of this group as well. Everyone got very concerned. She formed a group much like the one sitting here today. Her niece Sandy was very instrumental in this search. It was beneficial also that Sandy was a renowned psychiatrist in Madison."

"So what did they find?" one of the other dreamers Mitch found asked.

"Nothing," Beth lamented. "Absolutely nothing. And it drove Sandy mad, downright mad. Sandy became obsessed with finding answers, but there were no answers to be found. She spent her entire life devoted to solving this problem, answering the equation, and stopping Them. It was almost as if she was engulfed in darkness, like a dark storm cloud was constantly hovering over her. I think many of you in this room knew Sandy, so you probably know how her story tragically ended as well."

She took a deep breath and said, "I need you all to listen to me now, and listen to me closely. I was the little blonde girl in the story. I lost my best friend to the darkness of this world. I watched my own niece drive herself crazy pursuing the same search you all are on right now. I then had to look my sister in the eye and feel so much guilt for years now because her daughter-- my niece, Sandy-- took too many pills when the pressure of this unanswered question and the weight of the darkness and negativity consumed her because of a question I planted in her head when she was young. I have lived a long and amazing, yet tragic, life. I have learned a lot over the years.

"All of you gathered here today are so young, with so much life ahead of you to live. *You all aren't living right now.* You are dreaming. You are hoping, wishing, praying, and dreaming you will find answers. Look at you, you've assembled a group to do what exactly? If you ever found Them, what did you plan to do? A fight to the death? Outsmart them? What then? They will just come back. This is not an action film where the solution is an epic battle with explosions and fire and only the good left standing in the end. This is real life, my dears."

"I don't understand," Addison said, frustrated.

"Honey," Beth said, walking up to Addison and staring her in the eyes. "You are so very special. I can tell; I can see it in your eyes. You are meant for so much in this life. You will do so much good. You will help so many people."

"That's what I'm trying to do," Addison protested, looking close to tears. "I'm just trying to help people."

"Not like this, dear," Beth told her. Her voice sounded like a grandmother giving advice to her granddaughter, full of love and full of longing for the granddaughter to have a better chance at life than she did. Maybe she felt this was her chance to give the advice she never got to give her own niece.

She sighed and crouched down, so she was eye-level with Addison. "Addison, listen to me. When you came by the other day, you reminded me of a younger me or even of Sandy. You were so determined to find answers. You travelled across the country following a small lead you had, for crying out loud. At first that scared me. I left that life behind me years ago. Yes, I still own my gift shop, but that's just to make a living. Dreaming seems to be a very *"in"* topic lately, and it is a topic I know well. But in my shop, and the customers who usually visit, it is just that-- a fad, a hip topic. No one knows it's my real life. It feels more like fiction than truth at work. But then you two showed up, and I could see it in your eyes that you were dreamers. I wanted nothing to do with that. I couldn't let myself get roped in again. But after you left, I felt it was my duty to stop you from going down the same path my niece did. I couldn't stop her and I can't get those years back in my life...but I can help you."

"Help me how?" Addison asked, quietly.

"Honey, you just got married. You should be enjoying time at home with the man you love. You should be planning for a future together, building a home together. You shouldn't be out, traveling the world and chasing wild geese. You should be traveling because you want to, because you want to see the world together. You shouldn't be traveling because you're searching for answers to a question that can never and will never be answered."

"Thank you!" I told Beth, throwing up my hands. "I've been trying to tell her that for months now." I looked at Addison, "I love travelling the world with you. I would go anywhere with you. But I want to visit places we want to, not places where we have leads. I want for us to go to those lavender fields you dream of someday or back to Hawaii or Paris. But not like this."

"Me too, but--" Addison mumbled, barely above a whisper.

Beth stood and looked at the whole group. "We are all dreamers in this room. We all have felt that feeling of the heaviness in your chest when you wake up from a particularly horrible nightmare. We all have felt that uncontrollable smile after a pleasant and beautiful dream. We all have seen so much, in life and in our minds. Many of us have suffered various medical predicaments in addition to the ailment in our minds. No one on this earth thinks the way you do, my dears. Not even me. Not even the dreamer sitting next to you. We all have our own powers and abilities. We all have our own gifts.

"We also all have our own weights on our shoulders, weighing us down in addition to the nightmares. For some, like me, it's the loss of someone who was like a sister, someone who was a part of my childhood, suddenly and tragically. Or the loss of someone so young, who was like a daughter to you, and the burden of knowing it was all your fault. For others, like my friend or my neice, it was the loss of her life, of who she was, of her happy and bubbly personality. Please, please, do not make the same mistakes I did. Please stop what you're doing now. There is, in fact, a They or Them or It," she said with a knowing look to Addison. She continued,

"However, it is not the way you think. You can't just find specific people involved. The group itself does not exist."

"Bull!" Diane yelled at Beth, shooting up from her chair. Quickly, Diane was right up in front of Beth's face, pointing a finger at her and raising her voice. "We know the group exists. We have all heard the whispers of it."

"Exactly," Beth retorted calmly. "Whispers. Vague answers. Have you ever once heard someone say anything new? Anything concrete? Have you ever met or seen anyone working for this group?" Beth waited a second and then nodded. "Thought so."

Diane turned to Mitch. "Mitch, you better make this woman leave. All she's doing is upsetting everyone. You have no credibility," she said, wagging a finger at Diane. "None! Who are you to just come in here and tell some sob story? We ALL have sob stories, *Beth.* Sit down and I'll tell you mine! I can assure you it's just as tragic, maybe even more so."

"You do not have to believe me," Beth said, even-toned. "But what I am saying is the truth. I'm sorry if you disagree, but this needs to be said."

"Like hell it does!" Diane yelled.

"Let her finish," Mitch spoke, his voice firm and steady, the same tone he took with me when I did something stupid or talked back growing up.

Diane's face turned beet red. "Mitch! Where does your loyalty lie? You don't even know this woman! How long have we been working on this together? Years! That's how long!"

Mitch responded, and as he spoke, he narrowed his eyes, a sure-fire sign the discussion was over. "Diane, I may not know her. But I knew Sandy. Very well, actually. Better than I know you. I would like to hear her out."

"Thank you," Beth said proudly.

"This is insanity, Mitch! All of you! You're all just listening to this crazy old woman go on and on about nothing! I will NOT sit around any longer and waste my time here. You all are crazy. All of you! You'll never find answers listening to this woman babble."

Then Diane walked over to the whiteboard in the room. She picked up the eraser and began wildly erasing what little information we did have written there.

I stood up and walked over toward her. "Diane," I tried, reaching my hand out to grab hers.

But she pulled herself away and threw the whiteboard across the room, where it clattered to the floor after denting the wall.

"Diane," I repeated. "I think you should leave."

"Fine!" she yelled in my face. "You all are a waste of my time anyway!"

She stormed out of the room, knocking into people's chairs on her way out, yelling and yelling about what a mistake it was ever helping us and that we would be nowhere without her.

"Wow..." Addison said, walking over to me and rolling her eyes. "What *was* that?"

In all of the commotion, we had missed something else.

I looked over at the monitor. "Where's Jacques?" I asked.

Becky looked noticeably upset. "He agreed with Diane. He left in an outrage just moments ago." Then Becky squared her shoulders at the webcam and had a new look of determination in her face. "But not me," she said. "I wish to hear more. Please, Beth, continue."

So Beth did. She took a moment to compose herself again after Diane's outburst and then continued, "They are not a group created to torture dreamers. No. Dreamers and non-dreamers alike all have a 'they' that weighs on their heart. Every single person on this earth, all seven billion of them, all have their own thing that haunts them at night. Whether they have the gift of dreaming or not, everyone has their own fears and nightmares. It is sad, but it is true. Everyone has their own darkness in this life. The blessing, however, is that everyone has their own light. You just have to find it. You all need to stop searching for a cure and a quick-fix to end the darkness in the world. It's not possible. What you need to do instead, is turn this mission of yours around, starting today. Find that light. Find that something, or someone," she said, locking eyes with me and nodding at Addison.

Beth smiled. "Find that thing that is your light. Find something that makes you want to fight your way through the darkness. Find something to light up your life and make the darkness and nightmares a little better. We all have to deal with nightmares some nights. But we also get some sweet dreams once and a while if we let ourselves see the good. *It's all in how you look at it.* It took me years to figure this out. I don't want to see you all struggle the way I did. I don't want to see you alone because you spent so much time focused on this one, insignificant thing, that you miss out on life and love and family. I don't want you pushing everyone you love away in the hopes of finding answers. Because, let me tell you, the light lies in love. It could be the love you have in your faith, whatever you believe in. It could be your love of self, the way you finally respect and adore yourself for who you are, not just as a dreamer, but as a whole. It could be the love you share with that one special person who just gets you and loves you for who you are. It could be the love and bond between a mother and child. Don't you get it? Love and light wins. Love and light can block out all the darkness. Love and light, if you let them in your life, will slowly turn the black to gray, then the gray to white, and soon, you have a light as bright as the sun to cling to and keep the heavy darkness at bay.

"'They' exists," Beth explained, "But it could be anxiety, depression, a fear of flying, a fear of dying, losing a loved one too soon, abuse, heartbreak, self-image struggles, or anything that haunts your dreams and turns them into nightmares. The trick, my fellow dreamers, is to find something that holds you to this earth, grounds you, and keeps you going, makes you want to get out of bed in the morning. It's out there. I promise. So don't waste your time trying to find this group, Them...because They aren't a group of unknown people or things. Spend your time finding something or someone you love. Spend your time living, enjoying life for all of its beauty. Spend your time awake. Focus on your dreams as in your hopes for the future. Find them. Follow them. Don't focus on your dreams and nightmares and let them weigh you down. And please, lovelies, never let your nightmares stop you from following your dreams."

Two Years Later...

47

- Addison -

Tuesday, February 11th, 2025

I dream that I am running through that field of lavender flowers again. There's lavender everywhere.

This time, the colors are more vibrant, brighter, happier than I ever thought they could be.

I feel safe. I feel loved.

In my dream, I wear a flowing purple dress, made of a light chiffon fabric that blows behind me in the breeze. My hair is perfect, with perfect curls cascading down my back like gold-- the way I had it for our wedding. I am happy, so happy I look like I could burst.

The wind blows and the lavender waves in the wind, bending back and forth, gently swaying as if music is playing.

Zach is here. He is standing right behind me. Always there. Always with me.

This dream reminds me of the wedding, as we left, with our family tossing lavender as we headed off for the honeymoon. It was a beautiful moment. It was better than any dream I had ever had.

But that moment was not as good as this dream right now.

This dream is perfect and lovely.

The best of dreams are always in a field of lavender for me.

The best of dreams are ones like these, that show me what is yet to come, that I know is waiting for me someday, that show me love and light bright enough to drown out any darkness.

We both have been waiting for a dream like this. We have wanted a dream like this for years. Maybe even our whole lives have been leading up to this one very special dream.

Now, I can't be sure... it is a dream after all.

But...

I am a *dreamer.*

So when I have a dream like this, I can feel the overwhelming sense of joy deep within my bones. I know this one will come true. I can feel it. The love and light I see in this dream is coming to save Zach and me. I don't know when. But soon. Very soon.

I see that love and light running through the fields, giggling and jumping among the purple flowers.

There are two of them, two gorgeous little girls. They look about five. Maybe six.

They both wear little white eyelet dresses, with big bows tied around their waist. They both have light brown hair, somewhere in between the color of mine and Zach's. One has the most adorable little grin, with tiny little dimples on her cheeks that I already know her friends will wish they had. The other has dazzling blue eyes, bolder and brighter than Meg's or Zach's-- eyes with a blue so true you think they can't possibly be naturally that way, yet only nature could create a color so beautiful.

They're adorable and beautiful, and I know in my heart they're mine.

I can already tell these little girls will be the love and light Zach and I need. They will be that thing Beth talked about that grounds us to this earth and gives us the will to live. I thought Zach was that light for me amidst my darkness, but *boy,* I had no clue.

I know this is a dream. I keep telling myself that over and over again.

But I also know that these girls are *my* girls. *Our* girls.

My love, my light.

Our love, *our* light.

I can't wait for the day I get to see these two little dreams running through a field like this in real life. I decide that Zach and I should take the girls to that lavender field in France when they finally get here. It would be exactly like the dream right now.

I know truly having them in life will be a million times better than this dream right now.

But still, I will myself to stay in this dream, at least for a little while longer.

48

- Addison -
Tuesday, December 23rd, 2025

The snow fell in big, white flakes all around us. I looked out the windows, admiring how beautiful the snow-covered trees look outside our house. There was a big tree, right out this back window. It was big enough for a treehouse. When the girls get a little older, Zach wants to build them a treehouse. He's dreamt of building his children a treehouse for years.

When we were touring houses and found this one, the last one we looked at after three whole days of touring, I knew it was "the one" the second I stepped out of the car.

For starters, it was my dream house. It had light blue siding with crisp white trim. There was a white, wrap-around porch. There were dark navy blue shutters on every window. There was also a white picket fence going around the whole property. It was perfect. It really was a dream come true. I would later realize, once we had been living here for six months, that it was the exact house I had in my little dream book that I made back in high school. It truly was meant to be.

The second thing that solidified this was for sure our home was when we walked in the kitchen and Zach exclaimed, "This is the one! Look at that tree, Ad!" Sure enough, that tree, the one I stared at as the snow fell, was the perfect tree to build a treehouse in.

I heard a noise and turned, alert, to see what it was. I looked at the little screen on the monitor and saw that she was moving around a bit, but otherwise still asleep.

I walked over to the big table in our red kitchen. There was an envelope on the table with my name written on the front. It was filled with close to a hundred pictures, maybe more. My mom had recently gotten a new photo printer and was printing a bunch of photographs for me in colorful four-by-sixes and some black-and-white five-by-sevens. Before the girls were born two weeks ago, she had asked me to send her a bunch of my photos from this year so she could print them for me.

I removed the pictures from the envelope, flipping through them quietly as the girls slept in the family room in their little yellow and gray sleepers.

The first was a photo of me and Elijah, who was smiling so brightly it was like he knew what that day had meant, how important and loved he already was by so many, especially Jess.

Jess had been devastated for quite some time, knowing she could not have kids. She always dreamt of being a mom; she was heartbroken. Landon was incredible about it though. When she told him everything, he promised to always be by her side and that they would make it work. They got married on a beautiful beach in Alabama a few months later. She asked me to be her Matron of Honor. I was so touched. After they got married, they bought a little house on the outside of Madison and spent the weekends fixing it up exactly how they wanted. They bought an adorable labrador retriever, Rosie. In the meantime, they went to different doctors, and she tried many different diets and types of exercises, but nothing worked.

One day, Landon, who worked in medicine, was asked to go to Ethiopia on a mission trip. Jess decided to go with him, and they left for a month in Africa.

She came home madly in love. Not with the country, but with a little boy almost one year old. She showed me pictures the day she got home. "Isn't he beautiful? Look at him! His name is Elijah. Isn't he perfect?" I agreed he was and asked *who* the baby was. She told me they found him at an orphanage in one of the villages nearby where they were helping. He needed a family; he needed a home.

It took a while and there was a lot of paperwork and some worries that it would not go through. But three months ago, when this photo was taken, we all stood in Jess's backyard for a "Welcome Home" party, where all of us gathered to celebrate the official adoption of Elijah.

Jess was beyond happy; she was emotional the whole day. "Everything leading up to this happened to me so I could be this little boy's mom," she cried. "I know that's why. I knew there had to be a bigger purpose to why everything happened in the past."

"Look at Landon," I said that day, nodding to Landon holding little baby Elijah in his arms.

"He is *such* an amazing dad, Addison. Eli just smiles and smiles when Landon walks in the room. He was meant to be this little boy's dad, too."

"You both are already amazing parents," I told Jess, honestly. They were doing incredible with the adjustment. They were so good with him. They changed Elijah's life.

"And you're going to be amazing parents, too," she told me then, nodding at my belly that was still growing back then.

Now, I looked at the photo, smiling at the memory of such an amazing day. Elijah really was smiling the entire day. It was like he knew, too, how much he belonged there, how genuinely happy we all were that he was there. His blue-gray eyes had a certain sparkle to them and were so beautiful against his dark skin.

Yes, Elijah was a dreamer. I think that is what drew Jess to him in the first place. Of anyone on this planet, Jess understood this other world. She told me the day before she left to go bring Eli home, "I am going to help this boy to grow up in a house so full of love and light that he will never see the darkness that comes with the dream world. I will never let the darkness touch him the way it did me. If it's the only thing I do in life now, I know my job on earth is to protect him."

That moment really showed me what parenthood is all about, regardless of whether the child is biologically your child or not. What matters in a family is the love and light within it. Jess, Landon, and Elijah all definitely have that love and light.

* * *

I flipped through a few more pictures. I came across one of the day we found out it was twins! In the photo, Zach looked both terrified and overjoyed at the same time. He was hugging me tight, and I still remember him saying in my ear how amazing the news was.

There was also one of when we found out the babies were girls. Zach thought it would be boys for sure, or one of each.

But I knew. Those little girls in my dream months ago were mine, my little girls. From the moment we found out it was twins I just knew it had to be two girls, just like in my dream. The girls in my dream seemed to be the same age, and they looked very similar.

In the picture, my arms are raised up above my head, and I am mid-squeal. I was so excited. My dream was coming true. My little girls were coming.

* * *

In another photo, from about two months ago, I am crying, with my arms tightly around Cammie. Cammie is standing in front of a big mirror, hugging me back, in a blush-colored (not white!) organza dress.

"It's the one! This is the dress!" she had squealed right before this photo was taken, with tears in her eyes. "I'm going to marry Billy in this dress!"

She had looked at me, biting her lip and looking for approval. "What do you think, Addie?" she asked.

I had flashbacks in that moment of the two of them growing up together, of Billy asking me if he should ask Cammie out finally junior year, of them getting back together at our rehearsal dinner, and of the two of them finding so much happiness and strength in one another these past few years. This wedding of theirs was a long time coming.

"I think you look incredible, Cam! This is definitely it! This is the one!" I agreed, tears then flooding my face. I was just so happy for her!

"Don't cry or I'm going to cry!" Cammie wailed, waving me over to her and pulling me in for a hug.

"I'm sorry!" I had sobbed. "I'm having twins soon. I can't stop crying lately." But that wasn't all it was. It was that my best friend was getting married soon to the guy of her dreams, and I was just so insanely happy for her to feel as happy and loved as I did with Zach.

"Gosh! I cannot get mascara on this!" Cammie said, waving her hands under her eyes and looking up at the ceiling.

"You're right!" I pulled away and stepped back, watching as the bridal consultant went and added a short veil to Cammie's head, completing the whole look. "I'm just so happy for you! You and Billy...your love story is just so sweet. You two belong together. You're perfect for each other. I'm just so happy for you!"

Cammie's cousin, one of her bridesmaids, had snapped the photo I was looking at now while we hugged each other and cried. When Cammie saw it later, she had smiled and said, "This is my favorite photo of us. Ever. I love you, Addie!"

* * *

There was one from a while back of the two of us in front of our dream home, holding up the keys we just got. There was also one of us standing in our new kitchen once it was completed.

I remembered spending the next few months after we moved in shopping with my mom on the weekends, trying to pick out the perfect things. The kitchen in the house had been older and had very dark cabinets and bright green walls. Our kitchen was mostly white, with little bits of red everywhere. My mom had taken me to a kitchen design place where, Dave, the sales rep, worked with us to find the perfect cabinets. I got the kind with glass doors on the corner cabinet so that the red dishes Zach and I had picked out before the wedding were proudly on display, a bright pop of Zach's favorite color to keep the brightness in our home.

* * *

Another is of the dinner party for my parent's thirtieth wedding anniversary. We had rented a room at Zambini's, their favorite restaurant to this day, and invited all of our family and friends. We all surprised them when they thought they were showing up to just meet Zach and I for dinner. They were so touched, and my mom loved that I got the local bakery to make a replica of their wedding cake for the event. It was three layers, all white frosting, with blush-colored sugar roses and rose petals all over it.

I'll never forget the moment, toward the end of the night, that I was walking to the bathroom and overheard my aunt and Mitch talking in the hallway of the restaurant. Of course I had to stay and eavesdrop for a moment. They had been talking a lot ever since their trip to Georgia to try to find the other dreamers.

"So," Mitch said that night of my parents' party.

"So," my aunt replied.

"How have you been?" Mitch asked.

"Wonderful," Carrie replied. "I feel like a weight has been lifted. Honestly, for all those years, after my journey when I was Addison's age, I didn't 'get rid of' my dreams like people thought. I just chose to see the light in my life. I focused on me. I did yoga, meditated, and ate a clean diet. It really helped. Then for a while, recently, I got away from all of that, and the darkness started creeping back in again. But when Beth said all of that...I don't know, Mitch. It resonated with me. I got back into all my good habits. I'm focusing on me again. I'm choosing to see the light again. I feel great."

"You look great, too," Mitch said. "Really. Happier, maybe."

"I am." Then Carrie smiled. "What about you? It seems like the old Mitch DeMize I used to know is back?"

"I think he might be," Mitch replied with a grin. "I'm feeling great, too. I've seen too many dreamers get hurt from all of this... my sister, my mother, Sandy...I don't really care for any more darkness."

"Agreed."

Mitch sighed and said, "Diane is still on that search. She won't give it a rest. I spoke with her a few weeks ago, and she was a mess. She roped some other dreamers into following her and trying to reassemble a group."

"That's a shame," my aunt said. "However, Addie said Becky still emails her from time to time. It sounds like Becky is doing so much better! Addie said Becky has even been helping other dreamers in France to 'see the light.'"

"That's great!" Mitch said. "Did you hear about Meg?"

"I did! I'm so glad she's been getting better and better. Mitch, that's incredible! I think having Zach back in her life and knowing that he was okay was the light she needed."

"I can't believe I helped Adam take that light from her. I thought I was helping her," Mitch said, shaking his head.

"See," Carrie told him, "the Mitch I know *is* still in there."

"Would you like to grab a coffee some time...and catch up?" Mitch asked, sounding slightly more nervous than I would have thought possible.

"I don't drink coffee," Aunt Carrie replied, her tone flat.

"Oh, okay." Mitch turned to leave.

"But I love herbal tea," she offered.

He turned back around. "Really? That stuff is awful!"

She laughed. "You just haven't found the right kind yet. It takes some getting used to. But soon you won't even want coffee any more. Trust me."

"I do," Mitch told her.

There was a pause. "How about tomorrow?" she suggested.

"Sounds great."

Wow, I thought. *I wonder what will happen with those two...*

* * *

The girls arrived two weeks ago exactly. They came a week early, on December ninth, my grandmother's birthday and my birthday. They were the most amazing birthday gift I could have ever wished for and, if I do say so myself, picked a lovely day to arrive.

They were perfect and healthy and precious. They were little and their little arms reached out for each other when they slept. They already had the sweetest bond. They would be the best sisters.

The first minute I held them both, I completely agreed with what Jess had said the day she adopted Elijah. Everything that had ever happened to me in my life was leading me to this moment, to being these two beautiful little girls' mother. Everything within me just wanted to see them happy and to protect them with all that I had.

They were truly love and light. Everything about these two was happiness. They were our little miracles.

Zach and I couldn't stop staring at our daughters, with their tiny little faces and tiny little toes.

The first baby to be brought into the world weighed a few more ounces than her younger sister and had close to a full head of hair already. She was a very snuggly baby from the beginning, always closing her little fist around my finger or nuzzling her little head into my neck.

We named her Aislin.

Zach and I had found the name in one of those baby names books only a few weeks after we found out we were expecting. We were lying on the couch, and Zach was reading through some of the names, while I made a list of options we liked.

Suddenly, he sat up and said, "Ad, listen to this one! It's perfect!"

"What is it?" I asked, putting down my pencil and notebook.

"Aislin," he said.

"Aislin," I repeated, testing it out. "That's really pretty." I wrote the name out under the list of "To Consider" names.

Then Zach said, "But, wait, Ad! You've gotta listen to what it means."

"Okay," I had said. "What does it mean?"

"It means 'vision' or 'little dreamer,'" he said with a glint in his eye.

"Little dreamer," I repeated. "That is perfect! Zach, I love it! That's the one! No question!"

I picked up my pen and circled the name "Aislin" five times on the page.

So the first little girl, the one who would later have the bluest eyes either of us had ever seen, was named Aislin because she was our little dreamer, and I had seen her in a vision.

And she was our little dreamer. Within the first few nights, we could tell she was powerful. Zach guessed she had more natural talent than the two of us combined. "She's one special little dreamer," Zach said.

And she was. She really was. We would never even know how powerful she was, or how many lives she and her sister would change. Beth was right in what she had told us, there was more purpose to being a dreamer than chasing after something that wasn't really there. My purpose as a dreamer was to help my little dreamer through it all so that *she* could be the one to change the dream world.

The meaning of her name was painted in script with gray letters on the soft yellow wall above her white crib.

On the opposite wall, above her sister's crib, read the words Aria: Lioness of God.

It was another name Zach and I had loved, and from the moment our second little girl was born, we knew the name was the perfect fit for her. It was truly like she was our little warrior. Aria may not have been a dreamer -- a shock to us all-- but she had a unique power of her own that we could never even grasp the importance of.

Anytime Aislin had a nightmare, it was almost as if Aria could feel it, like she knew. Aria would reach out her tiny little hand and place it gently on Aislin's cheek. Suddenly, Aislin's stirring would stop and her breathing slowed back to a normal pace. Both of them would settle into a deep and happy sleep with a lovely dream that brought a tiny smile to both of their faces.

Zach and I watched amazed a few nights after we brought them home. "Did she just stop Aislin's nightmare?" Zach whispered to me.

"Yes," I whispered back. "I think she just did."

We gave them their middle names after both of our mothers. Their full names were Aislin Anne and Aria Megan Walker. They both had a piece of the dream world and a piece of reality in their names, which is exactly how they both seemed to be.

The last bunch of pictures in the stack were ones we took in the hospital the day they were both born. They looked so beautiful and peaceful, sleeping all bundled up in their pink little blankets.

My favorite picture, though, was one that hadn't been printed yet, as I just took it an hour or two ago.

It was Zach's mother, Meg, sitting in the corner seat of our gray tufted sofa in a purple sweater and jeans, rather than the wardrobe she had been used to for the past twenty years.

She had Aria in her left arm and Aislin in her right.

She was beaming so proudly, I don't think there could ever be a word to describe it accurately.

She was happy.

She was a grandmother to two little girls.

She was happy, but most importantly she is here.

She was alive, and she is awake.

I gathered up all of the pictures and walked into the living room, feeling almost dizzy with happiness and all of the emotions. Meg was kneeling next to the girls, humming a lullaby and gently rubbing her hand over the tops of their heads as they slept.

"I love you, my little angels," she whispered. "Grandma loves you."

49

- Meg -

Tuesday, December 23rd, 2025

She packed up her belongings into a very small leather bag.

The other residents looked on, questioning looks covering their faces. What? they would gasp. Is Meg going on a trip? We never go on trips! No one ever leaves The Haven.

Meg was not going on a trip.

No.

She was, in fact, leaving The Haven.

It was history in the making. Meg was one of the few individuals to ever be granted permission to leave The Haven. Meg was one of the only ones to seemingly get better over the years rather than worse. Meg was one of the best recovery stories The Haven had ever had.

But Meg wasn't like the other residents at The Haven.

Meg was different.

Meg was a dreamer.

Meg was a fighter.

She walked around her small room, the place she had called home for over a decade, and wondered how her life ever got so dark.

She was thankful, now, to have her little boy back in her life again. Although, he wasn't so little anymore. So many years had been lost to the darkness.

But they had the future now.

There were years and years to come of memories with her son and her new granddaughters.

She vowed she would make up for the time that was lost by spending as much time as she could with her family. She would spend more time being thankful and appreciating little moments, because there were years where she was locked up in this very room believing she would never have happy little moments like seeing her only son get married, hearing her baby granddaughters cry, or seeing their little smiles.

Her baby boy came to pick her up today and bring her home to stay with him and his family for a while.

He seemed so happy when he arrived that afternoon. He was talking about the little ones. He sounded so proud and happy. He was a wonderful father already.

Then her baby, who now has babies of his own, picked up her small bag of belongings and turned off the light in the room.

He smiled at her and said the words she never thought she would hear in her life. They were the most beautiful words. "Hey, Mom, ready to come home?"

And she was.

She was so, so ready to leave this place.

They said once you go to The Haven, you never leave.

They said all dreamers go crazy, that it's only a matter of time.

They said she was dead.

They said her son was dead.

They said there was nothing left to live for.

They said all hope was lost.

She used to believe them.

She used to let the darkness cover her.

She used to let my nightmares stop me from living, stop me from seeing the good in life, stop me from trying.

She used to think giving up was the easy thing to do.

She used to listen to the whispers of everyone around her.

She used to believe she would never leave this nightmare of a place.

But now she knew...

They didn't know anything.

They didn't know her.

Epilogue
- Addison -
Wednesday, December 24th, 2025

"Sweet dreams," I whispered, gently kissing Aislin on her little forehead and setting her down in her crib.

"Sweet dreams," I repeated, this time kissing Aria goodnight and smoothing my hand over the top of her head because that helps her fall asleep.

"Sweet dreams, my girls."

I turned around and saw Zach leaning against the doorframe of the nursery.

"Hi," I whispered and then set Aria down next to her sister. They liked to sleep next to each other.

"Hey, babe," he replied. Then that grin spread across his face. *Kills me every time,* I thought.

I walked over and stood beside him, falling into the curve of his body. He wrapped an arm around my waist and rested his chin on the top of my head.

"Look at them," he said, and I could feel him smile.

"I just hope Aislin gets some sleep tonight," I told him, taking a deep breath.

"She'll be fine." He hugged me tighter. "Plus, she's got Aria there for her."

"I know, I know. I just--"

"Ad,"

"Yeah?"

"Look at them," he repeated.

I took another deep breath and rested my hand over Zach's. I opened my eyes and took in the view.

My girls were sound asleep, Aria somehow sucking on Aislin's thumb again which made me smile. *My girls.*

"Thank you," I whispered, glad to have Zach there reminding me to take a step back and be in the moment.

"Anytime," he told me, staying still, not moving, just letting the two of us live in this moment for a little while longer. *Our girls. Our little dream come trues.*

A few moments later, Zach whispered by my ear, "Have you ever noticed no one ever says 'Sweet Dream'?"

"What?"

"Everyone always says 'Sweet Dream*s*'. Plural, more than one. Because it's always better to have more than one good dream, more than one sweet dream." He turned me around, so I was facing him. His blue eyes had a certain twinkle to them as he smiled and said, "Everyone always says 'Sweet Dreams', and we get two. Two of the sweetest dreams ever. Aislin and Aria. The sweet dreams we've been waiting for."

Wow, I thought.

I stood up a little taller on my tiptoes and kissed him. "Zachary Walker, I love you."

"I love you, too, Ad."

"Thank you for always fighting off my nightmares," I told him. He smiled.

"And thank you, *thank you,* for giving me my sweet dreams."

In that moment, I knew that no matter what nightmares life threw my way, I would make it through because I had my wonderful family, the man of my dreams by my side, and two of the sweetest little girls to get me through it all.

Life truly is the very sweetest dream.

And They Lived
Happily Ever After...
The End

Acknowledgements:

I have found in recent months that although I am a writer and have filled all of these pages you just read with words, I often cannot express my gratitude for this writing journey life has taken me on. I will be forever grateful for this story and every person who encouraged me to follow my dreams two years ago and publish Illusion. This experience has forever changed me. I am so blessed to be a writer.

There are so many individuals who have helped me throughout my writing journey. I'd like to thank take a moment to thank a few of them:

First and foremost, **all of you!** Wow. You have shared in this story with me for three books and three years. You have emailed me, come to meet me at book fairs, reached out, and read my books. My readers and their kind words and the love and light they've shown me are such an inspiration and are the reason I continue to write. Thank you to all of you who leave reviews and recommend the book to friends! Your support amazes me.

My Nonna. For always encouraging me to follow my dreams and for reading a page of my writing every night before bed. You are such an inspiration to me. Thank you for everything you've done to make me the person I am today. I will always treasure when you call me on the phone each night to say "Sona Dorro" ("sweet dreams"). I love you! Thank you!

To the other local authors **Dana Falletti, J. D. Wylde, Lillie Leonardi**, and **Stephanie Keyes,** for your mentorship. Thank you for taking me under your wings and helping me become the writer I am today. Your friendship and advice mean the world to me.

Thank you to the teachers who inspired me to follow my dreams as a writer and as a person: **Mrs. Lois Titus, Mrs. Nicole Maxwell, Em Lyons Bouch, Mrs. Marta Zak,** and **Dr. Elaine Hockenberger.** You all have no idea the impact you have had on my life. I published these books because of your belief in me and your encouragement.

Thank you to the online **literary community** of bloggers and authors! You all have been such an encouragement to me and are so amazing at what you do!

To **my Beta readers** and editors (Lisa, Maria, Wendy, Matt), thank you for catching all the little details and for being my sounding board throughout this process. This book would not have been possible without the four of you!

To **my family**, for coming to all of my book shows and sitting there with me for hours, for being the first to read my stories, and for being the ones who told me to dream big. You are the reason this book is in print. You are my light and love in life. Thank you. I love you!

To **all of my family and friends** who have been a huge support to the book. Thank you for your excitement about the books, your questions, your calls, and passing the book along to others. I so appreciate you all encouraging me and helping me to follow my dreams. I am so blessed to have you on this journey with me.

And thank you, **God.** As you can probably tell after reading this book, my faith is something that is very important to me. I know I wouldn't be where I am today without the gifts God has given me. So thank you, God, for putting these wonderful people mentioned above in my life. Thank you also for giving me this gift of writing and the words to share Addison's story. I am forever blessed to be an author.

Thank you, thank you, thank you!

May you all have light, love, and the sweetest dreams,

-Nadette Rae Rodgers

About the Author:

Nadette Rae Rodgers is a young author who published her first novel, *Illusion*, at just eighteen. She can be found with her nose in a book or a pen in her hand in Pittsburgh, Pennsylvania or Naples, Florida. She has been writing since she learned read and is so grateful for the opportunity to get to share her words with others all around the world. The idea for this book trilogy came from Nadette's interest in dreams and dream analysis. She hopes that her books will inspire the dreams of her readers, not just dreams like Addison's, but their hopes and dreams too.

Sweet Dreams is the final installment of The Illusion Trilogy, and Nadette's fourth published work. Her children's book, *Hoo Loves You*, is a Finalist in the 2018 International Book Awards.

Her books are available online at Amazon and Barnes & Noble, in both paperback and Kindle editions. They are also sold at Riverstone Bookstore (Pittsburgh, PA) and some Barnes & Noble's locations.

Sweet Dreams Playlist

Many readers ask where I find my inspiration. The answer? I am so inspired by nature. I often write outside or, if I'm inside, by a window so I can see outside. The sound of the ocean inspires me, beautiful flowers inspire me, the sound of the rain inspires me, and so much more.

I am also very inspired by the music I listen to while I write. There were so many amazing songs that inspired me to write this series. For some songs, the lyrics remind me of the story or my characters; for others, the instruments and music of it inspire me.

So, I wanted to share the songs that inspired the writing of this trilogy with you all in hopes that their lyrics and melodies might inspire you too.

Much Love & Sweet Dreams,
Nadette Rae

* * *

- When You Look Me in the Eyes by the Jonas Brothers
- When I Look At You by Miley Cyrus
- You Found Me by Kelly Clarkson
- Little Do You Know by Alex & Sierra
- Somewhere Only We Know by Keane
- From the Ground Up by Dan + Shay
- Heaven by The First Theft
- She Is Love by Parachute
- Thinking Out Loud by Ed Sheeran
- Turning Page by Sleeping At Last
- In My Daughter's Eyes by Martina McBride
- Isn't She Lovely Glee Cast version
- H.O.L.Y. by Florida Georgia Line
- I'll Be by Edwin McCain
- Marry Me by Jason Derulo
- Work Song by Hozier
- Die a Happy Man by Thomas Rhett
- More Than Anyone by Gavin DeGraw
- We Are Man and Wife by Michelle Featherstone
- Unchained Melody Glee Cast version

- Because You Loved Me by Celine Dion
- I Met a Girl by William Michael Morgan
- When You Say Nothing At All by Alison Krauss & Union Station
- When I Said I Do by Clint Black & Lisa Hartman Black
- Tenerife Sea by Ed Sheeran
- All I Want by Kodaline
- I Won't Give Up by Jason Mraz
- All-American Girl by Carrie Underwood
- Perfect by Ed Sheeran
- Cinderella by Steven Curtis Chapman
- I Loved Her First by Heartland
- Yours by Russell Dickerson
- Endlessly by The Cab
- Grave by Thomas Rhett
- Sway by Dan + Shay
- Slipping Through My Fingers from "Mamma Mia"
- I Have a Dream from "Mamma Mia"
- Honey, Honey from "Mamma Mia"
- Where You Lead I Will Follow by Carole King
- It Will Rain by Bruno Mars
- Mercy by Brett Young
- Olivia Mae by Brett Young
- Colder Weather by Zac Brown Band
- Never Stop by SafetySuit
- Long Year by Jackie Lee
- Dream by Imagine Dragons
- Speechless by Dan + Shay
- When I Pray For You by Dan + Shay
- Where I Stand by Mia Wray
- Live Like You Were Dying by Tim McGraw
- Walk with Me by Bella Thorne (Midnight Sun soundtrack)
- When the Sand Runs Out by Rascal Flatts
- She will be loved by Maroon Five
- Come Away with Me by Norah Jones
- Like I'm gonna lose you by Meghan Trainer ft. John Legend
- If I Ain't Got You by Alicia Keys
- You are the Reason by Calum Scott
- Wanted by Hunter Hayes (also cover by Boyce Avenu

Connect with Nadette:

Nadette's Blog: nadetteraerodgers.wordpress.com

The Official Illusion Trilogy Website: **illusiontrilogy.weebly.com**

Instagram (author): **@nadetterae**
> If you want to see what Nadette is currently reading,
> check out her other Instagram account
> **@NadetteRaeReads** for book reviews and more!

Twitter: **@nadetterae**

Goodreads: **https://www.goodreads.com/nadetteraerodgers**

Facebook: **https://www.facebook.com/theillusiontrilogy**

Amazon Author Page: **amazon.com/author/nadetterae**

Nadette loves to hear your thoughts on the book, so feel free to email
her (**nadetteraerodgers@gmail.com**) or leave a review on
> **https://illusiontrilogy.weebly.com/news–reviews.html**
> Amazon, Barnes & Noble, or Goodreads